Christmas at Frozen Falls

Christmas at Frozen Falls

Kiley Dunbar

San Diego, California

 Canelo US
An imprint of Printers Row Publishing Group
9717 Pacific Heights Blvd, San Diego, CA 92121
www.canelobooksus.com

Printers Row Publishing Group is a division of Readerlink Distribution Services, LLC. Canelo US is a registered trademark of Readerlink Distribution Services, LLC.

First published in the United Kingdom in 2019 by Hera. This edition originally published in the United Kingdom in 2019 by Canelo.

Published in partnership with Canelo.

Correspondence regarding the content of this book should be sent to Canelo US, Editorial Department, at the above address. Author inquiries should be sent to Canelo, Unit 9, 5th Floor, Cargo Works, 1–2 Hatfields, London SE1 9PG, United Kingdom, www.canelo.co.

Publisher: Peter Norton • Associate Publisher: Ana Parker
Art Director: Charles McStravick
Editorial Director: April Graham
Editor: Angela Garcia
Production Team: Beno Chan, Julie Greene, Rusty von Dyl

Library of Congress Control Number: 2024934491

ISBN: 978-1-6672-0860-2

Printed in Faridabad-Haryana, India

28 27 26 25 24   1 2 3 4 5

For Mouse, with big wiggly hugs and love.

Chapter One

It's December the sixteenth and all over the little market town of Castlewych (that's where I live, in one of the posher bits of Cheshire, where I am incongruously 'not posh') all the gift shops and tearooms are packed with Christmas shoppers and the streets are bejewelled with bright twinkling lights of every colour.

I am definitely the least colourful thing about this scene. I know my face is pale and washed-out without even having to look at my reflection in the shop windows. Even with my getting-revenge-on-my-ex-fiancé bright red dyed hair (which is supposed to be a symbol of how completely fine I am and how well I have already moved on), it's obvious that I'm fooling precisely no one and I am abso-bloody-lutely knackered and still, frankly, heartbroken. But, it's the last day of term and I'm off work for three whole weeks and I am *ready* to tackle Christmas head on.

Mum and Dad are away, of course. They organised their once in a lifetime New York break to coincide with my honeymoon, never imagining that their little girl would be embracing solitary spinsterhood this holiday, but that's OK because I've got it all planned – and it isn't at all tragic. No, it isn't.

There's still umpteen bottles of the bubbly that Dad bought in bulk for the wedding that never was, and I've mail-ordered one of those woolly blankets shaped like a mermaid's tail (hey, don't judge me; the home shopping channels have been an enormous comfort, and I'm now the satisfied owner of an array of vegetable peeling and vacuum storage devices), and then there's all the end of term seashell truffles and chocolate oranges from the kids and their parents (a really decent haul this year; I can't help wondering if it's because they feel sorry for poor jilted Ms. Magnusson). Come Christmas day I'll be happily ensconced in my flat with the *Strictly Come Dancing* Christmas Special on repeat; a drunken, woolly mermaid with record-breaking blood sugar levels. *What?* I'm not crying, *you're* crying.

In another life – in the parallel universe where Cole didn't ditch me one week before our gorgeous, romantic summer wedding – my passport reads 'Mrs Sylvie Magnusson-Jordan' and we've spent the past six months engaging in bouts of blissful newlywed Olympic-gold-medal-winning sex, and now Cole's got Christmas off work and me and him are busy packing our matching His and Hers suitcases with my tiny thong bikinis, his tighty-whitey speedos, and a mega sized box of condoms, getting ready to fly off on our honeymoon to Mauritius. Round about now I'd be having a spray tan and getting my eyelashes tinted and Cole would be engaging in some serious manscaping on that hairy chest of his.

Come on, Sylve! Get it together. What did you say at the school carol concert today? The parents loved it… Oh yeah… These are the heady, chilly, joyful days of Advent when the coming holiday is full of possibility and promise, and the old year has stored up its very best and brightest moments for the bleak midwinter as it bids farewell in a fanfare of carols and charity, kindness and kisses, yadda yadda yadda. I must buy some gin on the way home: bubbly won't be enough to get me through to New Year.

Right, here we are: the travel agent's. I push my way inside, making the bell over the door ring, to be met by the sight of a substantial queue and the panicked expression of the frazzled young guy behind the desk. He looks like he's thinking, 'Shit, not *another* customer.' He shouts to me, 'Madam, you'll be number five in the queue,' and I take a seat beside a giant cardboard Mickey Mouse who's failing to tempt me to spend my Christmas in The Happiest Place on Earth.

Hold on! Did that travel agent just call me *Madam*? For crying out loud, I'm only thirty-four. Do I really look careworn enough to have transitioned from a 'Miss' to a 'Madam'? I'm working hard on ignoring my own answers to this question when I hear a beeping sound coming from somewhere about my person. A text.

I rummage in my coat pockets trying to retrieve my phone and making crumpled tissues, ponytail bands and Chapsticks tumble onto the floor by my feet. I scrabble to gather them up and tell myself I wasn't always this shambolic. This is all Cole's fault.

> You're NOT really doing it, are you?! WTF happened to the Beyoncé Protocol?

It's a message from Nari, my best mate and the co-creator of the, admittedly very drunken, break-up survival

3

strategy we named after Nari's all-time favourite singer-slash-goddess-slash-inspiration. It had all sounded so positive on that Saturday night back in August – on what should have been my wedding night. It was too late to cancel the classy spa hotel, not without losing all the money so, feeling defiant, me and Nari checked in to the bridal suite and immediately devoured the contents of the minibar.

'Little vodkas! My favourite. And look Sylve, *tiny nuts!*' Nari had called out as she ransacked the fun-size snacks. 'Remind you of anyone?'

Admittedly, it wasn't as bad as I'd feared. We ordered room service and lounged around on the four-poster bed in fluffy robes and those white hotel slippers they let you keep. I held it together and managed not to cry but only because I had wept solidly all week long and was utterly exhausted and ready for some mind-numbing drinking and serious pampering.

The Beyoncé Protocol had taken shape over the course of that evening, and Nari, being Nari, typed it all out onto her tablet and emailed me a copy in case my memory was hazy the next morning, which it was. This is how it went:

1. Cole can *eff off*. You don't need a man to be happy. Plus, he was very, very hairy for a thirty-five-year-old (and *not* in a good way).

2. Move out of your mum and dad's on Monday and come to live at Nari's 'House of Win' for as long as you want. Tell Cole you want your contribution to *his* mortgage payments back.

3. Nari will take you out every Friday night, when she's in the country, to a place of your choosing – but there must be cocktails and hot waiters.

4

4. First thing tomorrow – hotel salon hair makeover. New Life: New Look.
5. DO NOT cancel your December honeymoon. It was your wedding present from your folks, so it's yours. Go anyway. Take someone amazing like, say, Nari? Get drunk, get a suntan, dance the night away, and live off rum cocktails and coconuts all week long.
6. Nari will flog your lovely wedding dress on eBay. You can put the money towards a deposit on a dog friendly place for you and Barney.
7. And remember, if Beyoncé has taught us anything – and, of course, she has – it is to remember that you are a QUEEN. Don't ever forget it.

And the plan had worked too. Well, it worked during those first few gut-wrenchingly broken and humiliated weeks when I was still off school for the summer break. The headmistress took pity on me and let me skip the summer planning meetings, so the whole of last August felt like one long holiday – albeit the kind of holiday where you catch your reflection in a mirror, see how sad your eyes look, and start up again with the snotty ugly-crying.

Nari made sure I was rarely sober and never alone for much of the summer, planning Netflix nights or taking me out to the cinema (sassy chick-flicks), or booking nice restaurants (gourmet cheeseburgers and ice cream sundaes), and then we'd hit the gym, chasing the endorphins. Cardio Bootcamp is much, much harder when you've just downed a Jack Daniels and Coke with lunch, but still, we worked out like daemons. The music blaring in my earphones and the adrenalin coursing in my veins obliterated all other thoughts and feelings, anaesthetising everything, if only for half an hour.

When I was with Nari I didn't have to face the pity-visits from extended family, and all those lost deposits, and the awkward questions about what I'd like my wedding guests to do with the presents they'd bought from my carefully curated gift registry and never had the chance to give me. I'd had to bite the inside of my cheeks to stop myself yelling into their well-meaning faces, 'Bloody well *give them to me*, Auntie Brenda! I really wanted that toastie maker.' But instead I'd smiled and told everyone to return them for refunds.

Basically, what I'm saying is that without Nari I'd probably never have dragged myself out of bed again. She orchestrated all of the clichéd break-up survival stuff, including making me dye my mousey, blah-coloured hair this luscious red, which I'm still not one hundred per cent sold on, and it *did* all help, but after the strange excitement and shock that comes with being unexpectedly single started to wear off, I realised I was simply alone again and had to make the best of it.

I went back to work at Castlewych Academy in September, back to teaching truculent teenagers about history, and life went on. Only now I have to carry around this dull, empty, aching feeling in my heart where once there was a bridegroom, our lovely home, and a Happy Ever After.

More people have joined the queue behind me. When did they come in? I must have been miles away. I'm half looking at the winter holiday brochures on the shelves with their snowy alpine scenery, smiling skiers, and cosy gingerbread cabins when my phone buzzes again.

It's another text from Nari.

Ghosting me? I'm on my way.

Feeling slightly panicked, I power off my phone and slip it into my pocket. She'll never find me. Will she? I am cancelling this honeymoon and that's that. Back in the summer and fuelled by Bacardi and Beyoncé, our single girls' winter 'honeymoon' had seemed like a good idea, but as it's come around I've realised, deep down, that a plan B beach holiday with Nari isn't actually going to feel fun and rebellious; it's just a bit sad, especially at Christmas.

Mum and Dad offered to cancel their New York trip and host their traditional Christmas at home, which is so like them, but that made me feel sadder than anything. No, I can do this. I'm a grown-ass thirty-four-year-old woman, and I can't carry on with the jilted bride routine forever. I'll beg this poor travel agent for a refund – even if I can only get some of the money back – and I'll repay my parents, even though they insist they don't want a penny of it back.

They think Nari's right and that we should be treating ourselves to an exotic yuletide adventure. I sometimes think it's been worse for them than it has for me; they're so heartsore that the shitbag they've called 'son' for the last decade could up and leave the way he did.

I'll ask Nari if she'll spend Christmas with me at my new flat. Normally she'd be in some far-flung location for Christmas, or sometimes when it was Mum and Dad's turn to have me and Cole for Christmas, she'd spend the holiday at my folks' too. Her mum and grandmother live in South Korea and Nari isn't flying out to visit them until February, so I know she'll be up for it, once she's gotten over the disappointment of missing out on Mauritius – hence this impromptu trip to the travel agents to cancel the whole sorry honeymoon shambles.

I shove my growing-out fringe off my face (I was never a fringe sort of girl, I should have been firmer with Nari about that) and let out one of my newly perfected Eeyore sighs.

I can just about make out the Christmas tree in the town square through the steamy glass of the travel agency windows; the condensation is making its lights shine out like stars. Their colourful glow sets me thinking about my bare little flat and all the unpacked boxes and how I haven't even sorted out a tree yet.

Oh, come on! What's the hold up? I usually try to avoid having time alone to think, it isn't good to dwell on it all.

'Next, please? Madam, it's your turn,' the travel agent calls out.

I'm not moving fast enough for him and he's not even attempting to hide his annoyance. Deep breath. Here goes.

'Sorry about your wait,' he says unconvincingly.

Why do shop assistants always say that? As though they're commiserating with you over your body mass index.

I hand over the crumpled booking confirmation. If I say it really fast maybe it'll hurt less. 'I know this is late notice, and I've read the terms and conditions so I know I'll get next to nothing, but I need to cancel this,' I tell him.

The young man, Nathan his badge says, starts reading it out aloud without a shred of interest.

'Luxury beach hut, seven nights, bridal package with champagne and rose petal welcome…'

It's at this point that Nathan pauses momentarily and glances up at me. There's a curling smile at the side of his mouth that isn't sympathy; it's salacious interest and somehow mocking too. I'm trying to assume what I hope looks like an air of quiet dignity. He carries on in a too-loud voice that everyone in the queue behind me can surely hear.

'Full board, spa treatments, scuba diving experience, private boat transfers, leaving on the *twenty-second of December*? Oh! *No way* should you cancel this… You and your… um… husband will lose the lot.'

Am I allowed to thump this supercilious little creep? He's dressed in a cabin-crew-style blue waistcoat and tie with flying wings on his lapels as though at any moment he'll have to check the doors for landing and offer around the boiled sweets as opposed to spending his days flogging cheap deals to Benidorm and shuffling his brochures. And he's *still* talking.

'Your only option is to transfer onto another holiday if you don't want this one. You'll lose your deposit and there'll be a whopping great admin fee but at least you'd get a holiday *of some kind*.' This is said with a note of patronising faux compassion.

By now my cheeks are burning with the effort of not crying in front of him. *Why* have I left this so late?

'I hadn't thought about transferring,' I say weakly, just as the door behind me flies open and the piercing note from its little brass bell makes me flinch. It's Nari and she's out of breath. *Dammit*, I knew she'd track me down.

'You haven't done it, have you?'

I try to explain Nathan's idea, fleshing it out a bit so she doesn't kill me with the incredulous, harassed stare she's directing towards me. 'I might be able to transfer the holiday… maybe we could go somewhere nice in the summer with the money that's left. Rome maybe?'

Nari's shaking her head and motioning for me to get out of my seat. Nathan's bloody loving this.

'Right. You need a brew. Come on, let's go. She won't be needing your help, thank you very much.' She turns her death stare on Nathan, making him jump up, panicked.

As I'm gathering my things, Nathan stuffs brochures and leaflets for last minute Christmas escapes into a carrier bag. He shoves them towards me before Nari marches me outside.

Nari lectures me all the way to the cafe about how last minute holiday cancellations and transfers are financially crap decisions, and I just nod because she's right and, frankly, I'm a bit scared of her when she's got a point to prove. She knows what she's talking about though; she runs a pretty successful adventure travel blog, boasting over fifty thousand followers on Instagram, and I'll bet she's written for more off the beaten track style travel books than any other woman in the industry. So whatever she's going to say about all this, I'd better just keep schtum and listen to the expert.

The coffee shop windows are steamed up and streaming. It's one of the big chains and is cosy despite the corporate uniformity. There's only two free seats right in the middle of the cafe and there are people surrounding them on all sides. I pick my way around the chair legs and bags of Christmas shopping, only stopping to pat the heads and boop the noses of every dog and pup in the place (one Weimaraner, two pugs and a beagle: pretty good dog-booping haul for today – happily, Castlewych is the kind of posh, doggy-friendly place where even the big chains have jars of dog treats by the tills), and I plonk myself down with a huffing sigh. The last thing I want is an audience of earwiggers overhearing Nari's words of wisdom; she can be pretty brash.

Nari waves from the counter by the entrance, mouthing, 'Want a muffin?' before dismissively waving a hand as if to say, 'Of course she does.'

The baristas are bashing spent coffee grounds into a metal bin and refilling the espresso machines in the blink of an eye. Stream is hissing in great white clouds into the air and countless red cups are being filled with the festive gingerbread lattes that always taste a bit artificial to my (simple) tastes.

I've got time to ponder the contents of the carrier bag in front of me, thinking of the surly travel agent's advice. I edge one of the leaflets out and gaze down at it.

Last-Minute Christmas and New Year Deals Flying from Manchester Airport.

Hmm, do any of the destinations sound appealing? Edinburgh, Stockholm, Dublin, Frankfurt, Tenerife, Solomon Islands… What's my problem? None of these jump out at me. I shove the leaflet into the bag as Nari appears with a tray.

'OK, I got a pumpkin spice chai latte with whipped cream and cinnamon sprinkles, or an English breakfast tea with skimmed milk.'

'You know me so well,' I say, lifting the teapot onto the table.

'And two red velvet muffins. And two mince pies. I have a feeling this is a two cake kind of emergency.' Nari grins with a softness in her eyes. 'Do you want to tell me what was going on back there? Can you *really* not face the holiday of a lifetime with your bestie?'

'Holiday of a lifetime, yes, I *do* want that, but this one was meant for me and Cole and now it's here I just can't face it. I'm so sorry. Let's go on holiday somewhere else, another time.'

Nari sips her drink, comically leaving a whipped cream moustache on her top lip just so I'll smile. 'For a start, I'm only free this Christmas break; I've got quite a few trips pencilled in for next year already, so that might not be an option. Look, there's more to do on Mauritius besides sex and couples' massages on the beach, you know? We'll be able to island hop, visit the national park, and see the waterfalls. The food is *amazing*. And the cocktails!'

I'm already halfway through the mince pie so can only shake my head at all this. Nari sees I'm momentarily speechless and takes the opportunity to present her closing arguments.

'It's only a week. You can pack some beach novels, your iPad, your vibrator, and you'll have a blast!'

The two elderly ladies at the table behind Nari (who've been listening intently to every word) suddenly splutter and cough over their ginger snaps and rattle their saucers in shock. That'll teach them.

Nari sees my dubious expression and gives up. There's no fight left in her and I watch her kiss goodbye to her dreams of a Mauritian island paradise.

'What is it?' she asks me. 'You've been much happier since you moved into your new flat last month, you genuinely looked as though you were moving on a bit, but now… you've lost your… *oomph* again. Is it just because it's Christmas, or is it Cole?' Her eyes flash and she gasps before saying, 'Oh my God, there hasn't been a Christmas miracle and he's finally had the guts to get in touch?'

I admit to Nari that I've had my head in the sand about the impending festivities, and now, here I am, dreading the days ahead. And no, I haven't heard from Cole. There hasn't been a peep from him since that lovely sunny day in August during my final dress fitting when, like a coward, he'd rung my mobile and shattered my world into a thousand tiny pieces – the only contact we've had since was letters sent via his solicitor informing me that I would receive precisely nothing from the proceeds of the sale of the house we once shared and that I was to clear my stuff out of *his* garage ASAP.

'He'll be at his mother's for Christmas, no doubt,' I offer with a grimace.

Nari reaches for the only silver lining to be had. 'Well, at least you never have to see Patricia Jordan ever again.'

They're welcome to their family Christmas, I think to myself. I always felt horribly out of place at their celebrations. My would-be mother-in-law's exacting standards were obviously far higher than I could ever have hoped to live up to. Ten years ago, when I was a graduate with a newly acquired teaching degree and freshly in love after four exciting months with Cole and already moving in together, Patricia came to our house-warming party to meet 'the new girl'. That's what she called me. *To my face.* Back then, I had no idea that in real life people actually ran their finger along surfaces disapprovingly looking for traces of dust. But when I met Patricia that day she did exactly that and presented a (only very slightly) dusty Finger of Shame to me with an imperious, smug look I would come to be very familiar with. It had rather taken the shine off our Love Shack house-warming bash.

The Love Shack: that's what Cole had named our four-bedroom new build out by Manchester Airport, back when I thought he was so glamorous and exciting and charming, and I'd laughed at all his funny ways; back when I'd imagined us populating the spare bedrooms with adorable little Jordans, and when I'd given a damn about mollifying my near-miss monster-in-law.

The mince pie's somehow been demolished and it's obvious I'm sinking into the break-up abyss again, the place where I spend hours just going over and over it all. Nari's calling to me from the edge of the void.

'No. No! Don't drift off. We've got work to do here. Focus, Sylvie.'

She's tipped the brochures onto the table and is fanning them out in front of me, swirling her hands above them like a demented game show beauty luring me into gambling away the holiday I already have in the bag.

'Pick one, then. If we're transferring to another trip I'll contact *my* guy and get you a full refund. Stephen owes me a favour actually.'

Nari's wearing a leery grin so I can only assume she's talking about *that* Stephen. The one that owns a few airlines and travel companies, no big deal. He's a flashy, brash Los Angelino now – only a handful of people know of his lowly birth in Grimsby, long since forgotten now that he's bestowed with a transatlantic accent, numerous tax haven homes and an English Bentley that never leaves its Saudi garage. He's Nari's favourite thing to do on a Singapore stopover. I've listened to way too many gratuitously graphic descriptions of his impressive love-making in his even more impressive skyscraper penthouses over the years. I try to block the more lurid details from my mind by setting to work on my red velvet cake and flipping through the brochures.

'Nari, I don't really fancy spending Christmas in a chilly off-season Mediterranean resort full of pasty expats, do you? And a frosty city break won't be up to much when all the museums and galleries will be shut for the holidays and everyone's preparing for New Year street parties and snogging at midnight. And I *definitely* don't want another trip to a paradise island populated by shagged-out newlyweds. I've already got one of those and the thought of going makes me nauseous. So, what do we do?'

'You missed this one.' Nari presents me with a very smart, shiny booklet. It says 'Santa's Enchanted Lapland' in glittery red letters and there's the most Christmassy Father Christmas of all time smiling out of the cover at me through half-moon spectacles perched on rosy cheeks.

'Ha ha, very funny,' I say, returning it to the bottom of the pile, but Nari's switched on the death stare again and I wilt a bit under her unrelenting gaze.

'Hold on a sec, Lapland's supposed to be gorgeous. And I've never been that far north in Scandinavia before,' she protests.

I flip through the pages again, holding them open to show Nari. There's nothing but mischievous-looking (read 'annoying') costumed elves with pointy ears, or cosy families, all blond hair and blue eyes, toasting marshmallows by snowy wilderness campfires.

'I'm sure it's *adorable* if you're six and seriously into reindeer.'

Nari's having none of this. 'Actually, Lapland is very chic. This stuff is just for the family market, ignore all that. Picture it, Sylvie... You and me sipping Christmas spirits in a fancy igloo ice bar under the aurora borealis. And there's all the skiing and fondue. Oh, and Jacuzzis and saunas... and hot Nordic men... although you'd already know a little about *that*, wouldn't you, Sylve?' This is said with a wink and a smutty laugh that makes us the centre of coffee shop attention all over again.

I know perfectly well what she's referring to and I'm not biting.

'Well... that does sound quite nice,' I say, looking with fresh eyes at the brochure.

'It's only a short-haul flight but we'd still be getting away from it all. We'd be miles inside the Arctic Circle.'

I must admit I take a deep breath at this idea. A bit of peace and total isolation.

'Keep talking. You're winning me round,' I say with a smile. 'Won't it be a bit chilly though?'

'Freezing! And dark. Totally dark. The sun barely touches the horizon in December.'

Hmm, I'm not convinced this is a good thing. I don't like the cold and dark. 'The total opposite of Mauritius, then? *Oh no*, Nari! I've just realised. What about your Mauritius feature for the website?'

'*Oh no!*' Nari mimics soundlessly, holding her hands to her cheeks *Home Alone* style. 'I'll just ring my boss, shall I?' Facetiously, she mimes dialling a phone. 'Hi Nari, is it OK if I switch our January feature from "A Girls' Indian Ocean Getaway" to "Two Go in Search of the Northern Lights"? Uh-huh? Uh-huh?' She dramatically hangs up on herself and says with a grinning wink, 'Boss says it's A-OK,' before shovelling a huge wodge of cake into her mouth. Christ, she's annoying. Brilliant and annoying.

As we pack up to leave (I've still got that gin and a Christmas tree to buy on my way home, and Nari's promised to ring Stephen the Sex God to sort out our travel plans), I pull up my collar and peer out the door into the street. It's gone five o'clock and the little boutiques all around the town square are staffed by harried workers bracing themselves for another round of late-night opening for the Christmas shoppers. My mum would say it's too cold for snow, though I've never really understood what that means.

Some of my school kids are milling around by the war memorial waiting to get into the first showing of the Christmas film at Castlewych's one screen cinema. Some of them spot me as I walk outside and shout, 'Merry Christmas, Ms. M!' and I wave back at them.

As I'm hugging Nari goodbye I notice over her shoulder that two of the sixth-formers have paired off alone under the town's light display (the council has gone for an odd mix of strings of trumpeting herald angels and dancing Santas this year), and I can tell the teenagers are totally oblivious to everything going on around them.

They're leaning their foreheads together and he's lovingly holding her face with his fingertips. They're utterly frozen in each other's gaze, intense and intimate, just the two of them alone together in a crowd of people, holding off, enjoying the moment before their lips will, at last, meet.

As Nari blows a kiss towards me and walks off across town, I can't help looking back at the kids, but I lose sight of them in the bustle of Christmas shoppers.

I plod homeward, dragging the last petrol station fore-court Christmas tree behind me and clinking a carrier bag of discounted booze, and I think about how, a long time ago, a boy kissed me like that. And then a name that I haven't spoken aloud in years crosses my chilled lips in a cloud of warm vapour.

'Stellan.'

Chapter Two

'Decorations... decorations... Where the hell are you?'

I'm attempting to ascend the cardboard box mountain at the foot of my bed. They've been piled up like this for three weeks – since the day I moved in – and it's getting ridiculous now. I ran out of pants back in week two and have been round at Mum and Dad's using their washer dryer more times than I'm proud of. I know that somewhere at the top of this pile there's a box full of tinsel, pompom snowmen and silver pinecones.

'*Ah-ha!*' I shout in triumph at the exact moment the mountain gives way beneath me and I slide down onto the floor sending the contents of the decorations box flying into the air. A corner of the Michael Bublé CD that Mum gave me years ago hits me on the temple. I've been listening to The Smiths a lot since the summer, but I suppose they're not exactly festive so I shrug off the undignified fall and put the CD into my ancient laptop. Out pours some Canadian Christmas crooning and the scene is set for tree-decorating.

Since leaving Nari in town, I've already downed three glasses of bubbly with my baked beans and oven chips and I'm getting down tipsy single girl style to 'It's Beginning to Look a Lot Like Christmas' when I spot it: a glittering vintage solitaire diamond on a thin rose-gold band. My engagement ring. It must have been in one of the fallen boxes and it's just lying there among the scattered silver bells and stars.

I don't know why I do it but I slip it onto my finger and hold out my hand, making the stone shimmer. It is still gorgeous. I wore this thing for nearly ten years waiting for Cole to set the date, but there was always something in the way. He needed to get his flying hours up, then he had to commit to the long-haul schedules in order to get promoted, then he moved airlines... Oh, did I mention Cole's a pilot? I know what you're thinking. Lucky me, landing a gorgeous, uniformed, suntanned high-flyer, but the truth is we barely saw each other and the Love Shack was a pretty lonely place out there under the twenty-four hour flightpaths.

I remember the summer day he slipped this ring onto my finger. As a romantic teenager I'd always dreamt that my future fella, whoever he might be, would propose over dinner in a classy restaurant; the kind of place I'd seen on eighties romcoms, with candles and tinkling piano music and white linen tablecloths. I'd imagined many times how my mystery man would secretly drop the ring into my champagne flute and as he made a quiet toast to our future his eyes would linger on my glass and I'd see the ring and weep tears of surprised joy.

But quiet romance was never Cole's style. Everything had to be a statement, reflecting him and his overinflated sense of himself – instilled at an early age, I've come to learn, by his doting mother.

At the time, I hadn't exactly minded the public question popping; at least, I had been taken by surprise, and I had wept, just like in the rehearsed fantasy proposals of my girlhood, and I'd smiled away the qualms rising up with the colour in my cheeks.

He chose to do it at his sister's wedding reception. This should have been my first clue.

His sister, Clementine, is a consultant cardiologist, just like her father was, and the wedding party was basically a gathering of the great and the good of Harley Street. To give Cole his due, I hadn't suspected a thing all day. All the way through the overly long service in the glittering Mayfair church and the delicious wedding breakfast in the hotel across the street, even during the speeches and elaborate rituals of cake-cutting and bouquet throwing, I hadn't the foggiest notion he was about to pop the question. Why would I? We'd only been together for four months, and I'd only met his mother for the first time a couple of days before at the Love Shack house-warming bash.

Poor Clementine clearly had no idea what was about to happen either. Just as the room was bursting into rippling applause and the quartet were readying them-selves to strike up a tasteful number for the couple's first dance, Cole had tapped at his champagne glass so loudly I thought it might shatter. Before I knew what was happening, he was dragging me – yes, me, the girl the bride and groom didn't know from Eve – into the centre of the room, coming to a stop directly in front of the perplexed happy couple.

I'll never forget the look on Clementine's face as, without any further warning, Cole sank to his knee before the gathered crowd and held the ring up to me. The diamond gleamed in the sudden light from the wedding photographer's flash.

That's when I looked from Cole's confident grinning face to his sister's. Clementine's expression didn't mirror my own blushing shellshock or my look of creeping embarrassment at Cole's ill-timed matrimonial fervour. Instead, she was hitching her bottom jaw a little to one side and, after glancing wearily at her new husband, raising her eyes to the vaulted ceilings. I watched her shake her head as if to say, 'I knew it. They couldn't let me have *one day*'.

The guests had broken out into a polite smattering of sudden applause – Clementine's set are nothing if not socially astute and smartly responsive. But, as Cole loudly declared his undying love for me and, with a struggle, forced the too-tight ring onto my finger, I glanced around the room to discover what I'd feared all along; that not one of Clementine's doctor friends was actually smiling, nobody was. Except for Cole's mother, Patricia Jordan. She was smiling, alright, with a look of defiant pride aimed directly at the shrinking Clementine.

I should have known then. If the pair of them could cook up a plan to upstage their own nearest and dearest on the best day of her life, they'd be capable of anything. But I'd managed to pack away all those reservations, and I performed a delighted 'yes', overwhelmed by what I chose to interpret at the time as Cole's impulsive largesse and his hapless enthusiasm to pile happiness upon familial happiness and bring me into the Jordan family in the biggest, showiest way possible, and as soon as possible.

I could count on one hand the number of times we met up with Clementine after that day, though I made sure to send gifts to their London home as each of our nephews was born, and I always made sure to remember their birthdays.

Yeah, I should have known then.

I realise I'm still spreading my fingers out, making the ring sparkle in the light of the bare, unshaded bulb on my bedroom ceiling. Michael Bublé seems to have shifted his attentions to Frosty the Snowman and either the festive season is finally winning me over or I'm teetering on the edge of the abyss of jilted brides again because I find myself racing to the living room sofa and tearing into a chocolate orange with frightening ferocity. The phone rings in the hallway as I'm six segments in and I let it go to voicemail.

'Hello, Sylvie love. Have you unpacked your stuff yet? Me and Dad are hoping you'll pop round for dinner tomorrow before we jet off to the Big Apple. I'm experimenting with chilli dogs and fries to help us acclimatise. Lots of love. Oh, and... bring a friend if you like. OK, bye, love.'

Bring a friend. That's Mum's not so subtle way of asking if I've managed to get myself a boyfriend for Christmas. Which, of course, I haven't, because this isn't a Richard Curtis movie and Castlewych Academy isn't exactly bursting at the seams with eligible bachelors. I've drank enough bubbly to laugh out loud at the thought of Mum's expression if I turned up tomorrow with old Mr Halcrow (the sweaty mathematician) on my arm.

It's getting late and even though I've taken a perverse pleasure in parading around with a few grands' worth of bling on my finger, I know it's time to take Cole's ring off. Even after he had it resized for me, it was always just a little too tight and wearing it now is making my skin hurt, not to mention my heart. Just as I resolve to send it back

23

to him in the new year I hear a jumbo jet flying over the flat. I raise my eyes, tracking its passing unseen above me, and I remember I have no idea what his flight patterns are now, or where in the world he might be. I don't even know where he's living nowadays. It's then that I feel the need to go lie down on the bedroom floor in the middle of the spilled debris of our shared life and the remnants of a decade of Christmases where I was Cole's metaphorical co-pilot and second officer. OK, *now* I'm crying.

-

It's pitch dark when I wake up and I seem to be dry mouthed and frozen on the floor. I want to say this has never happened before as it doesn't exactly cast me in a good light, but I'll admit it has.

I scrabble for the light switch by the bed and squint at the bare Christmas tree across the hall in my moonlit living room. Mary and Joseph, it's cold in here! So much for cosying up the flat for Christmas.

I can see my mobile flashing on the hall table and drag myself to my feet. It's gone four in the morning; Bublé and bubbly must have laid me out cold. I put the kettle on and dial my voicemail, and of course it's Nari.

'All right, Sylve? Well, I've given Stephen a good chatting to via FaceTime, and it was all *very* cordial. He's asked his PA to sort out a refund for you; it was all booked through one of his subsidiaries, apparently. The full amount will be back in your parents' account by morning. *And* he's got two Finnish Lapland options for us, both leaving on the twenty-second: there's a hotel in the middle of Rovaniemi, I think it was, or a couple of log cabins somewhere near a ski resort called Saariselkä.

Let me know which you fancy and I'll finalise the details tomorrow. Oh, and I think I've got myself a New Year's date in London. I guess Stephen needed a little reminder of what he's been missing; he's jetting in specially. OK, nighty night.'

As I sip my coffee and wander around the flat closing curtains, adjusting the thermostat, and listening for the boiler coming on with a whoosh, I think how nice it was of Stephen to sort everything out like that. Even though I'm grateful, I can't forget how much he hurt Nari, though I suspect he isn't even aware of that fact, and Nari just pretends it's all fine now. I wonder if this New Year's date means he's willing to commit this time? It sounds plausible if he's coming all this way to see her, but I'll believe it when I see it. Still, imagine having the power to just offer up two choices of holiday like that! I admit I'm impressed. What had Nari said? Rovaniemi or... and that's when it clicks. *Saariselkä?* I've heard that before.

I grab my laptop and settle on the sofa while making a start on a Christmas Toblerone from one of the school kids. 'Saariselkä... Saariselkä,' I say in an increasingly over pronounced and inaccurate accent. I'm sure that's where he was from. How many other Lappish towns has the average British woman heard of?

Right. Facebook. I'm in, and my fingers hesitate over the keyboard. 'Stellan... Stellan...?' What the hell was his surname? 'V... Vir... Virtanen!' That's it! How many Stellan Virtanens can there be on Facebook? Ah, just the one then, and he appears to be a very small, very cute dog. I click on the blue-eyed husky pup avatar and hold my breath. Holy crap! It *is* him.

'Stellan Virtanen. Saariselkä, Inari. Finnish Lapland. Studied Languages and Cultures at University of Lapland and Manchester University.'

Hmm, but that's all I can see. He's got his security settings on. Very sensible. You don't know who's creeping around your timeline and perving over your summer holiday snaps. Before I know what my stupid fingers are doing, they've sent a friend request, and I'm left feeling momentarily panicked, but the bubbly in my bloodstream simply shrugs and I let it go. Besides, my mind is busy elsewhere all of a sudden.

I know it's a bit sad, and I know I shouldn't, but it occurs to me that even though I can't get a peek at what Stellan looks like now (probably paunchy and balding, I tell myself), I at least know where there are photographs of him from way back then. I just have to scale Box Mountain again.

Half an hour later, I'm on coffee number two, the Toblerone is history and I've finally found what I was looking for in the bottom of a box marked 'University' which has followed me from my halls of residence to Mum and Dad's, to the Love Shack and now it's here, and in all that time it's never been opened.

From beneath ring binders filled neatly with my meticulously handwritten lecture notes (I was *that* nerd at uni; well, for the first half of my degree at least), I lift out the green faded T-shirt. It was his favourite. After we'd gotten to know each other I took to wearing it, wanting to stake my claim to gorgeous Stellan so the other girls knew he was with me. The T-shirt has spent the last fifteen years wrapped around a bundle of photographs. I crawl into bed with them and pull the duvet around me. OK, let's see if I'm remembering him correctly.

And there he is. Blond, very blond, and serious-looking. There's that furrow between his thick flaxen brows, and those pale brown eyes, the lightest I'd ever seen. As I inspect the image it hits me all over again, that familiar stomach flipping feeling I used to get when he looked at me like that. He really was something else.

There are a few more pictures of him taken at student parties, one where he is singing karaoke, his arms around his fellow exchange student friends' necks, bottle of beer in hand. He's at ease and grinning in that one and showing his deeply bowed lips curling over straight white teeth. He had the kind of smile people round here pay a fortune for.

And then I stop flipping through the images as my eyes fall upon one of us together. Who took this? I have no idea. It's me and him sitting by a table piled with empty beer bottles and glasses at some hall party or other. I look so young, only nineteen and effortlessly pretty, though I had no idea of that fact back then. And we're right in the centre surrounded on all sides by partying students. I can see someone's got a guitar and people are singing. But Stellan and me look oblivious. We're facing one another, the tip of my nose brushing his. His eyes are half open and his lips are parted for the kiss that was to come. He has that desirous, intense look on his face that I could have grown so used to, given half the chance. But what gets me in the pit of my stomach as I gaze into this glossy window into my past is the sight of Stellan's fist twisting the hem of my top into a scrunched knot, the muscles in his forearm flexed and taut. For a second, tucked up alone in my bed,

I can almost feel the graze of his knuckles on my skin as I, teenage Sylvie, sank into his kiss.

Placing the photo aside, I reach for what was once Stellan's T-shirt, holding it at arm's length as it unravels, and I read the faded lettering, 'Lapland–Manchester Cultural Exchange 2004'. Obviously, giving it a little sniff would be weird, wouldn't it?

I'd like to say that I *didn't* hold the soft material to my face and inhale it like it was cocaine and I was an addict falling way off the wagon; I'd *like* to say that, but I'm pretty sure I drifted back to sleep moments later with Stellan's T-shirt fully covering my face.

Maybe I was partially asphyxiated by the fabric, maybe it was the shock of finding him online, or maybe it was all the day's talk of Lapland and those old photographs. Maybe that's why Stellan Virtanen turned up in my sleep.

In the dream, I'm at one of those student parties. It's late at night, the room is packed with people and there are disco lights spinning and sparkling everywhere. Stellan is smiling, his lips swollen from kissing me, and he's leading me by the hand into one of the bedrooms. He lies back on the pile of coats in the dark as the door closes, and I lie down too.

My younger self's body feels long and lithe beside him, and he's so warm. He covers my mouth with his, and I let him, dizzy with the feeling of his full lips and the sound of his breathing. He takes his time, stretching the wide neck of my top down over my shoulder, and his mouth travels across my throat before placing a slow kiss into the hollow above my collar bone. He must be able to feel me trembling.

'Should I stop?' he asks in his heavenly accent as he pulls away cautiously, but I smile and shake my head, guiding his mouth back to mine.

His hand passes over my stomach and comes to a stop cradling my hip bone through my clothes before he shifts his body on top of mine and presses my legs apart with his thighs. He sinks down onto me, letting me feel the weight of his long muscular frame and his hardness through his jeans. I let my head roll back. I've never experienced anything like this before and I don't want him to stop now, or ever.

I pull his plaid shirt off his back, throwing it to the floor, before slowly lifting his T-shirt, letting my fingertips run up his sides, making him inhale sharply. As he breathes hot kisses on my neck, the ends of his clean scented hair fall against my face. My nerves prickle as his hand gently eases inside my jeans and I melt into the slow movement of his fingertips, wanting to arch my back under the weight of his body anchoring me down. In the dark I can see his eyes are open and he's watching me, tantalised and smiling.

And then I wake up.

I lunge for my mobile and quickly type a message for Nari.

> **You said there was a choice of two Lapland destinations? I quite fancy Saariselkä.**

Chapter Three

In late December I can usually hear the Christmas carols blaring out from the kitchen before I even get up my parents' garden path. Their house always looks cosy and festive at this time of year. There are usually two holly bushes decorated with luscious red bows and topiaried into perfect spheres on either side of the porch and long strings of coloured fairy lights running around the window frames, but as I unlatch the gate it strikes me that they may have broken with tradition this year. Maybe Mum's mixing it up a bit and the décor is all indoors for a change.

I ring the bell, knowing just what to expect. Even though it's only the seventeenth of December, Mum will have been cooking for ages, there'll be a big pot of mulled wine on the stove and a Christmas cake ready for cutting taking pride of place amidst the poinsettia and ivy decorations running the length of the dinner table. There'll be a sprig of mistletoe over the living room doorframe and they'll already have stopped a million times beneath it for a parental snog (I've spent my life swinging between extremes of thinking my parents are adorable lovebirds and recoiling in squirming horror – especially in my teenage years – seeing them kissing when they thought nobody was looking). Dad will have polished up all the silverware and a festive aperitif will be waiting for me in a twinkling champagne glass.

As I reach for the doorbell again, wondering why nobody's answering, I'm struck by the strongest memory, the thing I loved best of all about Christmases past, and I can see it now so clearly: an image of Mum and me stirring up homemade Christmas puddings and a humungous, boozy fruit cake on the last Sunday before Advent, adding a gleaming sixpence to each one before they were baked. The sixpences had once belonged to Mum's great, great auntie and were a treasured part of Mum's festive rituals long before I was born. I was supposed to place one of those sixpences inside my shoe on my wedding day; a little reminder of home, family and happy times as I walked down the aisle, a precious token of good luck from Mum. I'm in danger of having a weepy wobble right here on the doorstep, but Dad appears just in time.

'Sylvie! Come in. You're early and we're, um, not quite ready for dinner.' Dad's looking flustered as I head past him to the kitchen. 'Just a minute, Sylve…'

I tell him not to worry, I already kicked my gritty boots off in the porch, but he's still flustering behind me. There are some yummy cooking smells but, I notice, no music, no scented candles and no tree.

'Is Mum ill?'

'Eh, no, dear. Why do you ask?'

'Everything's… different,' I say, as I catch my reflection in the hall mirror which is neither frosted with spray-on snowflakes nor adorned with tinsel. Something's definitely up.

'We thought, since we're going away for Christmas, we needn't bother with the whole palaver this year. No

31

point letting a tree go to waste in an empty house, is there? Anyway, Sylvie...'

'I suppose not.' *Dammit!* Given the sorry state of my flat, I'd been hoping for a dose of familial festive cheer and, whilst I'm busy mourning the loss of Mum's traditional Christmas, I don't mind admitting I'd been looking forward to their obscenely expensive cheeseboard. Mum really goes to town for the holiday season, and I did too, until this year.

In Christmases past I'd have a six foot tree delivered to the Love Shack and even if Cole wasn't around to help decorate it – I can only remember two occasions where he was, now I think about it – I'd make it pretty with the baubles Nari brought home for me from the festive markets she visited on her travels. She knew how much I loved this time of year and always indulged my festive obsession. I just don't know where all that goodwill to mankind went after Cole ran off, but I've definitely lost my Christmas sparkle, and it looks like Mum and Dad have too.

'Hold on, Sylvie, there's someone...' Dad's trying to take my hand as I round the corner into the kitchen, clearly also a Christmas-free zone. I clock Mum looking harassed, standing over a pile of hotdog buns, brandishing a knife as she slits them down the centre. Dad overtakes me inside the doorway and hurriedly takes the knife from her. 'We've got a visitor, actually, Sylvie, love.'

Suddenly, Mum's stormy expression and Dad's agitated blustering make sense. Cole is sitting at the kitchen table nursing a cup of coffee. He's in his pilot's uniform. *Shit!* I hadn't spotted his car outside.

'I tried to tell you, Sylve,' Dad says quietly.

The shock of seeing Cole is overwhelming and my first instinct is to run, but Mum has already crossed the room and has my hand in hers. She's giving me a reassuring look but I know she's seething inside.

'Cole dropped by a moment ago, looking for you,' she says stiffly.

He's standing now and all six foot of him is slowly making its way over the floor towards me.

Don't kiss me, don't kiss me, don't kiss me. I'd hate to collapse in a stupid heap on the floor. Too late, he's bending down towards me. I hold my breath. But he suddenly stops, straightens up and takes a step back. He smells so nice, and so familiar; of spicy aftershave and somehow warm and indoorsy. There's a wary look on his face. Maybe he thinks I'm going to knee him in the balls. His instincts are sharp. I resist the temptation, strong though it is.

'I'm sorry to take you by surprise. I didn't know your new address so I called in to ask Lynn and Malcolm.'

'Oh,' I say.

That's it? Six months of plotting and planning my revenge, six months of imagining how this moment might play out, and all I can manage is 'Oh'. In my fantasy scenarios I'm usually on the arm of a dashing stranger, dressed in a revealing evening gown and towering heels, my hair piled up in a gleaming tumble of curls. We're at some fancy occasion, a Prime Ministerial ball or Royal wedding, you know the sort of thing. I smile viciously with blood-red lips as he crumbles at the sudden devastating realisation that he's passed *all this* up. He falls to the ground and I step over his limp, twitching body, my stilettos piercing his flying jacket. That's how it usually goes.

I hadn't bargained for our first meeting since he dumped me taking place in Mum's kitchen on a night damp and windy enough to have expanded my usually limp hair into a frizzy knotted nest-like affair, and I most definitely didn't plan on greeting him with an unwashed face while wearing a pair of baggy at the knees joggers and a chuffing elf jumper. I look down my body and cringe in shame, letting my carrier bags of Christmas shopping fall to the floor.

Cole looks even better than I remember. Nothing about this is fair.

'What do you want?' I manage, barely able to look at his face. Dad's by my side now too, looping his arm in mine.

'I, uh… I brought these for you; some leftover things I thought you might want from the Love Sh… from the house, now that it's sold.'

He holds out a lidless shoebox. I see dusty bottles of perfume, my cashmere bed socks, my unworn wedding garter belt – a confection of lace and white ribbon, still in its clear box – and a photograph in a frame, the sight of which sends me reeling all over again. It's a picture of Barney. Our dog. My puppy. Dad sees me on the brink of tears and comes to my rescue.

'Let me take your shopping, Sylve. Have a seat in the lounge and I'll bring you a drink. We're trying out some New York nosh tonight and I've got you some root beer to go with your chilli dogs.' He's circling a reassuring palm over my shoulders. 'Will you be staying for dinner, Cole?' he adds, with a curtness I rarely hear in Dad's voice.

'No he won't, thanks Dad,' I say, scowling at Cole who truly looked as though he were about to accept the invitation. Unbelievable! I can see I'm not the only one missing my parents' cosy Christmases. God knows, the alternate years we spent at Patricia's were so relentlessly grim and joyless, he really must regret losing out on the relaxed, cosy welcome of Mum and Dad's festivities.

Mum grabs the shoebox from Cole as we make our way to the living room where only a solitary candelabra on the windowsill lifts the gloom and signals that it's supposed to be the Most Wonderful Time of the Year.

Cole closes the door behind him and comes to perch beside me on the sofa. He's struggling to form his words and I have no intention of helping him out. I watch him as he nervously reaches a fingertip inside his smart collar and tries to loosen it. A big gulp moves his Adam's apple and I emphatically *do not* think about how sexy his throat is.

'So... how have you been?' he manages.

I'm not answering that. What can he possibly expect me to say? I glare at him in silence and pull one of Mum's cushions up over my belly, curling my legs beneath me, wanting to shrink from his gaze and make myself as small as possible.

'Listen, Sylvie. I've been doing a lot of thinking about what happened, and I know I probably owe you an explanation—'

'*Duh!* You think?' I butt in, enjoying being sarcastic when he's trying to share his feelings.

'Sylvie,' he chastises me. 'It's been really hard for me to accept what I did. You don't know what it's been like, living with this guilt.'

'Excuse me if my heart doesn't bleed for you, Cole. What do you think it's been like for me? Ditched a week before our wedding! And you just disappeared like that. Nobody would tell me where you were, not even your mother. What was I supposed to do? Mum and Dad had to deal with all the wedding stuff. They lost so much money, Cole. Where were you then? Then all I get are your solicitor's letters telling me not to expect a penny from the sale of *your* house. And now you rock up here as casual as you like and wanting to stay for dinner!' I don't mention Barney; if I do, I'll cry and I point blank refuse to let him see that.

'I know it's unforgivable, I know! I just freaked out. The wedding came around so suddenly and I panicked and I... I ran.'

'You don't think ten years was a long enough build-up to our wedding? You needed a bit longer?'

'I know that nothing I say will stop you hating me. I just... really needed to see you.'

He suddenly shifts over towards me and takes my left hand in his, running his thumb over the spot once encircled by his engagement ring. He frowns, stoops his head and, after a tiny hesitation, kisses the spot, still soft and bearing the smooth indentation from a decade of pressure from the golden band. His lips are warm and I feel a mood of defeat begin to creep over me as, at last, I look into his troubled eyes.

I'm going to try to brazen this out; he can't see me weakening. 'Cole. You can't just walk back into my life after six months.' Then it hits me. We'd be going on our honeymoon in five days' time. Is he here hoping for a reconciliation? Has he had some time to think and calm down and now he wants us to go on our honeymoon together, even though he skipped out on the actual wedding bit of the whole arrangement?

'I need to ask you one question and then I'll get out of your life forever, if that's what you want.'

I feel my eyes widening and my pulse picking up. He's struggling to find the words to say what's coming next and a tense silence spreads in the space between us. He squeezes my hand and I can't tell if he's trying to reassure me or himself.

I watch him take a deep breath. *I knew it!* He's come crawling back. He can't live without me.

Mixed in with the feelings of triumph and self-satisfaction there's something else, something I'm too delirious to recognise as trepidation.

'You see, I really *had* to come see you today,' he says in a low voice, his eyes still cast down at my hand. 'It's um… it's…'

'It's because you miss me.'

Cole draws his hand away.

'Um, I was going to say… it's my mum.'

What the actual fuck? My mouth clamps shut.

'She wants the ring back.'

Well, I was *not* expecting that. The world spins off its axis and my stomach lurches in response. All I can do is fold my arms tightly over the cushion and inwardly count to ten, trying not to scream.

He knows I'm counting, and he lets me – he's seen me do this often enough in the past, it's my way of calming myself down, though, it strikes me, I haven't needed to run through these numbers for months now.

Eventually I'm able to speak again. 'She what?' It's more of a growl than actual words but he gets my drift.

'You remember it was my grandmother's? Mum says it's a family heirloom, so I have to get it back. She wants to give it to her granddaughter.' He's sheepish now. At least he has the good grace to be ashamed of running this horrible errand. Bloody mummy's boy.

'Granddaughter? Not Clementine? She's already got the four boys! Poor woman.'

Cole shakes his head, and I think for a moment before laughing wickedly.

'Has *Kelvin* got someone pregnant?' The thought of Cole's weedy, layabout younger brother even so much as talking to a woman seems wholly implausible, let alone the idea that he might have impregnated one.

As I'm saying all this, I notice the look on Cole's face, like a bold little boy caught stealing in a sweetshop. He seems... not ashamed, exactly, but he has a look of cheeky chagrin, as though he's been rumbled and is enjoying the powerless shopkeeper's haranguing.

The world lists again and I try to rein in my shock so he doesn't see it. 'It's you. *You're* having a baby.'

I don't remember much else, just a few snatches of Cole's voice, weak and cowardly. She's a girl in his cabin crew... twelve-week scan... and the time's never really right to start a family, is it? But he's excited anyway and...

I'm half aware of Dad showing Cole to the door with a civil restraint he definitely doesn't deserve, and it's possible, just possible, that I shouted out something about fucking the fuck off and never coming back, but I can't be sure. And that was it.

Poor Mum and Dad's New York *bon voyage* celebration begins and ends with them cradling their daughter on her childhood bed as she wails her heart out for all that she's lost. The last thing I register before I fall asleep is Dad muttering under his breath to Mum, 'That bloody *bastard*! Why did I let him in?'

Chapter Four

Nari Bell, travel writer and lone adventurer.

This is my #nomadgirl blog. One woman, one great big world to explore.

I'm a romantic, I'm a realist, I prefer the road less travelled. I'm at home anywhere and everywhere but am especially close to Seoul and Glasgow (my parents' home cities) and Cheshire, where I hang my hat.

–

Welcome back, and a big Hello to all my new followers.

Today is my blogiversary! Ten whole years travelling the world, exploring the culture, art, history and food of other countries, sharing it all with you, my readers, through stories and photos.

If you're new to the site, expect blogs about independent escapes and all the ups and downs of flying solo with one aim in mind: inspiring you to venture outside your comfort zone.

I started this blog a decade ago, combining my old dating blog with my passion for international getaways. And I know some of you loyal fans miss the old days where the blog was more *Sex And The City* than city break travel hacks, but I'm very much your lone travel guru these days.

I'm feeling pretty proud of what I've achieved since me and my blog set off on that first trip a decade ago (spending a sunny winter discovering Agadir and Ouarzazate, and occasionally spilling the deets about hot dates under the date palms) but, even back then, the essence of my blog was there: I travelled alone, relying only on me, my passport, my camera and my GPS. I'll tell you what I wanted back then (and still want now) from travelling:

1. A window seat with a vacant chair beside mine
2. Unlimited currency (I wish) to spend on ALL the local food
3. Freedom to go any place I please (and to take you, gorgeous readers, with me)
4. A holiday romance (even if, nowadays, that's in fictional form. I'll always pack one romcom novel – or download one hundred – and let you know if I recommend them for your own travels)

So, who's coming with me as I plan a whole new year of adventure, starting with a snowy escape in Lapland? This one's a real departure for me as I'm going with my best friend, S, but I'll be sure to blog everything we get up to.

Remember to hit subscribe, and comment below with your own travel plans.

Kisses, Nari Bell.

#Celebrating #tenyears #solotravel #intrepid #Suitmyself #Nomadgirl #FemaleSoloTravel #beachreads #IndependentGetaways #adventuretravelgoals #fearless #female

Chapter Five

Cole's surprise visit was two days ago now and it's astonishing what you can achieve on emotional autopilot. I drove Mum and Dad to the airport yesterday and waved them off. We all managed to smile and I think they were close to conquering their concern for me and getting excited again about their big adventure. They suggested we have a family dinner on the thirtieth (Nari included) when they return and we'll exchange gifts then, so in a way I'll get two Christmases, which is something to be glad about, but even so, Cole really does know how to put a big fat dampener on everything.

I've had a couple of sleepless nights to think over Cole's baby news, wondering exactly how long he's been with this cabin crew girl if she's already three months gone. If I'd had my wits about me, I might have asked if she was the reason he called off the wedding, but the shock was just too much for coherent thought back at Mum and Dad's the other night, and I really, really don't think I could handle any more new information right now. Ditched Bride? OK, that's fine, I guess; but Gullible Cheated-on Fiancée? It doesn't bear thinking about. Though of course, I *have* been thinking about it, and have the sunken black eyes to prove it.

And that's not all that's been niggling away at me, if I'm honest. Since Cole's visit I'd known there was something I had to do and it had been making me even more anxious. Now it's over with, I suppose you could say I'm relieved.

On my way home from the airport I called in at Patricia Jordan's house. After making sure Cole's car wasn't parked outside, I summoned up all my courage to ring her door-bell. The wait for her to answer felt interminable.

She blanched noticeably when she discovered me standing on her doorstep. I didn't give her much processing time, I simply put her mother's precious ring into her hand and said in my biggest, proudest, most dignified voice, 'I believe you wanted your ring back? Consider it returned. Cole and I have no further business together so if you want any other errands running ask *the new girl.'*

She didn't say a word but I know she watched me as I walked back to my car. I kept my head up all the way, even though my legs were wobbling. Once I was safely back in the driver's seat with the door locked (irrational, I know; women like Patricia Jordan don't run after ex daughters-in-law so they can shout at them like fishwives in the street), I drove around the corner, pulled to a stop in the car park of a veterinary surgery, and I cried out all the nervous energy that seeing Patricia again had generated, hoping nobody was watching.

As I'd rung her doorbell, it had all came flooding back, all the strange tension that had hung in the air at every encounter we'd ever had, even when we were meant to be enjoying a family meal in her smart dining room or at one of Cole's legendary barbecues at the Love Shack – the only times he ever set foot in the garden of that

43

place. There was always something amiss, and I'd never fully understood what it was.

We'd hit it off relatively well enough, in the first moment that we met. She'd looked me over and told me she'd always known that one day Cole would 'bring home a supermodel'. I'd laughed and brushed off the ridiculous compliment at the time. It had taken years to realise that it hadn't been a compliment at all, but was, in fact, an affront. Patricia's weapon of choice was to think the worst of someone but smile and say the exaggerated opposite. Over the years I'd heard that kind of thing many times.

'Sylvie, you're working so hard at that school, the weight's just *dropping* off you, and I don't know *how* you manage to look so rested.' That's Patricia for: 'You're overweight *and* you're haggard through overwork'.

Or I'd be told, 'IKEA curtains, you say? Well, Clementine could learn a lot from you when it comes to scrimping and saving with the housekeeping.' A Patricia double whammy, flagging her dislike of my cheap and cheerful furnishings while also undermining poor absent Clementine and her elegant, expensive tastes.

The long and the short of the situation, I realised, was that there was no way of pleasing the woman.

When I worked part-time she teased Cole over seemingly never-ending lunches at her house about how wonderful he was for taking extra flights in order to 'keep me in the manner to which I'd become accustomed.' And when I moved to working a five-day week, she'd wondered aloud at how I was managing to run a house with only the help of online grocery deliveries and doggy day care for Barney: 'I don't know how you do it, Sylvie, always juggling. I'm sure if I tried it, there'd be absolute chaos and my home would resemble a bombsite.'

If I'd prepared us all a meal she'd tell me how she'd recently dined in a restaurant where she'd ordered the exact same dish and it had been 'cooked to perfection' there. If I talked about holiday plans with Cole she'd let me know how a couple in her extended circle of friends had visited the same resort and found it 'fuddy-duddy' but then would say, 'you never know, *you* might like it Sylvie, dear.'

And all the while, as Patricia smiled placidly and launched her little spite grenades, Cole would sit by her side, utterly unaware, shovelling a towering barbequed burger into his mouth, content in the knowledge that Patricia wholeheartedly approved of everything he did, and thinking how convenient it was that the women in his life got along so well.

Much later on, when I'd given up striving for an ounce of approval from her, I'd broached with Cole the idea that his mother might not be very keen on me, and that, in fact, she might be a perfectly permed, passive-aggressive narcissist with a smattering of son-worshipping Oedipal weirdness. He'd just laughed loudly with the usual slack-jawed incredulity that any of my protests were met with.

'Mum?' he'd say. 'No, Sylve, you're being paranoid. I know she loves you, really, and she's been *so good* to you over the years.'

So I gave up pointing out her little jellyfish sting asides, instead storing them up and spilling them to Nari during late night phone calls when Cole was away.

'You're in Bates Motel territory with those two, Sylve,' she'd said. 'If the motel were done out in Farrow & Ball "Wimborne White" and new season Laura Ashley chintz.'

–

Having at last faced my recent hideous past, I sat in my car, clutching the steering wheel with white knuckles. After sobbing for a good ten minutes, I attracted the concerned attention of the vet's assistant as he popped out to the shop on the corner, so I blew my nose and hurriedly left the scene.

Confronting the crinkly old bat had felt like one great big leap towards leaving Cole behind, not a great feeling exactly, but a positive one nonetheless.

After a short while in self-imposed solitary confinement (eight hours straight watching QVC with a box of Milk Tray – thank you, little Selina Dawson in year nine), I dusted myself down and put my festive game face on.

By this morning, the nineteenth of December, all my presents for Mum, Dad, the extended family and, of course, Nari, were wrapped and under my twinkling tree – my only concession to the season. Having sorted out the house, I turned to Cole's shoebox, tipping the contents into the kitchen bin, saving only the cashmere socks and the photo of Barney.

The picture was taken on the day I found him when he was just a few months old – nobody at the rescue centre knew how old exactly – and he's sitting on his fat, wrinkled little bottom and gazing up at me with big soppy Labrador eyes. It hurt to put his picture up there on my mantelpiece but I'm hoping in time the pain will ease a bit. Anyway, I'd resolved not to cry any more so I gave myself a stern talking to and locked away the memories, at least for a while. Thinking about what happened with Barney is just too much, given my December so far.

–

Nari took me to the out of town shopping mall to pick up some Lapland essentials this morning. With festive music and the smell of coffee and fast food in the stifling air, we made our way to one of those outdoorsy stores, the kind of place where you'd buy a tent and a tin mug. I've never set foot inside one before but Nari was clutching a list and was a woman on a mission, so I let her take control. As she inspected the microwavable hand warmers, I told her Cole's baby daddy news and her summation of the situation was, I must say, succinct, if a bit unpleasant.

'Good riddance to him, the great steaming turd.'

'Quite. But, honestly, I feel OK about it. In fact I don't really feel anything. I think it was the perfect closure.'

'Good. You needed some. Hopefully by the time we get on board that plane you'll be totally clear-headed and ready to chill.'

'Literally chill?'

Nari laughed and rummaged through a rail of thermal long johns. 'Yep! You'll need some of these, but buy a men's size small; they fit better than the women's ones under your snowsuit, less pinchy round the waistband.'

'*Must* they be this colour? They're godawful.' I inserted my finger into the beige flap at the front, pulling a squeamish face and realising this wasn't going to be a glamorous holiday. Of course, Nari's got everything she needs for snowy travel, having skied in Aspen, trekked in

Mongolia, and seen polar bears in Alaska. I'm the cold weather newbie. 'How many layers will I need? Two?'

'Try four... as well as a snow suit.'

'You're kidding?'

'We'll be outside for long stretches in minus twenty degree temperatures and waist-high snow drifts. You'll be glad I made you buy hideous flappy men's drawers,' Nari said, having bundled multiple pairs into the basket.

'What's next on your list?'

'Convert some cash into Euros. Then its balaclavas, ear muffs, merino vests and socks and then... you're sorted. And I think we should grab a hot chocolate so we can get in training for drinking pints of the stuff on holiday.'

I followed her dutifully to the checkout, mumbling as I went. 'Balaclavas and ear muffs? Ooh, I am going to look all kinds of hot in Lapland.'

—

Nari had been enthusing about Frozen Falls resort for ten minutes, telling me all about the husky-sledding and reindeer led sleigh rides through winter fairylands, and how our cabins overlook a wooded hillside, when she'd stopped suddenly. At first, I hadn't realised and I'd carried on fiddling with the candy cane that had arrived bobbing in my hot chocolate. We were sitting at the bar in a donut concession and I'd barely sipped my drink.

'Sylve? Sylvie? Wakey wakey!'

I looked up to see her eyes narrowed and suspicious. 'Sorry, I was miles away.'

'I could see that... and you were *smiling*.'

'No I wasn't!'

'And now you're blushing! OK, spill it. What's going on?'

With a groan I realised I'd have to tell her. 'All right, but promise you won't make fun of me?'

'As if I would.' This would have been more convincing if she hadn't drawn an invisible halo around her head with her finger and brought her hands together like a praying angel, but leery and desperate for some gossip.

'Do you remember Stellan?' I said.

'Was he the guy who fitted your new taps a fortnight ago?'

'Jesus no, Nari! I told you about him ages ago, back at uni when you and I first met? My first proper boyfriend, Stellan?'

The penny dropped and she was bubbling with intrigue. 'The Hot Viking? Of course I remember you telling me about him. What's his name, Stellan…?'

'Virtanen.'

'Ooh, fancy! What sort of name's that again?'

'Finnish, I guess? It means calm river, at least that's what he told me on the night we met, and he wasn't the type to embellish things. In fact he was so earnest and serious I doubt he could lie about anything.'

'Calm river? I like it.'

'That's how we met. Did I never tell you about that night?' I said, and she pulled a face that suggested she was unsure, so I filled her in. 'It was my second year at uni, the first week of the autumn term, and I was handing out the name badges at a social event for the new intake of exchange students – I always was one for volunteering, if it meant I got to meet new people and wield a clipboard – and he arrived with his mates. I ticked his name off my guest list and told him I had a Scandinavian name too and we got talking. His parents were both Finnish, but there was some Swedish somewhere along the line, if I'm remembering correctly, and he'd always lived in Finnish Lapland. I had to tell him that no one in my family really knew much about our Scandi roots, only the name Magnusson remained. Anyway, it was all a bit stilted at first; he was so reserved and hard to talk to.'

'That's weird, I remember you reminiscing about him that night we did the flaming Sambucas, and you said he was *without doubt* the hottest lover you'd ever had? It didn't sound to me as though you had problems communicating, at least not in the bedroom.'

A harassed mother sitting behind Nari reached over to her pre-schooler son and covered his ears with her hands, shooting a scowl at me.

'Keep your voice down, Nari! Yes, he was totally… what you said. I couldn't figure out why he was so awkward with me, and the other girls for that matter, and yet he was so relaxed with his mates. When I asked him, he told me that where he was brought up the boys were always a bit shy and they'd wait till the girls came to them, and then usually nobody approached anybody.'

'*Really?* That sounds awful!' Nari was wrinkling her nose and spooning whipped cream from her steaming cup into her mouth.

'It's a thing apparently; the boys don't get much practice chatting up girls, and I suppose that stayed with him into his twenties.'

'So you helped him out, did you?'

Laughing, I'd kept my eyes cast down at my drink. 'He didn't need much help once we got to know each other, but it took a while for him to thaw.'

'So... what about him?'

'Oh! Well... when you sorted out our trip, I remembered he was from somewhere near Saariselkä. His family owned hotels and a husky dog centre there, I imagine they still do, they can't be that old. And... I looked him up on Facebook and sent him a friend request.'

'Nice work, Sylve! And what did he say? Was he pleased to hear from you? Is he married? Got kids? Is he still blisteringly hot and brooding? Not that I ever saw him, his exchange trip ended just a few weeks before I met you, right? I remember you crying about him the very first time I spoke to you at the undergrads' Christmas lunch. But from what you told me, he was a real hottie...'

She was really enjoying this, I could tell. She was spilling mini marshmallows all over the bar and grinning madly. I took a long drink and left her in agony.

Eventually, feeling abashed because I realised I'd built this whole Stellan story up to a massive anticlimax, I had to admit, 'He hasn't responded, actually.'

'Maybe he's dead,' Nari offered unhelpfully.

'Right, well, thanks for that. Maybe he just doesn't remember me?'

My mind instantly flitted to my dream and I wondered if it was possible for someone to forget the kind of connection we had. My heart sank at the thought that maybe he had it with everyone. Maybe he travelled across Europe giving every woman he met multiple orgasms and a lifetime of yearning memories.

'I wish I hadn't looked for him on Facebook now. The whole thing's stupid and juvenile. It was, what, fifteen years ago now?'

'What happened with him? Apart from the Sambuca night revelations, you haven't talked about him for years. But he must have been pretty special to get you in a tizz like this.'

I'd tilted my mug towards Nari, showing her the froth at the bottom. 'If I'm going to tell you *that*, I'll definitely need another one of these. Mint chocolate this time, please.'

And so, I told her. The *whole* thing.

–

I've always been pretty easy to read, a heart on my sleeve kind of girl, but Stellan really took the wind out of my sails when my inept teenage flirting didn't seem to be getting me anywhere. I started to wonder if he liked girls at all, and then I was worried it was just me he didn't like.

One night I asked him straight out whether he fancied me – we'd had quite a few drinks at the student bar – and he finally opened up and told me that he *thought* I'd been flirting with him but was worried he had his wires crossed and he didn't want to disrespect me. By then, I'd been in his Friend Zone for weeks and was desperate for him to seriously disrespect me, but his concern was so sweet, and nothing like the other boys I'd been dating since I was seventeen (by which I mean snogging in dodgy nightclubs, and alright, that started when I was fifteen, but keep up with the story, please).

We started getting together after lectures and slowly he opened up, telling me about his family – who he really admired – and his hobbies back home. He'd cook for me and we'd make out and not do any exam revision. The thing was, he was only taking part in the exchange programme for one semester and I knew that come Christmas, he'd be gone. But, I didn't hold back, I liked him too much for that. Short-term relationship or not, I just wanted to make the most of the time we had together.

It took us nearly the whole semester to get really close, just getting to know each other's bodies slowly. I think that's what made it so special between us. Other guys would have been pressuring me into bed but he wasn't like that at all. And based on all previous experience, I'd had no idea a guy could be so hot *and* so considerate. Meeting Stellan was like expecting yet more bath salts and unwrapping a Fabergé egg. In the end though, I guess I rushed him. I wanted more and more, emotionally I mean, and he pulled away. I was so young, and we both had our degrees to finish, I wasn't thinking clearly about what kind of long-term, long-distance future we might have together, or anything like that, all I knew was I'd fallen for him, and hard.

He left early, at the beginning of December, right in the middle of the winter exams, and I carried on at uni alone, without him. I missed him so much. I just couldn't understand why he'd disappeared like that.

We'd known each other for a couple of months by then, ten weeks at most, and we'd only had actual, proper sex a few days before he took off, and that's when I'd told him I loved him. I'd even learned how to say it in Finnish – I thought it would be so cute and he'd say it back and we'd joke about my pronunciation and fall into bed laughing.

How wrong I was! He just looked at me, all sceptical, and told me that where he came from people only said they loved each other if they really, really meant it, or if they were dying or something.

The thing is, I *did* mean it, but I guess he wasn't sure of me. I was two years younger than him, which is a lot when you're a teenager. Maybe he thought I was some love-struck kid. Anyway, off he went, and I never spoke with him again. And I don't mind admitting, I was devastated.

At the risk of sounding like Old Mother Time, this was in the days before Instagram and WhatsApp, and we just didn't keep in touch. *What?* We were all too busy listening to James Blunt, wearing pashminas and following our Atkins diets. It was the early noughties, OK! An age ago. And he knew where I was. He could have got in touch, if he'd wanted to.

So I bumbled on, heartbroken. At the end of our degrees, me and Nari moved in together and she encouraged me to go on some (pretty unsatisfying) dates, and then I met Cole just before I graduated with my teaching qualification. I was twenty-four by then and already a part-time classroom assistant, and we quickly moved in together.

If I'm making comparisons, maybe there wasn't any great passion there, but he was bold and glamorous, and he arrived like a breath of fresh air at the end of what had become a stale, monotonous slog through my studies. We settled down and enjoyed blowing our combined incomes, and we got Barney, and snatched a few summer weekends in Cornwall and spent our Christmases – when Cole wasn't flying – snuggled up together. Perfect, right? Until his cold feet carried him away.

The stark reality of all those years wasted with Cole and the last of my girlhood squandered on him always brings back the familiar ache in my chest. And I'm back where I was at the start, only now I'm thirty-four, single and alone and, thanks to Nari and her clever travel ideas, I'm giving far too much head space to an old flame who was last seen hightailing it for the Arctic Circle faster than I could say, 'minä rakastan sinua'.

That's 'I love you' in Finnish, if you're slow on the uptake.

Chapter Six

Hello stranger! I'll be in your town over Christmas. Care to show a girl the sights? If it still is your town? You could be anywhere these days, but anyway, I'm coming to Lapland, Sylvie, xoxo

Oh my God, no! Delete, delete, delete.

Hi Stellan. Just letting you know I'll be in Saariselkä with a friend for Christmas, if you happen to be at your parents and free to meet up for a cup of glögi. No pressure, obvs p.s. my friend's a girl, with a boyfriend, well sort of, he's more of a shag-buddy than anything. What I'm saying is, I'm single.

His beautiful Finnish wife will love reading that, for goodness' sakes. Delete. This is impossible. OK, how about…

> **Hi, it's Sylvie Magnusson from Uni. I'm spending Christmas somewhere near your parents' resort. Maybe message me if you are around? All the best, Sylve**

And… send. It took half an hour and a stiff gin to compose that rubbish. I don't know why I'm getting so wound up. He hasn't even accepted my friend request, not that I'm checking every twenty minutes.

Right, I've had it with this! I've got to get some sleep. Nari's picking me up for the airport at four a.m. and I've still got to get Finnish sauna ready. Nari's already threatened to drag me to one, so I'd best shave my legs. And I've neglected my roots all winter, so I'd better touch them up a bit. There's a box of dye in the bathroom cabinet. I wonder if Stellan likes redheads, well, bottle-red heads?

Ugh! Why am I doing this to myself? He's in his mid-thirties, we haven't seen each other for fifteen years, and we were together for mere weeks before he bolted. It's hardly the love story of the century. I'm boring myself now, thinking of him – or what only really amounts to hazy memories of him. I need to remember he was the first guy to run out on me; my first broken heart, and it really did hurt. Why am I letting him get in my head like this? Time seems to have worn away the sharp corners of my memories of Stellan. It was so long ago, it's somehow easier to remember the lovely bits, and reminiscing over a gorgeous teenage boyfriend has made a refreshing change from moping over Cole, but this just isn't healthy. Right, I'm done. His name won't pass my lips again.

I go through my hand luggage one last time. Tickets, passport, euros. I guess that's it. I'm ready. My suitcase is positively bulging and I have to sit on it to get it zipped up.

Earlier today, me and Nari tried on all our cold weather gear back at her place, layering it up until I looked like the Michelin Man's pastel pink cousin. Nari opted for classic white instead and I'm regretting my choices now.

The dreaded long johns went on first with a thermal vest, then a black merino wool mid-layer like a baby's sleepsuit, then a thick pink fleecy top and bottoms, stretchy under-gloves with pink ski gloves on top, then a pink balaclava thing, a bobble hat and scarf. I was sweltering and that was *before* I put on my pink snowsuit. Nari says we'll be provided with proper arctic snowsuits and boots when we check in at the lodges, but I liked the look of the pink one in the shop and couldn't resist. Stephen's PA let Frozen Falls know our sizes and she's sorted out some on-resort surprises too, apparently. Nari said all this while still managing to look cool and glamorous in her umpteen layers of winter white wool. I, on the other hand, was an itchy, sweaty mess with a polyester induced static electricity problem. Why am I bothering shaving my legs for this?

After the year I've had, all I want to do is recline in a bubbling hot tub, see the snowy sights, and catch up on some sleep. Nari might have a similar idea. She told me she was packing her laptop for working on the blog, a bundle of steamy novels and a selection of Korean facemasks her mum sent her, so I guess she's got her evenings sorted. I'll pick up some magazines at the airport. Since the summer and all the upheaval of moving house and losing Barney I haven't exactly been able to settle to reading anything that requires much attention, which made marking the kids' exam papers and homework sheets pretty tricky. Unless, of course… There is something in my bedroom that would make interesting holiday reading.

I go in search of it. It's so spacious round here, now that I've finally blitzed Box Mountain and found a place for everything. In fact, the flat feels much more like home today. It was quite nice seeing all my old familiar belongings after so long, and I sorted through that box of Uni stuff too, and that's where I found it, my diary from 2004, the year I met… you know who.

All right, just a quick peek before I de-fuzz and retouch. Just a page or two. I turn my diary over in my hands. There are pictures of the boys from Busted stuck all over the covers, and here was me thinking I was all cultured and grown up at nineteen. I open it up somewhere around the centre pages. It's an academic diary so that just happens to be nearing the middle of the winter semester.

> *Twenty-ninth of November. Missed the history lecture again today. That's the third one this month. Not good. But it was sooo good having the flat to ourselves. SV made lunch, a sort of smashed chickpea thing on toasted baguette slices. He is so sophisticated. I offered to do him a Pot Noodle but he wasn't keen. He was, however, pretty keen on what I had planned for dessert. ME!*

Bloody Hell, Sylve! Back then I was sure I was a suave mixture of Sylvia Plath's searing intellect, with all the irresistible sensuality of Linda Evangelista, and the rock sensibilities of a north of England Courtney Love, but this is toe-curlingly cringe-inducing stuff. And I can't stop reading. Before I know it, half an hour's passed and I've devoured every salacious morsel about his wonderful kisses, and how amazing he smells, and how dreamy his eyes are. I obviously kept the details of my tentative teenage sexual shenanigans pretty brief – I'm not sure why I did this; Mum wasn't the type to go snooping in diaries when I was at home between semesters – but there's lots of none too subtle code words, such as me wondering if instead of just undressing each other and making out, we'd finally DTD (Do The Deed). Clever, Sylve. Real Alan Turing, Enigma code stuff.

But what really shocks me is how obviously good my Finnish boyfriend was for my self-esteem. I hadn't really thought about it before, but one entry in my embarrassing teenage journal really brings it home and I stop wincing and smile as I read.

> *This morning we were just lying in each other's arms in bed and I needed to get up for a drink of water. I was trying to find my clothes without getting out from under the duvet and he asked what I was doing. I told him I didn't want him seeing me naked in the harsh daylight and he said the sweetest thing to me. He said, 'Please don't hide your body away. You are a woman with a woman's body. Enjoy being this body. It is strong, it is feeling, it is you.' OK, maybe he didn't say*

exactly those words, I've made him sound weird,
but it was something like that. So I got up and
walked to the kitchen in the buff – bare arsed all
the way. He says this kind of thing to me all the
time.

I close the diary, a wave of nostalgia flooding over me as I remember how, that semester, I really took his words to heart. I was happier then than I'd ever been. And maybe it wasn't just his words; it was the way he looked at me, the way he touched me, like I was the most perfect thing he'd ever seen. And he wasn't shy about his own body at all. Quite the opposite.

Reading this reminds me how insecure I'd been as a teenager, like everyone else, but I *know* I wasn't born trying to hide my body. It makes me think of all those awkward formative years spent comparing myself to other girls, thinking how I'd be happy once I slimmed down this bit or waxed or tanned or straightened that bit.

As I head to the bathroom to apply the dye to my mousey roots it strikes me that over the years I've slipped back into those old bad habits and I realise that I can remember pretty much every single negative comment anyone's ever made about my looks or my shape, but I had no memory at all of him saying these nice things to me, or indeed of any of the nice things other people might have said to me over the years.

There must have been *some* compliments, but only the bad stuff sticks in my mind and I replay it all to myself every now and again when I'm feeling crap; like the time Cole suggested that I lay off the red wine and tea as he handed me a leaflet about cosmetic teeth whitening, or that woman with the tape measure in the bra fitting cubicle who told me I could 'minimise my back fat' with the right kind of support. Cheeky cow. So basically, I end up trolling myself with this stuff, which really isn't on. But he – oh, all right, *Stellan* – didn't believe anyone had imperfections or flaws, and he just saw me. I repeat this to myself in the bathroom mirror with a smile and a shrug as a blob of red dye plops down my forehead and onto the tip of my nose. He just saw me.

After I rinse the colour off and blast my hair dry, I quickly check Facebook once more, telling myself this really has to be the last time. And… nothing. There's some photos of Mum and Dad grinning in front of the Empire State Building and a message from them hoping I have a great trip, but there's no new 'friends'. I shut down my laptop, also trying to shut down the hopeful little butterfly feelings in my stomach telling me how much I'd hoped to hear from him before jetting off.

The thing about nostalgia for the past, I find myself thinking as I get ready for bed, is that everything is rose-tinted; you recollect the best bits and magnify them, and no wonder, really. I'd rather remember Stellan – and Cole for that matter – in those first exciting, happy days, when we were just finding out about each other, and when everyone's on their best behaviour and still very much wearing their nicest underwear.

Maybe the problem with all this Stellan nostalgia is that we never had the chance to get to the saggy old pants stage? I never saw him asleep and drooling on the sofa wearing sweaty gym gear on a Saturday morning. I never had to squeeze past his muddy track bike and umpteen pairs of his expensive trainers in the hall as I struggled inside with the groceries. I never had to accompany his grandmother on her trips to the chiropodist because nobody else could be bothered taking her. Yes, you've guessed it, all things I experienced with Cole.

Nostalgia only works for those with the luxury of never having seen the humdrum reality of how things would have turned out. And even though Stellan ran off and broke my teenage heart, I still manage to remember him making me supremely happy and being an utterly delicious human being. If I don't let myself think about how it ended, I can accurately claim the relationship was one hundred per cent blissful, until it suddenly wasn't.

I put the diary back where it belongs in the box marked 'university', folded away with the photos and Stellan's T-shirt, and I shove the box into the back of my wardrobe. It's been fun, in a way, looking back, but I've done so much of that lately. Stellan could be anywhere in the world now (goodness knows, he spoke so many languages, he'd be employable pretty much anywhere), and of course, he'll be in love with someone, and no doubt he's a devoted daddy too.

I shut the wardrobe door. It's for the best that I leave the fantasy of Stellan in the past where he belongs with the scatty, happy, drunk-with-love nineteen-year-old Sylvie. The grown-up me is going on a cosy retreat with her best mate to the land of Christmas trees and snow trails, husky dogs and hot spiced wine, and I'm so excited I doubt I'll get any sleep tonight.

Chapter Seven

Hello readers, Nari Bell here!

It's late, and I have an early flight to beautiful Finnish Lapland tomorrow, so this'll be a quick one.

After a conversation with S, my closest friend, I got thinking about Finland and one national stereotype in particular I feel like busting open…

But first. Researching this trip I discovered the following: A UN report has found for the second year running that Finland is the happiest country in the world (based on quality of life stuff, wealth and schooling). It's also the most forested place on the planet. Trees − happiness, no surprises there. It is also the safest country in the world (low crime, safe roads, good hospitals, that kind of thing). People don't mind paying higher taxes to get these things too. It all sounds pretty perfect to me: beautiful place, and kind, generous people.

Then I found a survey, and OK, it was a dodgy looking thing from an online news source from a decade ago, but it said that Finnish men who date women are twenty-five times less likely to tell their partner they love her within the first six months than Swedish men. I've also discovered that Finnish women are increasingly marrying men of other nationalities. Can the two be connected? Are my Finnish sisters getting sick of non-committal, undemonstrative boyfriends and hooking up with hot Americans, sexy Scots, or those declarative Swedes who are, allegedly, dropping the L-bomb all over the shop?

So, I dug a bit deeper, trawling dating and travel forums and YouTuber blogs so you don't have to, and there did seem to be plenty of anecdotal evidence supporting the theory that Finnish blokes really are more reticent about talking about their feelings, and this can be pretty frustrating for their significant others.

When it comes to generalisations about this kind of thing I'm cautious, but curious. I know the idea's blown out of the water by the mixed demography of Finland that shows us this tiny population's a melting pot like any other European place, a huge variety of languages are spoken there and, I guess what I'm saying is, there's no monolithic Finnish Man. And yet, Disgruntled Girlfriends of The Internet are telling me their Finnish boyfriends need to get with the programme when it comes to sharing their feelings. They describe attractive, calm, reserved, respectful, taciturn men who love nature, value solitude, have a connection to the land and the seasons, love to feed people, and are prone to joking at your expense as an easy way of showing affection. So, all in all, these Finnish Men, whoever they are, if they even exist, sound pretty good.

Now, you know I left my dating blog behind a long time ago, and I'm determined to get the *travel* lowdown on Lapland for you all, but if me and my friend, S, happen to discover if there's any truth to the myth of the shy Finnish fellas, all the better. Check back soon for an update when I'll be touching down in snowy Inari.

#NariInInari #Girlsholiday

Chapter Eight

'Just look at this place!'

Nari lifts up one side of her sleep mask in acknowledgement of my excited dig at her elbow. The flaps have just opened and the loud clunk of the wheels coming down somewhere underneath us finally jolts her to full wakefulness.

Low mountains brood over the Lappish plains. Stretched out in the grey-blue expanse below are the strange shapes of fir trees bent under the weight of snow and what I first assume are white roads, before realising they're frozen rivers. From up here it looks as though there are no motorways, no streetlights, and no buildings as far as I can see, just miles and miles of wide open, infinite space.

Back in Castlewych you can't walk for ten minutes without railway lines or canals dissecting your path. The town's horribly cut up by B-roads and claustrophobically cut off by motorways, housing developments, and the out of town shopping centres that are slowly replacing the real, old town centre. This place, on the other hand, seems endlessly wild and unpopulated. Everything looks barren and alien, and our flight is making its descent into the strange snowy world.

Nari barely glances towards the window. She's such a seasoned traveller. She even remembered to slather on moisturiser and down a bottle of mineral water as soon as she buckled her lap belt, and within minutes she was sleeping soundly, even during the bumpy six a.m. take off through blustery Manchester sleet. I tried to sleep too, but ended up uncomfy, crick-necked and grumpy, so I'd reaching for my battered old copy of *The Kalevala*, once a treasured possession during my nerdy early-teen obsession with Scandi myths and legends. I'd struggled to read more than a few verses in the low light of the noisy cabin, so I gave up, watching old episodes of *Friends* on the in-flight entertainment system instead.

Nari looks fresh and rested as the plane smoothly touches down and she slicks on lip balm and ties her hair back. I know I look a fright but it hardly matters, we'll soon be covered from head to toe in bulky snow gear.

As the plane door opens, the entire fuselage fills with icy arctic air and everyone, except the Laplanders travelling home for Christmas, exclaims at once.

Soon we're walking across the airstrip, breathing in the strange mixture of frigid air and jet fuel. Note that I didn't call it an airport. There's a terminal building – basically a large-ish glass shed – and that's it, the only building for what looks like miles around.

As I slide my feet along, trying not to fall over on the icy tarmac, I pull my pink bobble hat down over my ears and stuff my thin undergloves and snow mittens on as fast as I can. The cold is already biting and I'm shivering.

So this is snow. *Real* snow. There are ten-foot drifts of the stuff piled up at the sides of the runway. How the hell did the plane land in this? And how come this place stays open in these conditions when Heathrow seems to close after the lightest dusting?

There are Christmas trees alight with white bulbs lining our route into the terminal and they're glowing in the strange darkness of the morning. I check my phone thinking that time has stood still since our take-off in England and it's still somehow six o'clock – judging by the dark emerald sky shot through with cranberry pink, and the strange muted glow of a waning crescent moon half obscured beneath the horizon. I'm astonished to find it's nearly eleven, local time. Back home it'll be almost nine and light by now.

Even though it's oddly gloomy and there are curiously fine, glittering snowflakes falling rapidly from the sky, I'm struck by the feeling of the heavens stretching out above and around us, and my lungs seem to be expanding and my back straightening as I raise my head and look up. I've never been more aware of where I am on the planet. This is the kind of North that makes Manchester grimness seem positively equatorial and balmy. We're up in the stars here.

Entering through the glass doors and into passport control, everything is quiet, clean and calm, nothing like the hideous scrum this morning at Manchester airport, and the horror of the security hall. Was any place designed to be less Christmassy and exciting for travellers than that? This, on the other hand, feels serene and if not effusively welcoming, at least comfortingly inviting. I see Nari trying to coax a smile out of the serious official with ice-blue eyes who's examining her passport inside his glass box. He's immune to her flip vivacity it seems and I catch a flicker of surprise on her face as she gives him up as a lost cause.

My heart sinks a bit as I approach the only baggage reclaim carousel in the airport. There, straddling the suitcases, riding round and round and flapping their green and white candy-striped arms are three rosy cheeked elves. The bells on their drooping red hats tinkle as they greet us. One of them pats me on the head as they glide by on the conveyor belt.

It's mid-morning, I haven't had my first cup of coffee yet, and there's just NO NEED for this kind of forced jollity, and, *hell no*, is that a reindeer over there? Yep, another elfy toerag has arrived and is leading a very pissed off looking reindeer in a halter. He looks like he's been dragged reluctantly from a cosy shed somewhere and he's making angry huffing snorts through fuzzy nostrils. He has an antler missing but they've decorated the remaining one with silver tinsel. He and I exchange sympathetic, un-Christmassy glances. *I know how you feel, babe.*

Last Christmas, I'd have been over there posing for a selfie with Rudolf, grinning like a child on Christmas day. I used to love this kind of thing, but I've lost it this year. I hope this trip helps bring the Christmas cheer back. Once upon a time I had it in spades. Mum drilled it into me as a kid with her amazing year-round Christmas planning. She really went all out for Christmas. Looking back, I wonder how much of that was to do with me being an only child and Mum trying to make each year extra special for me. She'd buy posh crackers and discounted decorations in the January sales and squirrel them away for December. I'd catch her in her bedroom curling ribbons and wrapping gifts all autumn long. She always made sure I had a new party frock for Christmas Day, and we'd do the rounds of Santa's grottos in the Chester department stores. Even though I knew none of the Santas we saw were the real thing, I was still convinced they somehow had a direct line to The Big Guy himself, so I made sure to be as good as gold while we queued up.

I heave a sigh as I scan the room, looking for Nari. She's already wrestled her suitcase from between the knees of a particularly excitable elf and is marching briskly for the exit, presumably to see if our taxi's waiting. My case is nowhere to be seen so I step back from the carousel and wait it out.

A gaggle of screaming children have gathered around a lady elf dressed in an inappropriately skimpy elf-frock. She's handing out sweets from a basket. I notice a few of the mums and dads helping themselves to the sweets too. I could do with a chocolate. I guess I don't qualify for one, as I don't have kids with me.

Through the glass, I can see a coach out on the road, its engine idling, ready to whisk the families away to their various resorts and the Christmas of a Lifetime spent searching for Santa, singing carols in hotel restaurants, leaving out bowls of porridge for magical elves on Christmas Eve, and excitedly tipping out the contents of overstuffed stockings when the Big Day finally arrives.

It comes out of nowhere and hits me in the gut as I watch the misty-eyed parents snapping photo after photo of their children's awestruck, elated faces. I'm all alone here at the top of the world. No husband, no babies. My own mum and dad are miles away and I suddenly miss them so, so much. Meanwhile Cole's at his mother's house with his gorgeous, pregnant trolley-dolly girlfriend and Patricia's probably snapped up the entire range of The White Company newborn clothes already, and oh, how they'll laugh and chatter about the new life waiting to come into the world and what a perfect daddy Cole's going to be…

One of the elves has put her arm around my shoulder and is giving me a gentle hug. She must think I'm overwhelmed by the magic of Christmas and their enchanting Lapland welcome, but honestly, I'm just tired and grouchy and feeling sorry for myself. The nice lady elf in the too-short dress stuffs a handful of her candies in my coat pocket with a wink that tells me I'm not the first recently dumped woman to blub in her arrivals lounge, and I give her a grateful nod before grabbing my errant suitcase and making a run for the taxi.

'Please don't tell me it'll all be like this,' I say to Nari who's waiting for me outside.

'Like what?'

'Like Christmas on uppers and cooking sherry. It's too much.'

Nari just laughs. As the driver helps her load our cases into the boot, I look around.

So this is Lapland. It's absolutely glacial and I'm aware that my thick jersey trousers, perfect for chilly days in Cheshire, are never going to cut it here and my legs are prickling with cold.

We seem to be on a raised plain overlooking lowlands on all sides. Lights from a small city bleed into the late dawn light far in the distance to my left.

'Is that where we're going?' I ask the driver, who is, oddly, wearing little more than jeans, jumper, and a thin beany hat despite the arctic chill. He chuckles knowingly to himself.

'No, you're going that way.' He points a gloved finger along the road to our right where the dark lowland stretches on and on into nothingness and the road seems to disappear in a swathe of white.

As we drive I share the nice elf's sweets around and I think about the waterworks back at the airport. Those happy families really got to me, but it's not like I want to have Cole's baby, not now, obviously. And I don't even resent him having a family of his own. If anything, I hope he falls head over heels for that little baby and he gives it all the love and care he couldn't find in his heart for me and our hypothetical future rugrats.

It's just that babies were all part of our plan, you see? Get a house, get a job, get married, and hopefully be lucky enough to get a take-home baby one day, giving Mum the excuse she's been itching for to knit a thousand pairs of pastel booties and tiny matinee jackets. But when your plans are all torn up and chucked back in your face it takes a while to readjust.

For the immediate future I have no plans other than to *make no more plans*. I'm simply determined to enjoy this holiday and hoping it does the trick of putting some more distance between me, Cole and the past six months… and if I *can* bring back a little Christmas sparkle, all the better.

I reach into my pocket and pull out the two silver sixpences Mum gave me as I dropped my parents off at the airport ahead of their American adventure.

'Here you are, Nari,' I say, as I hand one over. 'A talisman for a happy Christmas.'

Chapter Nine

'Now this is more like it!' I squeal as I barge around my cabin, flipping lights on and opening cupboards.

Nari's behind me in the doorway. She's accustomed to luxury travel, but I get overwhelmed at the opulence of a Premier Inn breakfast buffet, so this spacious, wooden cabin with its fur rugs and roaring fire feels *really* special. There's a kitchen with a proper stove and a huge fridge stocked with food for our arrival.

'Thank you, Stephen the Sex God!' I exclaim as I peer at the bottles through the glass door of the wine cooler.

Nari's joined me now and is nodding with a knowing smile. 'He did promise us a few extras, remember?' Her eyes glaze over and a devilish grin forms. I know she's thinking of all the ways she can thank him for his generosity come their New Year rendezvous in London.

Leaving the lounge with its towering chimney and bushy – but bare, I notice –Christmas tree behind me, I push open a wide door at the far end of the lounge, revealing a smaller room like a glass house with a white bed and a towering pyramid roof and a view of the sky above. My shoulders collapse as the mood of relaxation hits me.

The taxi took about an hour to get us here through terrifyingly snowy, slippery roads and I was gripping the seat with my fingernails the entire time. Our cabby was, actually, amazing. Nobody would go out in conditions like this at home. I can't imagine a Cheshire Uber driver even venturing down Castlewych High Street in a snow-storm, let alone setting off on a cross-country trek in a blizzard that's entirely obscured not only the road mark-ings but all sign of the road itself. I still don't know how he did it without us ending up in a ditch. It had felt as though we were climbing up to the top of the world, which I suppose, we were, and all the time my neck was getting shorter and stiffer as my shoulders lifted in tense knots.

But here I am in a silent, cosy haven. The bed, covered in a pristine cable-knit throw and plump white quilts, looks unbelievably tempting.

'Dive in!' I yell to Nari, who's standing at the door behind me wrestling a cork from a bottle of red wine.

Soon we're snuggled up, bare foot, in my enormous bed, sipping the really yummy wine and scoffing iced ginger biscuits in the shape of tiny stars and looking out of the wide pane before us at the grey afternoon. Big fluffy flakes are beginning to fall and I'm trying to resist the urge to sleep that's stealing over me.

'Won't people be able to see in?' I worry.

'What people? There are only eight cabins out here and their occupants will be doing exactly what we're doing, gazing out at the world.'

'I know but didn't your mother ever read you fairy tales about dark Scandinavian forests and the granny-eating wolves and axe-wielding woodsmen who live in them? Anybody could pop up at that window.'

74

'What? And get an eyeful of us in fleecy pyjamas and facemasks? God forbid!' Nari laughs and rolls her eyes, and we both settle into silence for a while.

I've never heard quietness like this before. No traffic, no planes overhead, not a bird singing. Nothing.

'This is the closest to heaven I've even been,' I tell Nari. 'Pass us another biccie.'

'Will you be OK?' she asks as she hands me the bag, unable to take her eyes off the view of the dense snow-covered forest just beyond the glass.

'What do you mean?'

'Sleeping here on your own.'

This is when I remember that the cabin is all mine. Nari scored us two of these beauties and hers is next door. 'I think I'll manage,' I say, stretching out my achy muscles against the soft mattress. 'What did you do to Stephen to wangle this?'

Nari simply smiles and sets to work untying the strings on a complimentary bag of marshmallows.

'You must really like each other... freebies like this, meeting up at New Year?'

She shrugs and pops a marshmallow in her mouth. I wait expectantly as she chews.

'He's a lot of fun. We enjoy each other's company. Neither of us asks for too much. It suits me.'

'And you don't mind that?' I say. Not that I'm being judgy, it's just that I've long had a sneaking suspicion that Nari, in spite of her Samantha Jones bravado, would secretly quite like a more permanent set-up with someone a little more available. 'You really are happy drifting in and out of each other's lives? A quickie in Singapore here, a dirty weekend in Chelsea there?'

'Sounds pretty good to me.' Nari holds her glass up to mine with a wink. 'Cheers, Sylve. Here's to our Northern adventure.'

We clink glasses and I know she's already forgotten about Stephen, for now.

Nari's eyes look heavy, we're both stifling yawns and it's not even dinner time. I watch her close her eyes and smile to herself with her trademark inner calm and poise. Not many people have seen Nari crack or caught a glimpse of the vulnerability she keeps well hidden. Trying to get her to open up about Stephen is nearly impossible now, but there was a time, years ago, when I could hardly stop her talking about him. She was smitten, though she wouldn't admit it now.

I remember the shock of her turning up at the Love Shack and seeing her in tears for the first (and only) time as she told me the story of how she came to discover Stephen was very much keeping things strictly fun and informal.

They'd been at a party in London all evening, a travel industry thing with lots of work talk and exchanging of business cards. As it was coming to an end, a group of Stephen's friends had suggested they go on to a club where they had a VIP lounge waiting for them. One of the men had casually remarked, 'Does your girlfriend want to come?' As quick as a flash, Stephen had smiled politely and replied, 'Nari's not my girlfriend.'

At the time Nari had smiled too, as she let it sink in that what she had hoped was a growing connection between them was in fact exactly what they had promised each other from the beginning: a zero strings, maximum fun hook-up if ever they happened to be in the same time zone. In fact, the whole thing had been her idea, as she wasn't interested in a long-distance relationship, or so she'd thought.

She was always on the move and she was still, at that point, writing her popular dating blog – the one she'd set up as a new graduate from uni trying to break into writing – and had yet to find her feet in the travel industry. For years she'd tried every dating service available and written her tongue-in-cheek dating diary with exaggeratedly comic examples of her own dating disasters, persevering only in the half-hope of meeting any real potential boyfriend who might signal an end to her increasingly lucrative single-girl blogger persona.

But, three months after meeting Stephen in a designer clothes store in the Gangnam district, she'd stopped blogging about her dating escapades and fully devoted herself to cultivating her travel blog.

She never told Stephen she'd started to have feelings for him, so, according to Nari, it was easier to stifle her affections, until there was nothing left. And she often tells me she's glad to be part of their informal, glamorous, jet-setting arrangement.

Of course, she'd left that industry bash without joining Stephen and his VIP friends at the club – Nari's nothing if not dignified under pressure – and she hadn't called him, waiting for the inevitable message after an interval of a month or two letting her know there was a jet at her disposal ready to whisk her off to meet him in Malibu or Miami, or wherever she wanted to go.

And so now I only hear about the fun they have on the few occasions each year when they meet up, and I have to admit that Stephen genuinely does sound charming, considerate and romantic – sweetly shy even, which rather goes against my image of billionaire travel execs, but there you go, people are surprising, aren't they?

Still, I often find myself hoping Nari will meet someone else who might like her enough to call her his girlfriend, and she'd let him. One fact fills me with hope on this front: Nari is just as devoted to romantic novels as she's always been. She gets through hundreds in a year and knows of every new release on the market. If she ever gives up on *those*, then I'll give up my hopes of her finding love.

I take the wine glass from her fingers which are crossed over its stem and resting on her chest, and she opens one eye.

'I'm not sleeping,' she says. 'Just recharging.'

'So what should we do first then, once you hit full power?' I ask. 'You are, after all, the travel guru.'

'How about a sauna followed by a plunge into an ice hole in the frozen lake?'

I can't tell if she's joking or not. 'Not for me, thank you very much. I'm thinking of a snooze, followed by a steak in the resort restaurant. You don't really want to do the cold plunge do you?'

'Nope! The most energetic I'm going to get on this break is drinking cloudberry liqueurs and making drunken snow angels with you.'

She's reaching for the overly complicated remote control by the bedside. After some random button pressing and some very un-festive language she manages to send the flames roaring in the minimalist gas fire built into the corner of the bedroom (which I'll admit, I thought was a telly) and the lights by the bedside slowly fade out.

'Snooze it is,' she says, as we rub our shoulders into the plump pillows.

As I'm drifting off, I hear her say, 'I'm glad we're doing this, Sylve. Thank you.'

I'm too tired and wine-warmed to reply, but I reach my pinkie out to hook around hers under the covers, and I can tell she's already contentedly fast asleep.

–

When I wake up I think for a moment that I'm at home in my flat, except this bed is so much softer than mine and there are no traffic sounds from the road outside my front door. In fact everything is eerily silent, except for Nari's gentle breathing beside me. As I open an eye I'm met with a strange sapphire darkness. I make out the thick snow on the glass over our heads, obscuring the sky. It must have fallen heavily while we slept and the silence feels somehow damped down by its weight.

I'm thirsty with a red wine headache and a rumbling stomach. I can't read the time on my watch. The trouble with these long dark days above the Arctic Circle, I'm beginning to realise, is that you have no idea what time it is just from looking out a window. We might have slept for half an hour and it's nearly dinner time or it could be midnight now. I have no idea.

The fire is still flickering away in the corner and kicking out the most incredible heat. It's stifling actually. If I could find that remote control thingy, I'd turn it down.

As I'm rummaging under the covers around Nari's snoozing body, a bright flash of light momentarily blinds me. It's coming from beyond the glass somewhere among the trees. Another bright flash hits me and a second beam of light joins the first.

'Nari. Nari. Wake up. There's something outside the window.'

Nari groans and slaps my frantic hands away.

'God's sake woman, wake up! I knew this arctic wilderness thing was a mistake. It's probably robbers after our euros and passports or a yeti looking for its next meal. Do they have yetis here?'

Nari sits up, rubbing her eyes. 'Maybe it's your elf mates from the airport checking to see if you're being naughty or nice,' she says dryly, refusing to panic.

Whatever it is, the lights are getting closer and they seem to be scanning across the windows of the surrounding chalets. The beams settle on us once more, lighting up the room.

'This isn't funny. If it *is* elves, they're getting their candy canes snapped,' I quip, but my voice is beginning to waver.

We hear the sound of men arguing outside, deep and loud, and Nari whips her head round to face me. Her eyes are perfectly round with fear. If *she's* panicking, now I really am afraid. Nari's reached for the remote control and is brandishing it as though she's ready to throw it through the triple-glazed windows and I'm cowering under the covers hoping they kill me first.

The first tap at the glass makes us scream. The second, accompanied by two faces pressed close to the pane, turns us bloodless with fear. That's when I realise there's no phone in here to ring reception in the resort hub a few hundred yards away down the snowy road, and I remember we haven't yet worked out how to get a signal on our mobiles, and they're in the kitchen anyway. This is how I'm going to die; killed in my bed by two of Santa's little helpers.

Another tap. One of the figures is waving a huge gloved hand. Their faces are covered with scarves which are layered over with snow; only their eyes show through the gaps between hats, scarves and hoods. The tallest of the pair is shouting something but the sound is muffled. He's pointing to the side of the chalet, indicating that he's coming round to the door, and with that, the light from their torches fades. Nari and I share incredulous glances.

'He wants us to open the door,' says Nari.

'He can get knotted then!'

Nari, who always did have more of a sense of adventure than me, is making her way through the lounge already, her bare feet padding on the polished wooden boards. I follow a few paces behind. The heavy bang on the cabin door makes me flinch.

'They could be lost in the snow. I have to let them in,' Nari shrugs, a daring little gleam in her eyes.

I join her by the door, concealing the empty wine bottle behind my back. I've never smashed a bottle over an assailant's head before but it looks like fun in films and there's a first time for everything.

A sub-zero gust hits us as Nari throws the chalet door open. Nobody speaks and we peer expectantly out into the dark.

There stand the two men. One is tall and broad, the other smaller but solid-looking. Both are dressed in elaborate, layered clothing with colourful embroidered belts and cuffs. I've seen this traditional type of clothing in the Lapland holiday brochure. The taller man is wearing an incongruously modern snow jacket over his costume and has loops of thin rope slung across his body. The smaller guy looks resplendent in a long, thick reindeer hide coat and grey fur boots which curve into points above the toes.

Nari breaks the silence, and uses her fiercest voice, though I suspect she's enjoying this now. 'What do you think you're doing, scaring the life out of two defenceless women?'

Neither of the men reply. Instead of barging into the cabin and garrotting us with our own bootlaces, they take a step back further into the darkness. They're right to be afraid of Nari. Very wise.

At last I hear a voice, slow and deep, coming to me through the thick wool of the taller man's scarf. 'It *is* you.'

It takes a moment or two to register. Then I hear him say my name and even though it's muffled by the layers over his face, I know that voice, as smooth and tempting as spiced hot chocolate. Its owner reaches thick mittens to his face and tugs the scarf away and I recognise those full lips and that jawline, broader now and more bristled than when I last saw them.

'Stellan?'

I'm aware of Nari's wide eyes burning into the side of my face and I just know she's smirking. I step forward, trying to get a better look at the man I haven't seen since I was a teenager, not easy in the polar darkness and with snowflakes flurrying between us.

'What are you doing here?' he asks, in a not entirely friendly voice.

'I'm on holiday with my friend, Nari.'

Nari offers Stellan her widest grin. She's put a steadying hand on the small of my back.

82

'I was on a reindeer trail with some tourists. I just got back and found your message on Facebook,' he says.

I'm nodding and trying to gauge the look on his face, something between caution and annoyance. It suddenly strikes me that I shouldn't have come here. There's a reason we haven't spoken for years. What was it again? Oh yeah, he ran off and abandoned me. Story of my life. I look down at my feet, embarrassed, and also a tiny bit pissed-off that he's being so hostile.

Nari's the only one smiling and she's looking back and forth between me and Stellan like this is a highly entertaining Grand Slam match point. She's nudging me and I realise it's my turn to say something. Stellan stares at me, his eyes screwed up against the snow.

'Do you want to come in for a coffee?' I say.

'No,' he replies, and it's so abrupt I stiffen my neck in shocked response. I remember him being a cool customer but was he always rude like this?

The second man hurriedly steps forward at this point, pulling his own scarf down, revealing an apologetic smile. 'Welcome to Lapland. I am Niilo Oskal. I work with Stellan on the wilderness trails. I am at your service.' He makes a charming bow and I just know Nari's as struck by his beautiful features and soft, kind voice as I am. She reaches for his hand and pumps it enthusiastically, introducing us both with a broad smile.

Niilo nods shyly, not quite making eye contact with her and occasionally directing his smiling dark eyes somewhere down towards her feet.

'How long are you staying?' Stellan asks, his voice softer now, cowed by the polite example set by his friend's warm welcome.

'Until Boxing Day.'

He receives the information without a sound, so I add, 'That's the twenty-sixth.' He still doesn't speak, though his eyes are set disconcertingly on mine. His golden-brown irises are still the lightest I've ever seen and they're framed by white, frost-covered lashes.

'OK,' he nods sharply, and then turns to leave. 'Enjoy your vacation.'

Niilo shoots another sorry smile towards us as he makes after Stellan, before turning back suddenly and speaking directly to Nari, who's still grinning in amazed disbelief.

'*Hyvää joulua,*' he says.

And with that Niilo follows after Stellan, who has already stalked off and been swallowed up by the dark treeline. Nari and I watch the light from Niilo's torch as it dances and jerks before finally fading out.

Closing the door with a heavy shove, Nari laughs. 'What the hell was all that about?'

'I have no idea,' I reply, realising I'm still gripping the wine bottle, my would-be weapon, and feeling utterly ridiculous.

'Rude, much?' Nari remarks, as she reaches for her suitcase handle.

'I'm sure he used to be nicer than that. *Much* nicer. Sweet even,' I say, wondering why I'm defending the clot.

'His friend was nice though, wasn't he?' Her eyes glisten and her lips hitch up at the side a little. I've seen this look a lot, but she's all smart talk, smirking, and no action when it comes to blokes these days, so I let it go.

I watch Nari struggling to drag her case over the lip of the door frame. Before she heads next door to her chalet she throws a glance towards the deep footprints in the snow made by our strange welcoming committee. 'Get ready for dinner. Maybe they'll be back at the resort restaurant waiting for us.' She waggles her perfect eyebrows up and down.

'I doubt it. Stellan looked positively irate with me. I'd rather avoid him, if you don't mind.'

Nari's shaking her head and laughing as the door closes and I'm sealed into my cosy cabin alone.

The evening passes without bumping into Stellan or Niilo again, and I can't say I'm very upset about that; I'm still reeling from Stellan's oafish rudeness.

'Why shouldn't I be here? He doesn't *own* Lapland as far as I'm aware,' I say to Nari as I make short work of a tender steak in the resort restaurant. The pleasant Christmassy music tinkling over the speakers above our cosy booth feels at odds with my frayed nerves.

The walk from our cabins out on the edge of the resort along a snow-ploughed road beneath gleaming stars did nothing to help me recover the calm and serenity of our cosy, boozy afternoon nap. Neither did having to wrestle off my snowsuit and boots in the restaurant lobby whilst the other diners calmly watched me.

The holiday makers way up here in the remote North seem to be mainly rather sophisticated-looking couples or families with children old enough to cope with the freezing temperatures and treacherous conditions, certainly better equipped for the cold than the toddlers and primary school kids we saw back at the airport who were heading for the big family friendly resorts further south.

The restaurant sits just off the lobby of the resort's main hotel and the entire place has an air of rustic Scandi cool.

Four snowy paths radiate out from the hotel to each point of the compass and at each one stands a little cluster of cabins among the trees.

As we trudged along the path from our cabins towards dinner I didn't spot a single building; no souvenir shops or ski centre, nothing. Over our meal Nari told me those can be found a few kilometres away in Saariselkä itself and that, if I want, we can take the resort bus there tomorrow for a mooch around, but somehow I'm struggling to make meaningful conversation tonight.

'Earth to Sylvie Magnusson, do you read me?'

'Sorry, I was...'

'You don't need to tell me. I know what you're thinking. I'm disappointed too. From everything you told me about him, I thought your Stellan would at least be pleased to see you.'

I shrug and set to work on the creamy potatoes and broccoli. 'Maybe I'm misremembering him.'

'You were crazy about each other once upon a time, and your face lit up every time you mentioned him, so he must have had some redeeming qualities way back when you knew him.'

I think of the Stellan I'd written about in my diary and sigh. 'Oh well. Let's change the subject. He's not glad I'm here and that's all I need to know. Let's try to enjoy our Christmas without arrogant, puffed-up Viking men spoiling our fun.'

'Niilo didn't seem very puffed-up to me. I wouldn't mind bumping into him again,' Nari says, with a grin that tells me she's surprised even herself by saying this out loud, before she straightens her mouth and contentedly places her cutlery on an empty, sauce-streaked plate.

'What about Stephen?' I say.

'What about him? What goes on above the Arctic Circle stays above the Arctic Circle. He wouldn't mind anyway.' This is said with a dryness I pretend not to notice, for Nari's sake.

And I couldn't agree more. Let's leave my humiliating encounter with my surly ex-boyfriend here, buried under a ton of snow.

Even with the surprise of seeing Stellan again, dinner is good. The waiting staff are incredibly friendly and they bring us everything we want, including some particularly amazing chocolate cake and the strongest coffee I've ever tasted. And it is wonderful to sit by the window gazing out at the snowy world beyond, feeling warm and cosseted in our booth beneath the thick garlands of greenery and red bows that criss-cross the restaurant ceiling. But I still can't help occasionally looking around for Stellan, wondering how he'd found his way to my cabin door.

Is this his hotel? I know his parents ran a resort and husky centre somewhere near here back in the early noughties. Maybe our cabins are part of their business? I guess Stellan could have read my Facebook message and quickly checked the guest list. But why come out in the dark and snow looking for me only to trudge off into the night again after a few gruff words?

I think about our encounter during the slow walk back to our cabins after dinner, the dark night penetrated only by the slim moon, the stars overhead and the flaming torches lining the road and placed at ten or so metre intervals. Nari's busy telling me that the torches are typical of the ones used by Sámi reindeer herders on their long walks between villages, but I'm ashamed to say I'm not taking much of it in.

'Maybe *he's* the one that's disappointed, Nari?' I blurt out, interrupting her. 'Did he rush out to see me, hoping I'd still be a cute, perky nineteen-year-old and what he found was… well, me?'

'Bollocks. It's not that. It's that he's a rude Neanderthal who's spent so long in the frozen North it's turned him into a cold-hearted old beast. Although, he did *look* pretty good. From what I saw of him anyway.'

The history teacher in me rankles – and maybe so does the Stellan's Ex-Girlfriend in me – and I find myself pointing out to Nari that calling someone a Neanderthal isn't much of an insult as they were actually a highly advanced species. This goes down as well with Nari as it does with my Year Nine kids, so I get off my high horse and let my shoulders slump in defeat.

'Why are we doing this?' I say as I stop at the steps of my cabin. 'We're in the most beautiful place I've ever seen, it's Christmas, we're together, and we're talking about another one of my dickhead exes.'

'Hmm… Maybe he's not as frosty as we first thought,' says Nari, her eyes fixed on something over my shoulder.

Confused, I follow her gaze to the top of my cabin steps. Beside my door stands a tall glass jar with a flickering candle inside that definitely wasn't there before. The candlelight casts its glow over a carved wooden animal nestled in the snow. And there's a note.

Nari nearly knocks me off my feet in her haste to grab it. She's terrifying in everyday life but now she's wrapped in four inches of padded snowsuit and can actually rugby tackle me, I'm left defenceless. I stand aside and watch her struggle out of her gloves and tear into the envelope with glee. She dramatically clears her throat before reading.

> *Sylvie, I apologise for earlier. I was shocked to find you here in my resort and I was very tired tonight. I've been guiding tourists through the wilderness with Niilo for five days. I was rude, and I am sorry. Please allow us to show you and your friend around Frozen Falls resort. It would be our pleasure. We will meet you after breakfast in the hotel lobby.*
> *Stellan.*
>
> *P.S. The reindeer is for your friend. It's from Niilo*

If there *were* any armed yeti men hanging around the cabins with murderous intent, Nari's delighted screams would have seen them off into the arctic wilderness. Even so, once I hug her goodnight and lock myself into my cabin alone, I don't have it in me to brave a night by myself in the glass-box bedroom. I half consider knocking at Nari's cabin door and asking if I can sleep with her but I know she'll already be drawing a steaming hot bath and getting her face masks out of her case. I suppose this is technically a working holiday for her and she needs her quiet time to think about her blog.

No, I'll be OK, but I'm sleeping on the sofa tonight. I throw more logs onto the fire beneath the towering stone chimney in the living room, giving the embers a bit of a poke with the brass stick thing like I know what I'm doing, and make myself comfy on the deep sofa, pulling a furry blanket over me. The Christmas tree towers above my head and I notice there's a big basket of baubles and carved wooden snowflakes waiting expectantly beside it. I thought I'd done all my Christmas admin for this year. Tree-trimming will have to wait until tomorrow. I've got dancing flames and glowing logs to gaze at.

As I settle myself, listening to the crackles and sparks from the hearth, Stellan's note still clasped in my hand, I think about how tonight must have felt for him.

He must have been horrified to learn some old flame was staying in his resort. No wonder he raced out to find me. He must be wondering what I'm doing here, what exactly it is that I want, though I don't actually have any answers. We were lovers long ago, yes, but time has passed. *I've* changed, even if he's gone back to his old ways. He was as disarmingly taciturn and economical with his small talk as he was on the day we met. Maybe he was worried I'd have a blond-haired, pale-eyed fifteen-year-old in tow. God, he must have got a real fright! I should have tried harder to reach out to him before now. But, he's thirty-six now and not a brooding twenty-one-year-old, all shy and reserved around strangers. I'm hoping he'll have thawed a bit more by morning.

Nari certainly didn't think much of him, even after I'd reminded her at dinner about what she wrote in her blog: that Finnish men are sometimes more formal and less cocky than English lads. She just raised an eyebrow at that. Though Stellan's friend Niilo didn't exactly hold back, did he? Nari's only been at the resort for eight hours and he's sent her a gift. I drift off feeling hopeful for tomorrow's sightseeing. Whatever Stellan's like now, I'm determined to enjoy my Lapland escape.

Chapter Ten

At Stellan's simple cabin out in the woods, far from Sylvie, Nari and the other tourists, Niilo pads into his friend's kitchen and grabs a pack of beers from the fridge.

'Stellan, *mä meen saunaan tänään.* You coming? I've got the beer.'

'Sure, give me a minute.' Stellan drags his eyes from his phone, which he's been silently absorbed with for the last half hour. Standing, he lifts the loops of rope from across his body up over his head and hangs them on a hook by the door.

'The dogs are fed and asleep already. Did you lock them in?' asks Niilo.

'Mm-hmm. You ready?' Stellan brushes past his friend as he gathers up two towels from a basket by the door. He looks back at his phone on the kitchen table before throwing off his thick jacket.

Niilo knows to give Stellan his space. All he needs is a quiet beer and a good sweat and he'll soon be back to his usual self. Stellan always finds the wilderness trails tough but tonight he seems especially weary and in need of their daily sauna ritual.

Niilo follows his friend out of the cabin and along the raised wooden platform to the sauna door where Stellan is struggling with the key. The building has been locked up and cold for five nights and the lock is frozen, but after blowing hot breath into its chamber, Stellan slips the key inside and the mechanism is freed.

Stepping inside, the men shut out the night-time world and all its coldness, stripping the many layers of clothing from their tired bodies in companionable silence, something they've done almost every night of their friendship.

It has been five years since Niilo arrived at Stellan's resort looking for work, and slowly over the months and years that followed, the quiet, reticent Stellan had become his firm friend. In all that time Niilo has never seen Stellan so shaken and uncomfortable as he was tonight when the red-haired English woman and her beautiful friend flew in for Christmas.

They take turns using the sauna's shower. Stellan goes first. By the time Niilo has washed away the grime of the long wilderness trail his body feels lighter and his muscles are beginning to relax. As he steps up and in through the smoked glass door of the sauna room he feels the heat has already built up from the *kiuas*, the electric heater in the centre of the room, constructed to resemble the traditional wood burner.

'It's already cosy,' says Stellan as he cracks open a beer can and hands it to Niilo who nods his gratitude, sitting down beside Stellan on the wooden bench.

'*Kippis*,' the men say in unison as they touch beer cans together before taking long slow swallows.

After agreeing long ago that it felt inappropriate to drink alcohol while guiding the tourists on the trails because they needed to stay sharp at all times, they haven't touched a drop in almost a week. They never know when one of their charges might turn ill or injure themselves and they need to be in control if anything did happen. So far they've been lucky, but Niilo, always mindful of the scar across his cheekbone, never underestimates how easily an emergency could arise. For now they are back at the resort, warm and safe.

The cold beer slips down their thrown-back throats, refreshing and sharp, as the temperature rises. The glass door is already obscured with condensation. Stellan closes his eyes and stretches his arms out along the back of the bench, bringing his feet up to rest on the low wall edging the *kiuas* pit, but Niilo can tell his friend isn't fully able to surrender himself to the warmth and relaxation as he usually does. Tonight Stellan is troubled and needing time with his thoughts, so Niilo turns the dial on the wall, feeling the surging heat, and sits back against Stellan's forearm, breathing in the hot dry air. He has his own thoughts to process.

'Stellan?' he asks after a long silence.

'Hmm?'

'Tonight I met my soulmate.' Niilo offers this up with confident, smiling certainty.

Stellan opens his eyes and sniffs, hunching his body forward, crossing his arms over his knees.

'Sylvie's friend? How can you know she's your *soulmate*?'

'I just know. I knew Nari was on her way to me before I even set eyes on her. I knew out on the trail that she was coming.'

Stellan smiles wryly and shakes his head, perspiration beading around his temples. The thermometer on the wall has reached ninety degrees and is climbing steadily.

93

'What is it?' says Niilo, knowing his friend is brooding over an objection. 'Tell me.'

'I'd just be careful with that one, OK? She's exactly the kind of woman you usually steer clear of.'

'And what kind of woman is she, Stellan?' Niilo asks, amused.

'I found her blog, and she's just more... worldly than you.'

'You're already stalking Sylvie and her friends online?' Niilo laughs and runs his fingers through his choppy dark hair, which is glistening with sweat in the low sauna light.

'I was just getting up to speed. It's a long time since I've seen Sylvie and I don't remember her talking about Nari, so I guess I just... looked her up too.'

'And what did you find? A string of convictions for man-eating?' Niilo laughs.

'No, I just looked at her blog. Granted, it seemed kind of old, but she talks a lot about dating men from different countries and compares them and, you know, that kind of thing?'

'I don't, actually. So she travels a lot. She meets a lot of people. She finds people interesting. So do I.'

'Yeah, but when did you last go on a date with anybody?'

Niilo shrugs. 'I didn't meet my soulmate until tonight. Why would I waste my time dating lots of different people? Besides, when was the blog you read published?'

'I don't know, 2010 or something like that. I didn't have time to look for more recent ones. I can only imagine they get worse as they go on,' Stellan says gruffly, closing his eyes once more.

Niilo falls silent, thinking about his friend's warning and how one of the American tourists back at the resort had propositioned him only the weekend before, asking him to show her the aurora with a meaningful glint in her eyes. She'd smelled of oily perfume and hairspray, and her thick black lashes seemed to have been attached with something cloying and sticky.

He'd made sure to let her down gently but firmly. There was no way he'd be baited and reeled in, yanked out of his elemental arctic home, not by one of the tourists set on a holiday romance with a pretty, exotic, spiritual stranger. He knew that was how they all saw him. No, he'd long ago resolved that he belonged here in the peace and silence where he was safe and unburdened. The fleeting tourists from the resort, with their return tickets and their penchant for Sámi men, were not for him.

Stellan interrupts Niilo's pensiveness. 'Niilo, you slept with that tourist from Sweden, didn't you? The one that wanted to see your cabin in the woods?'

Niilo simply smiles. He doesn't talk about the rare exceptions to his rules. Only he knows about the few people he's made love to and the memory of each one is sewn up in the quietest quarters of his heart. Apart from the fleeting lovers of his youth who he met during Southern migrations following his herds, the rest – all tourists – had got on planes and flown home to their real lives soon afterwards. He had learned his lesson with those few strangers. They don't really want to know who he is, and they never stay long enough to find out anyway. But Nari is different. She's the one he's been waiting for.

Niilo veers away from the subject and back to Stellan's reservations. 'An online blog is not a person. She must be much more than the public persona she portrays. Once I know her, I'll read her blog. Anyway, who are you to judge? At least I'm *open* to life's possibilities.'

Stellan huffs out an exasperated breath, but Niilo talks on. 'Aren't you glad I talked you into apologising to Sylvie? Doesn't it feel better now you've written down the words, told her how you feel?'

'You don't understand. Sylvie and me… it's more complicated than you think. Look, I'm not like you. You suddenly seem to have a lot of faith that this kind of thing will come right for you. You hide away, and you abstain, and you wait for a sign from some snow fairies or whatever—'

Niilo interrupts with a gentle laugh and a dig of his elbow in Stellan's ribs.

'You do! You say you've seen a sign and now you're mated forever with some woman you've said five words to.'

Niilo nods and pulls a face that says there may be some truth in what his friend is saying, but he doesn't regret telling Stellan out on the trail about the bear and how he'd seen it again.

The creature had ambled out of the darkness towards him, stood up on its hind legs, revealing its grizzled chest matted with icicles, and lifted his head, turning his black eyes to the sky. That was when Niilo saw the plane, the first that had passed overhead in four days out on the trail. He knew it was coming in to land at the airstrip fifty kilometres to the south, and he'd understood then. He'd closed his eyes and filled his lungs with arctic morning air, and the bear had disappeared, its message delivered.

Niilo had described his premonition to Stellan as they'd prepared the tourists' breakfasts, and Stellan had simply smiled. Niilo had always had a vivid imagination and powerful, colourful waking dreams that he'd come to rely on as a way of breaking the monotony of the snowy reindeer migrations and the long white nights of summer. They offered him a kind of comfort Stellan couldn't understand.

'You think I'm a romantic fool?' said Niilo, watching Stellan through the heat haze.

'Well, yes.'

'I think *you're* a pig-headed pragmatist.'

'You're going to get hurt.'

'Maybe. But I'll have loved.'

'Oh my God, you're crazy.'

'Just be polite to them both, OK? They're only here for a few days. You told me you were in love with this Sylvie once, so let's show her and Nari *our* Lapland, make this a really special time for them. OK?'

Stellan drains his beer. 'Don't say I didn't warn you.'

Niilo laughs again and hands Stellan a fresh can.

Chapter Eleven

My heart's pounding under all these layers. I don't know why I'm so nervous this morning, but I hardly touched my breakfast of yogurt and muesli. I gulped down two cups of that strong coffee, though. I'll need it to fortify me against the cold. The thermometer outside the restaurant tells me it's minus nineteen degrees, the kind of cold that kills if you're underprepared.

I glance at my reflection in the revolving door of the lobby, through which, at any second, Stellan is going to appear. I'm dressed in three layers underneath the padded pink snowsuit I bought with Nari at the mall, and hey, who's to say I wasn't going for the well-lagged boiler look?

Nari's looking business-like and is taking notes on a pad about all the food she just sampled in the hotel restaurant; mainly sliced cold meats, cheeses and various pickles and sweet pastries. She looks elegant all in white, and her black hair and red lipstick create quite a contrast with the white landscape and the late arctic dawn.

'Are you wearing false lashes?' I ask her, incredulously.

She gives me a slow Marilyn Monroe wink just as the door spins and delivers up first Niilo, then Stellan.

I search Stellan's face nervously. Is he pleased to see me this morning? Or is this a duty visit to the mad English woman who he thinks might be stalking him? I'm relieved to see he doesn't have the same cross expression he wore last night. I smile broadly at him in the hope that he'll be warm and welcoming in return. 'Morning.'

'Good morning, Sylvie. Did you sleep well?'

Thank goodness, he's being friendly, though he's not exactly smiling.

'I was afraid to sleep in the glass bedroom in case some scary men appeared out of the wilderness and shone their torches in at me,' I say teasingly.

Stellan cracks a tiny smile, but without showing his teeth, and he nods with an amused sniff down towards his feet. I recognise the shy formality of all those years ago when he was boyishly handsome and we were both so young. I realise with frustration that he's not going to reply.

'I'm so sorry we frightened you both,' Niilo offers with a gentle laugh. 'We didn't know which cabins you'd been assigned. But we found you.'

'You sure did, and you took a decade off poor Sylvie's life,' says Nari, keeping her eyes on Niilo. 'But *I* wasn't a bit afraid.'

'I'm glad to hear it. I hope you don't mind if we act as your guides today? We'll give you VIP access to Frozen Falls resort, show you the stuff only a privileged few get to see,' Niilo says.

After the briefest moment of silence as Nari and I exchange delighted glances, Stellan sweeps a hand, indicating the doors. 'If you want to make the most of the coming light we need to go now.'

Nari's face falls and I cringe at how abrupt Stellan seems. As I make my way past him, I can't help casting him an anxious look which I know he catches as he looks down again with a brisk nod of his head, like a sentry on duty.

Outside the restaurant I see tourists dressed for a day on the ski slopes clambering on to a minibus heading for Saariselkä, but there's no sign of our transport. It's nearly ten o'clock and the sky is only just beginning to lighten. Through the silhouetted bare branches of the snow-laden trees I can make out a cool pink tinge creeping over the horizon and into the sapphire blue. The moon hangs low in the sky, a thin sliver like a curved blade.

'It's so beautiful!' I say in Stellan's direction. I seem to be saying that a lot on this trip.

'This way,' says Stellan, seemingly ignoring me, as he stalks past, setting a brisk pace a few feet ahead of me. I suppose he must be used to mornings like this, they're not a beautiful novelty to him, but to me the landscape is making my heart swell and my senses tingle. I follow after Stellan as he stretches out his long legs, striding through the drifting snow.

Nari's dawdling behind with Niilo and they seem to be chatting away to each other like *they're* the old friends in this scenario. Occasionally Nari laughs and throws her bobble-hatted head back, making her long hair splay out over her shoulders and down her back. Niilo seems transfixed by her. This is going to be a long day.

'Stellan, wait up.'

At least he stops and turns to wait for me. He watches me with an unreadably blank expression as I amble along through the snow. Even with its layer of grit the road is lethally slippery so it's safer to walk through the piled snow in the gutters. I'm so glad I have these heavy snow boots that Stephen the Sex God's PA arranged for us, and my puffy snowsuit is doing an OK job of keeping out the wet and cold, though I'm already wishing I'd put away my vanity and worn the big black super thick suit the resort provided. I mistakenly thought the pink suit would be cute, but instead I'm feeling a little chilly and somewhat marshmallowy.

'I don't fancy being the third wheel for those two.'

Stellan casts his eyes back along the road just as Nari loops her arm through Niilo's. They're walking painfully slowly. He makes a sort of grumpy snort and shakes his head. Maybe I detect a hint of a smile, but it isn't amusement; it's something else. Something I don't like. He's judging her, and unfairly too. I can't remember ever seeing her react like this with a guy, other than Stephen. She must genuinely like him, but I'm not wasting my breath explaining this to Stellan; it's none of his business.

'So what are we doing today?' I venture, as Stellan turns sharply off the road and into the woods.

We seem to be heading for a shed in a distant clearing, and I can hear... *wait!* I can hear dogs yelping as we approach.

'Are we *husky sledding*?' I clap my mittened hands together and attempt to jump up and down, not so easy in these boots.

That's when Stellan smiles, an actual proper smile, and I get a flash of his white straight teeth. 'You always did love dogs.'

I can't help grinning back at him. He's right. '*Yes!* I was always a sucker for a pupper! Are they *your* dogs?'

'Uh-huh. Well, they belong to the resort, but yes, I look after them, and I train them.'

He's searching in his black padded jacket for a big bunch of keys to open the metal door of the shed. 'You ready for this?' he grins, gripping the door handle. His barley-wine eyes are gleaming.

'How many dogs are in there?'

'Thirty-six, and there's seven pups.'

A lesser man might have blanched at the squeal I let out, but Stellan seems excited too somehow. I've never met a dog I didn't like, except for that big German Shepherd that snapped at me in the street when I was a kid, but I like to think he was probably just confused and didn't really mean it.

The excited barks build as Stellan opens the door and I hustle past him to get a glimpse of the animals. The shed is warm and well lit. There are large cages all around three walls and in the centre there's an area separated off with bales of straw where I can see a very tired-looking husky bitch lazily wagging her tail. She's lying down surrounded by her tumbling puppies.

My words must have been unintelligible to Stellan, since they came out in a jumbled rush, but he made a decent attempt at trying to decipher them.

'That's Kanerva. She gave birth almost ten weeks ago. She's a really good mother. Go ahead, she won't mind you petting them if you give her a good fuss and let her sniff your hands first.'

'Kanerva?' I ask.

'It means heather.'

'Heather,' I repeat in a whisper. 'She's gorgeous.'

I approach her, sitting by her side on the bale wall, scratching her ear. She simply reclines and lets me fuss over her whilst Stellan, smiling placidly, makes his way to the back of the shed, unlocking each cage door as he passes them. Dogs rush out and crowd around him rubbing their heads against his knees and almost knocking him over in the sheer joy of seeing their master.

He unbolts a sliding door that takes up half the back wall of the shed and heaves it aside revealing a fenced exercise enclosure covered in snow. The dogs bound outside running in every direction, but always excitedly looking back towards Stellan and barking.

One of Kanerva's pups, who seems less timid than the rest, clambers up over the tumbling bodies of his brothers and sisters in order to get as close to me as possible.

'Can I give this little one of yours a cuddle?' I ask Kanerva, who's dragging herself up and making her way towards the long food trough at the other side of her enclosure. 'I'll take that as a yes.'

The puppy is probably the cutest little thing I have ever beheld. Except for Barney, of course. I sigh as I lift the little black and white panting creature up onto my lap. He has one shocking blue eye and one ice white. I'm just expostulating on how he's the best boy – 'yes you are, yes you are' – when Niilo leads Nari in through the door behind me. She's not a dog-lover like me, but her face lights up with glee.

'Nari,' calls Stellan from over by the big open door. 'Come help me with this?' He holds out a plastic trug full of tennis balls. Nari doesn't have to be asked twice and within seconds the huskies are racing out into the snowy yard chasing the balls she's pitching for them. Their happy yelps are excruciatingly sharp and loud. Niilo joins her, offering to hold the trug.

I watch as Stellan lifts a sack from a shelf before reaching into his snowsuit pocket for a long curved knife to make a slit across the top. There are wide bowls for dog food all around the shed and he fills each one.

'These huskies eat a lot, five times a day they get fed,' he says as the dogs rush back into the shed, jostling each other for prime position. Then, joining me and Kanerva's pups in the enclosure, he fills their long food trough and sits down directly opposite me on the bales.

I wonder why he hasn't sat closer, and I feel an achy little niggle in my chest at how much I resent his reserved conduct. It's not the frigging eighteenth century, Stellan Virtanen!

I look over at Niilo and Nari, surrounded by happy wagging tails. Niilo's showing Nari how to hose water into the big drinking bowls by the door and they're still smiling animatedly at one another. How come Stellan's got all the famous Finnish formality and Niilo's so vital and alive with warmth?

'Do they have names?' I ask, placing the puppy back in the enclosure so he can eat alongside his siblings.

'That one's Finn, he's easy to recognise with his white eye, just like his mother Kanerva. And that's Čáhppe, Miyuki, Lumikki, Aleksi, Yanni and, erm…'

'Bob?' I joke, but Stellan seems confused.

'Bob?'

'Yeah, Bob McLuskie the festive husky.' Oh well, at least I made myself laugh. 'Don't mind me, I'm just high on puppies. I can't believe this is your life.'

'Yeah, I'm in here a lot, morning and night. They spend the days playing in the yard with the tourists or out on the sledding trails. That's why they eat so much; they work really hard.'

I watch Stellan lean into the enclosure to lift the smallest of Kanerva's litter away from the food. He's already eaten his fill and is nodding his little black and brown head and falling asleep. 'This one's Toivo. He's a little scraggy one. How do you say it, he's the…?'

'The runt of the litter?' I offer.

'That's it, the runt. Poor baby.'

Baby? So Stellan does still have his soft side! My heart crackles and bangs like popping candy as I watch him lift little sleeping Toivo to his lips and place a delicate kiss on his pink nose. He's better with dogs than with people, I think to myself.

'I guess they're a lot of work?' I say.

'Yeah. But Niilo's often out here too,' he says, casting a glance over his shoulder towards his friend. 'He's my partner in the business, has been for five years. He's been a huge support. For a few years after my parents retired to Helsinki I ran this place by myself. It was hard work. And we have so many tourists coming through, three or four hundred a week in the snowy season, and we need to ensure everything is perfect for them. Then there's the reindeer too. But they're Niilo's herd and he has his own herdsmen working with him. I'm better with the dogs.'

He tails off just as I'm getting used to his beautiful thick accent. I want to urge him not to stop talking now, not as he was just getting warmed up. Speaking of warm, it's definitely getting hot in this snowsuit and all these layers. Stellan seems to read my mind, or maybe it's my face turning as pink as my bobble hat that gives me away.

'Unzip your snowsuit and remove your outer layer. You'll find you do this often. One minute you'll be cold, the next warm. It's the heat from the walk and all these animals.'

Not just the animals, I think, as I fumble for the zip by my throat. Just as I'm wondering if he's going to watch me, he averts his gaze, which is ridiculous because I'm wearing the equivalent of three duvets here. He won't get as much as a glimpse of bare wrist.

I pull my pink and cream Fair Isle jumper off over my head, making my hair stick up and buzz with static. Stellan stalks away as I'm smoothing it down and comes back with something small and silvery.

'Take a sip. You need to stay hydrated, even in the cold.'

I reach for the little flask and when I unscrew it, steam curls in the air between us. He sits down again, closer now than he was before, but still, maddeningly, at a respectful distance.

'Cheers,' I say as I take a drink of what turns out to be berry juice. It's hot and sweet and I can't help but heave a sigh as it slips down my throat.

'*Kippis*,' he says seriously, and I assume that's some kind of toast. This time he *is* watching me, so I take another slow drink and enjoy his pale eyes on me.

After a quiet moment where we both pet the puppies and pretend this isn't totally awkward, Stellan breaks the silence.

'So, the dogs are fed and watered. In ten minutes my staff will arrive and take the tourists out on husky trails around the resort. Would you like to join me and Niilo on a ride a little further away?'

'Don't you have to stay with your tourists?'

'I do. I mean, usually I would, but I'm going to let my staff take care of everything on their own for once. Would you like to help me harness the dogs to our sleds?'

It doesn't take long to get ready to set off. Niilo and Nari bring out the two sleds, long and thin and bundled with blankets, and five excitable dogs are carefully harnessed to each one.

Stellan takes my hand with an encouraging nod of his head and I clamber down onto the sled. I'm seated right at the back with my legs stretched straight out in front of me, watching Stellan checking the ropes and giving each dog one last pat and some words of encouragement, which makes me smile. Stellan's dressed all in black and has a thick black beanie hat pulled down over his ears and a wide furry hood encircling his face like a halo. The fur is blowing in the cold breeze. I watch him treading through the snow with that serious look of earnest concentration on his face and I can't help wondering whether his hair still falls in sleek blond perfection around his cheekbones like it used to.

I'm distracted by Nari's voice a few feet away. She's settled into her own sled and Niilo's crouching in the snow by her side pulling thick blankets up over her legs, tucking her in like a parent would a child. I watch them surreptitiously out the corner of my eye, half expecting Niilo to plant a goodnight kiss on Nari's head, he's so attentive and tender. Nari's giving him a dopey grin and I think to myself how I've never quite seen that look in her eyes before. I cannot wait for a full post-sledding debriefing about her date with Niilo. I mean, she is on a kind of date, right?

I look around for Stellan, who pointedly *hasn't* tucked me up in my sled. He's over by the dog shed giving instructions to his staff. Behind us on the road a minibus has pulled up and some tourists are spilling out and approaching the dog yard. I can hear loud, happy American accents exclaiming about the cold from all the way over here. I pull the covers up over my chilled legs. Just sitting here is making me cold again, even though I scrambled back into my jumper and zipped my snowsuit right up to my throat before leaving the shed.

'Get your balaclava on, Sylve! It's going to be freezing once we get moving,' Nari shouts across at me.

I'm going to pretend I didn't hear her. The last thing I want is for Stellan to see me in a woolly pink balaclava with its weird little eye and mouth holes that make me look like some kind of giant worm. No, I'd rather my nostrils froze up completely than wear that thing. I glance over at Nari and she's putting hers on. It's white and snood-like with a cowl neck and has the whole face cut out so it reveals her pretty features. Why didn't I go for one of those? I pull my pink bobble hat down over my ears and forehead, then I gather my scarf up around my mouth as best I can.

'All set?' asks Stellan from behind me as he steps onto the sled's long runners.

'Aren't you sitting in front of me?'

'I steer the sled from back here.'

He says it so curtly I feel stupid. Of course he steers this thing. I try to laugh off my embarrassment, palming my forehead and shaking away the sneakily intrusive vision I'd had of Stellan clambering under these blankets with me as I nestle up against his broad back – my legs wrapped around him, maybe. He doesn't laugh and so I turn away, settling in for a long morning's husky-sledding.

'We'll head west and stop at the lake for lunch. Yes?' he shouts.

I can barely hear him over the sounds of the dogs barking and through his carefully arranged scarf layers. Only his eyes are showing through the black slit beneath his beanie.

'Yes,' I manage but he shouts over me with a sharp '*Mush!*' and the dogs strain and yelp and prance in their harnesses. The ropes go taut and I feel the sled start beneath me. I have to grab the handrails so I don't fall backwards onto Stellan's legs. We're off!

The dogs stop their barking immediately and lean into their yokes, already panting with the effort. I'm in awe of their strength and the smooth motion of their shaggy legs powering us along the narrow track in a jolting stop-start motion.

I can just see over the snowy walls of the sunken path as we race along, picking up speed with every second. It takes only moments and we're out in the wild again, and I remember how remote the resort is. There's nothing more than blackened bracken and stunted bare trees jutting out from the deep snow as far as I can see.

There's a low range of jagged hills in the distance and I'm realising it's impossible to tell how vast they might be without buildings of any kind to offer a sense of scale. A strange feeling of smallness and stillness settles over me as the arctic silence falls, broken only by the crunch of gravel beneath the sled runners and the soft sounds of the dogs' feet on snow, mingled with their panting breaths.

It's so quiet I'm increasingly aware that I should probably say something to Stellan. I quickly glance up and find him staring commandingly out at the landscape ahead like a particularly shaggable Sir Ernest Shackleton on the prow of the *Endurance*.

'How fast are we travelling?' I ask.

'Around twenty-five miles per hour.'

'I thought Europeans used kilometres instead of miles?'

'You could use the old Sámi measurement of distance? The distance a reindeer can travel before stopping to urinate.'

I laugh and look up at Stellan's inscrutable eyes. Is he joking? I remember his dry sense of humour and how he liked to tease me. He told me once it was the Finnish way. If you make fun of someone it shows that you must be good friends. Is that what we've become? Friends? If that's the case, shouldn't he be chattier than this? I realise I'm going to have to work pretty hard to get to know Stellan again after all these years. I'll ask him about the dogs. He definitely came to life back at the dog shed surrounded by cute mutts.

'Don't they mind the cold? The dogs, I mean. Poor guys, what a hard life!' Although, I think to myself, they don't exactly look unhappy.

Every now and then a dog turns back its head and glances at Stellan as if to check he's pulling his weight, which I know he is; I can hear his boot scuffing the gritty ice as he helps push the sled along whenever we hit a slight incline. The dogs are bright-eyed and focussed. Would they be so keen to pull us along if they didn't enjoy racing through the snow?

'They could *live* outside permanently if they needed to. They can withstand temperatures of minus fifty. Not that they'd ever have to. And they have lots of company and food, and they cost me plenty of money in vet bills each year, believe me. They're the most pampered pups in Lapland.' Stellan says this with fondness in his voice.

'So how long have you been doing these trails for?' I ask, only having to raise my voice slightly over the sound of the runners, but this isn't graced with a response.

I glance up and find Stellan is still staring ahead. There's that little furrow between his eyebrows again. His eyes pinch and crinkle against the ice cold air rushing against our faces. I'm about to ask him again – it's possible he didn't hear me – when he briefly lets his eyes fall to mine.

'Just sit back and take it all in,' he says. 'Talking is silver, but silence is golden.'

So, that's me told. I look ahead at the dogs leading the way into the white beyond. I'm stung, if I'm honest. Cheeky sod. But he might have a point. The landscape seems to call for peace and solitude. There's something about these dramatic wilds that renders small talk very small indeed.

Stellan seems to know I'm brooding as I feel a tap at my shoulder. He hands me down the silver flask of warm berry juice. There's nothing else for it but to graciously accept it again, unscrew the cap and pull the blankets high over my chest. Settling back on the little pillow, I let myself be whisked away into the grey arctic light.

We make our way in silence out onto a wide plain and I suddenly realise we're crossing a huge frozen lake. I panic slightly at the idea of the frigid water beneath us but resist the urge to ask Stellan if we're safe because I know how capable and sensible he is. He wouldn't put us at risk.

I'm passively watching the white world slip by again and sinking back into the cosy stupor when I make out a dark, hunched figure on the lake ahead. Stellan seems to be steering the dogs in their direction.

'*Woah*,' he calls out into the silence. The dogs skip to a graceful halt and I hear the crunch of the brake behind me. Nari and Niilo pull up behind us. They're still chatting happily. Good for them. I'm guessing Niilo doesn't agree that silence is chuffing golden.

'Come round here and stand on this brake, Sylvie.'

I like how he says my name. *Sylvie*. So soft and romantic in his accent…

'Sylvie? Are you asleep?'

'No, no, here I come. What do you want me to do?' My legs have seized up a bit with the cold and it's surprisingly difficult to swing them up and over the side bars of the sled, but I only wobble slightly as I get my balance.

'You stand on this. If you step down, even for a second, the dogs will be gone.'

Transferring my weight for his, I slip my foot onto the brake as soon as Stellan steps off, keeping the sharp metal blades pressed firmly into the ice. I'm nodding seriously and hoping I look confident because I certainly don't feel it as Stellan stalks off across the lake towards the man who seems to be fishing over an ice hole.

The scene looks ancient, more like an echo of the past than something that could possibly happen in this day and age. I mean, where has this guy come from? He has no sled and there isn't a building, or even a tent, anywhere to be seen. How can he spend his days alone on the ice? How strange. Whilst I've been in my superheated classroom and nipping out at lunchtimes to Costa, he's been out here. I shake my head in wonder. My little flat and everything I know feels a million miles away from this world.

I watch as Stellan exchanges a few words with the man and stoops to offer him something from a paper bag, which the man accepts with a nod, and then Stellan turns back towards the sled. Within moments he's back in charge of our transport and I'm back under my blankets and we're off again. I wave to the fisherman as I glide by and he raises his gloved hand in silence.

'Who was that?' I ask as the dogs pick up speed.

'He lives beyond the fell. He's caught only two fish this morning so he didn't have any to sell me.'

'But you gave him something?'

Stellan snorts a reply as he tosses the same paper bag down onto my lap. '*Salmiakki*. Try it.'

I peer inside at the black diamond-shaped pastilles. I do like a wine gum or two, and my stomach's grumbling, it's been so long since the breakfast I was too nervous to eat. I pop a couple of the hard sweets into my mouth, not easy in these enormous gloves, and I scrunch the bag closed again.

Christ on a bike! These are no wine gums. I've got salty liquorice cloying to the roof of my mouth and in between my teeth, and something about the taste is taking me back to the dental hygienist's chair. And why is my tongue going numb? It would be rude to spit them out, wouldn't it? So I work and work at the evil cough medicine flavour chews until they gloop down my throat with a berry juice chaser. *Yuck!* Not everything in Lapland is what it seems, I'm learning. So much is shockingly unfamiliar.

I squint up at Stellan and notice he's laughing, his shoulders rising and falling.

'You knew I'd hate those, didn't you?'

'*Salmiakki* is an acquired taste, I know. I'm sorry.'

'Yeah, you look sorry. I'll remember this, Stellan Virtanen.'

'I'll make it up to you, I promise.' He's still laughing, with teasing in his voice, and something else, I choose to imagine, vaguely suggestive. Instead of looking up at him again – I don't want him to see me all flustered – I settle down for what remains of our journey.

We pass between two gently sloping hills and suddenly we're turning off the main trail onto a rougher, narrower path leading towards what looks like a big tipi tent in the far distance. I can smell wood smoke from a fire. The scent travels on the unpolluted air and makes my nose prickle. I hope this means food. I'm starving.

'This is it. Niilo's herding *lavvu*,' says Stellan as he slows the dogs to a stop and steps off the sled, immediately tying the ropes to a gnarled, stunted tree. The dogs all immediately lie on their stomachs and lick the snow to cool themselves, their breath rising in little clouds around the frosted fur of their muzzles.

Stellan comes round to stand in front of me and offers me a hand, pulling me to my feet.

'*Lavvu?* The tent, you mean?'

'Uh-huh,' he says. 'This is the first stop on our wilderness safaris for the tourists, and it looks as though one of the herders got Niilo's message to light the fire.'

After a few moments spent feeding the dogs crunchy biscuits from a sack and loosening their harnesses, Stellan walks ahead, carrying boxes he's lifted from the front of

Nari and Niilo's sled, interrupting their long, involved conversation.

It's obvious Nari had forgotten me and Stellan were even on the trail, and she beams at me after a moment of slowly dawning recollection.

She heads straight for me, her arms outstretched and gives me a hug and we laugh and break into a run as best we can through the deep snow towards the tent, our stupid, huge black leather Santa mittens preventing us from holding hands properly.

'What's the *lavvu* etiquette? Do I knock?' I ask Nari, realising that Stellan's disappeared inside. Nari shrugs.

Niilo's running to catch up in his reindeer hide coat and his big fur hat. He's got the blankets from the sleds bundled under his arm and looks glamorous and other-worldly somehow. The knife on his leather belt glints in the already fading daylight. How can it be getting dark again already, it's only just past noon?

Just as Niilo reaches us, Stellan pushes his hooded head through the tent flap, pulling the scarf from his face, and says with a grin, 'Come inside.'

Everything suddenly feels fun and adventurous, and I'm aware that we're young – well *fairly* young – and we're on holiday and its Christmas. What with being raised on MTV and cheesy eighties' pop songs, I can't help thinking of my favourite Wham! video where the gorgeous gang of skiing couples arrive at some sophisticated alpine resort for the holidays and they spoil their permed mullets messing around romantically in the snow.

The coming days suddenly feel full of possibility and I realise that, for the first time in a long time, I'm really enjoying myself.

And the fun carries on as Stellan leads us all into the surprisingly spacious interior of the tent and indicates for us to sit on the reindeer hide covered benches around the crackling fire, and we all help to unpack the food from the boxes he carried in.

I'm a little disconcerted to find we'll be eating elk meatballs, though the pasta and buttered bread accompanying them is very welcome. Just as I'm about to ask what exactly an elk *is* – is it like a moose or a reindeer? – I'm stunned into goldfish mouthed silence by the sight of Stellan pulling the black beanie from his head. I watch in dazed shock as he musses his fingers through thick, choppy hair.

All this time I've thought of him as I last saw him, with his jaw-length surfer's waves, and I've been secretly praying he hasn't changed them. The sight of his now messily cropped short locks, all Scandinavian blond and dark honey, makes me want to do a dramatic movie-starlet swoon. Instead, I offer to help stir the big pot over the fire and try to pull myself together, not helped by the whispered, '*Wowzers*, talk about a blond bombshell,' from a mercilessly teasing Nari by my side.

Niilo is the last to sit, after deftly dishing up our lunch and handing out the steaming bowls.

'Thank you, I'm famished,' Nari says as Niilo settles on the seat next to her.

Elk, it turns out, is delicious and lean, and not unlike my mum's beef hotpot.

'The cold burns calories faster than any workout. You need to up your carbs on this kind of trip, keep your strength up,' Niilo replies, matter-of-factly, and I watch as Nari's face lights up. I saw her slipping a jumbo bar of

Galaxy chocolate into her backpack this morning so I'm guessing its days are numbered now.

There is something magical about sitting in the firelight with the aromas of wood smoke and rich, hearty food in the air, and I find myself feeling surprisingly festive, even in the sparse simplicity of the *lavvu*.

Stellan produces a big bottle of something carbonated and black which, I naturally assume is some kind of Finnish cola drink, but which turns out to be orange flavoured. Of course it does. I should have learned by now to expect the unexpected here.

As I'm remarking upon the curious unfamiliarity of so many of the things we've encountered since our arrival, Niilo serves up something from a frying pan that smells delicious. He simply calls them 'pancakes' as he offers them around.

'*Pink* pancakes?' I ask, nudging mine with my fork.

'Blood pancakes,' he replies.

I laugh, knowing this must be another of the famous jokes Finns make when they tease a friend, and I slice a bit off and take a bite, only to be struck by the savoury, floury, meaty taste; a little metallic, a little sweet.

All three of my *lavvu* companions, I notice, are watching me as my jaw works and I try to figure out what's happening to my taste buds.

'Tastes like… tastes like… black pudding?'

'Like I said, blood pancakes,' Niilo smiles. 'Made from whipped reindeer blood and… are you OK, Sylvie?'

I swallow, nod politely and wonder how on earth I can sneak this thing out to the huskies without anyone noticing. But everyone else seems to be tucking in, enjoying this course of our meal, and Nari's engaging Niilo in friendly chatter every now and again.

Stellan, I notice, is eating quietly, staring into the flames. I never could tolerate someone being awkwardly silent, so I put my plate down and try to catch his eye, building up to saying something, but what, I don't yet know.

'Do you get used to the cold, Stellan?' That's not a bad opener, I think. 'I'm guessing it's a lot different to the winter you spent in Manchester?'

He looks shaken for a moment but lifts another forkful to his mouth. All three of us watch him chewing slowly and I'm aware of Nari and Niilo casting furtive, amused glances at each other. Maybe I shouldn't have mentioned the exchange trip? Maybe it irritates him, confirming his suspicions that I'm here to conduct a post-mortem on a love affair that's been dead for fifteen years.

'It's not so bad if you dress well. It's the darkness that's hard to cope with,' he says, and the whole time I'm analysing his voice.

He doesn't sound cross or suspicious. He's just neutral. I guess we're just like any other tourists to him; nothing special or out of the ordinary.

Niilo laughs, and I see a slight shake of his head aimed at quiet, stuffy Stellan.

'People wouldn't come here if it were not for the cold and the dark. Think about it,' says Niilo. 'Most people fly in, head straight for their hotels, then they eat in heated restaurants, they sleep under glass domes or in cosy cabins, locked away from the outside world. A few venture out hiking, or husky-driving, or to the reindeer sled safaris. And mostly, they fly home straight afterwards with their souvenirs and their phones full of pretty pictures. They get what they came for, a taste of Lapland in winter, but I don't think they're seeing the real magic of this place. They want the tourist treatment mainly, and that's fine, it's lots of fun. But, for me, I welcome the cold and the dark when it stays around in January and February, when the flights are less frequent and Father Christmas has gone back to his workshop.' He winks at Nari, and neither of us can help smiling. 'I get my world back. The resort's so quiet and I'm alone with my thoughts and the dogs and the herd. That's when I can feel my family around me again.'

'You can feel them? But... they're not here?' Nari asks cautiously.

'No. I have nobody left, just friends, good friends. All my immediate family are spirits now.' He looks into the fire, and Nari glances at me, alarmed, as we realise Niilo's a man in mourning.

'I'm sorry,' she offers.

'That's OK. The landscape, my history, the dark nights and the snow, these things are very comforting. I have everything I need, now. And I have cousins in the south, and of course, I have Stellan.' He laughs suddenly, coming out of himself again. 'And, as you can tell, Stellan is full of entertaining stories and jokes to make the evenings fly.'

'Oh! I could tell a few stories about you, if you like, Niilo, enough to make our guests' hair stand on end,' Stellan says. 'Which shall I tell first?' he adds. 'The time you nearly got yourself trampled to death in that reindeer stampede, which you caused by dropping that bale of hay, or shall I tell them about the day you fell from the spa roof trying to clear the snow off?'

'As long as you don't mind me mentioning how your beer brewing experiment ended with your wardrobe doors getting exploded clean off?' Niilo replies, with laughter raising his voice.

It's heart-warming to see Stellan and Niilo face each other off with good-humoured camaraderie, like brothers.

I guess Nari's thinking the same thing because she's drawn her camera out from the pocket of her snowsuit and she quickly snaps a picture of our two hosts. Stellan notices and instantly clams up.

'Be careful with that,' he says, snappishly.

'Oh, I'm sorry, I usually ask first, but you two were laughing and it all looked so natural and festive, I guess I didn't think. I instinctively snapped a quick picture for my blog. I'm sorry, I'll delete it.'

'He means be careful of letting your camera get cold. The batteries will drain away in minutes in these temperatures,' reassures Niilo, but as I watch Stellan return to eating his meal without saying another word or meeting their eyes, I'm not so sure that is what he meant. The jollity of our shared meal seems to have been shattered and we silently drain our glasses.

Soon after, Niilo rises to his feet and clears away our empty dishes. There's a basin of water by the fire and I offer to help him wash up. As I dry our plates and pack them away in one of the boxes, I listen to Nari trying to get Stellan to chat about the logistics of running the tourist wilderness trails. He answers and even accepts a few squares from her slab of chocolate, but I notice she's treading carefully, and she doesn't write down any quotes or take any more photos, and in spite of Nari's unharacteristic blunder – goodness knows she's travelled enough to observe the etiquette for taking pictures – I'm still cross that he's making her so uncomfortable.

–

'You and Niilo are getting along all right then?' I say, once me and Nari are finally alone outside petting the dogs after lunch.

'He's adorable, maybe a little bit shy though.'

'Shy? You two haven't stopped talking since we set off from the resort.'

'Somebody had to fill the silence. Has Stellan used up his word ration for the year and he's spinning out five a day until January?'

'Silence is golden, apparently.'

'Is it now? You didn't say very much over lunch either. You OK?'

I nod and concentrate on smoothing the scruff of one of the dog's thick necks. I don't want to tell her how much I had hoped that Stellan's note last night had signified a break in the ice and that today I might get a glimpse of the old, charming, caring Stellan. If I'm honest, I'd been hoping for a reminder of the flirtatious, provocative Stellan I once knew too. But I daren't say anything, not until Nari's opinion of Stellan improves a bit, if it ever does. He's not exactly trying to win us over. I cringe as I remember the tension that had threatened to spoil our lovely meal and I tell myself to avoid the topic of Manchester for the rest of the day, in case dredging up the past again makes things even tenser.

I decide to stay with the dogs when Nari says she's going to get some pictures of the exterior of the *lavvu*, and

I watch her peep her head inside the tent first, presumably asking Stellan's permission.

Niilo stops by me on his way to the sleds with the blankets, and he hands me some of the leftover scraps of our lunch to share out amongst the huskies. He crouches beside me as we crumble bread, which the dogs hoover up in seconds, and he says confidingly, 'Don't let him worry you. He's not being rude; he just doesn't throw words away.'

I smile, a little abashed that he can tell I'm wounded. 'Nari thinks he's rationing them.'

'She might be right. Look at these leftovers from our meal. We ate, now the dogs eat, and then the birds will find the crumbs in the snow when we're gone. Nothing is wasted here. Every little thing is precious. And Stellan has taken this lesson to his heart. But his heart is kind. Remember that.'

I watch Niilo walking off to find Nari and accompanying her all the way back to their sled with gentlemanly attentiveness.

I think about Niilo's advice as I divide the rest of the scraps between the hungry mutts. No words wasted or thrown away. That's our Stellan, all right. But why does he think talking with me is wasteful, after all this time, when it feels as though there are things that need to be said?

Ugh! I could kick myself! All this awkwardness could have been avoided if I'd either a) ignored Nari and not let her talk me into this walk of shame down memory lane – we could be in hassle free Lanzarote right now. I haven't, to my knowledge, got any awkward exes hanging around there, or b) not thrown away the words 'I love you' on Stellan that day all those years ago.

Stellan had told me those aren't words you bandy about – you should use them sparingly when you really need them. It makes me wince to think about it. He thought I was brainlessly squandering my feelings, faking it, and all along I was completely madly devoted to him. In fact, I'm not just wincing, I'm getting cross.

Minä rakastan sinua, I'd said. I'd compressed my entire heart and soul into those little words and offered them up to him, and he'd done a runner. Back then, if he'd just let me, I'd have said those words to him ten times a day, every day, for the rest of our lives. I thought I had gotten over all this angst a long time ago, round about the time I met Cole, but here it is, hitting me in the feels all over again.

Maybe teenage breakups affect you forever, even if you aren't aware of that fact. I imagine my situation's rather unusual in that I'm here, thrown together with my first love, and it's increasingly clear there's still lots of messy emotions scattered all around us, love-bomb debris from the day I said 'I love you' and Stellan ran.

Right, Sylvie, New Plan. For the rest of this holiday, in fact, for the rest of my life, I've got to hold on to that mortifying, hideous memory, because when it comes to any old feelings I might still have for Stellan, it's a case of waste not, want not. He thinks I'm an emotional spendthrift and that I say too much? Well, I'll show him how bloody golden silence can be!

'Time to go.'

I jump up, startled at the sudden appearance of Stellan behind me, and I make one of the huskies jump too. Poor thing.

'OK,' I say, remembering my resolution. I'm not going to give this guy any further opportunities to make me, or Nari for that matter, feel ridiculous. When we arrive back at the sheds I'll politely say thank you and goodbye, and I'll steer clear of him until Boxing Day. Easy.

I settle myself in the sled and we make our way back to the resort, neither of us uttering a single word. Even when the darkness falls completely before three o'clock and I can't quite believe the day is over so soon, I don't exclaim aloud. And I have to bite the insides of my cheeks when I see the pink moon on the horizon, seemingly racing up into the sky. Is that some kind of arctic illusion? I can't ask him. I keep my thoughts to myself, and the dogs run us all the way home across the frozen lake and through the great drifts of snow as fine flakes fall like glitter upon my face.

Chapter Twelve

'I'm going to my cabin to turn some of these notes into copy for the blog. You'll be all right getting to your cabin with Stellan, won't you?' Nari shouts out with barely concealed amusement once she's finished saying goodbye to the dogs back at the husky shed.

Niilo instantly offers to walk with her and the pair of them shuffle off into the dark. I hear Nari laughing as they go.

Stellan's just finished expertly coaxing each dog back into the enclosure behind the shed and now, I'm left looking at him and feeling ridiculous, because he seems to be pretending he hasn't heard Nari dumping me on him. She thinks she's matchmaking. I could happily run after her and shove her in a snowdrift.

Alone with Stellan. This was not part of my plan. I'm about to say, 'Well, I'll be off then,' when he strides over.

'Do you want to help with the dogs?'

'Sure.' *Dammit!* Here's me aiming for aloof and disinterested and he's offering me canine nirvana. 'Just for a bit, then I'd better get ready for dinner with Nari.'

Once we're inside again beneath the shed's fluorescent lights and all the dogs are munching happily on something that looks like strips of beefy jerky, Stellan indicates that he wants me to sit down on the bales beside Kanerva's puppies. He's produced two steaming mugs of hot chocolate from a neat little kitchen inside a glass cubicle in the corner of the shed, and we settle on the straw bales, looking intently at the dogs as they chew.

I don't want to be the one to break the silence, but he really is just sitting there staring into his drink. I clear my throat and he glances up with what looks like hopeful relief in his eyes.

'Stellan,' I say. 'I know it must be weird me turning up like this at your resort. Would you believe me if I said it was a coincidence, at first?' You shouldn't, I think to myself. I chose Saariselkä hoping, deep down, you'd be here, like a fool.

'It's not weird. I'm glad you're here. Are you happy you came?'

'Yeah. Yeah, I am.' I nod. 'But please don't feel obligated to show us around or anything. Me and Nari can see the sights on our own. You should probably be getting back to your tourists. It *is* Christmas Eve tomorrow, it must be your busiest day of the year, what with all the preparations for the big day.'

Stellan nods, and I wonder if he looks a little wounded.

'I mean, obviously, it was nice spending time with you,' I say quickly. 'It was good to catch up after all these years, wasn't it, with an old friend?'

The moment of silence that follows is so excruciating I almost ask for another of those disgusting *salmiakki* sweets just to break the tension. I feel a bit churlish and rude now I've said all that out loud. I take a drink of chocolate and think about saying something about how I'll get out of his hair now, leave him to finish his work, when finally Stellan speaks.

'Why *are* you here, Sylvie?' He meets my disconcerted eyes for a second then looks down again.

'Well, I'm on holiday, aren't I?'

'Alone?'

'I'm not alone, I'm with Nari.'

'I meant, with no family, or...'

'Oh! Right. No, I don't have anyone like that. No partner or... anything.'

Now he's looking right at me. If I don't ask now, I never will. Here goes nothing. 'And what about you? Does your... partner live here too? On the resort, I mean?'

He shrugs his broad shoulders slowly. 'No partner. Just me. It's kind of hard to meet someone out here – someone who's sticking around after the end of the season, that is.'

'Right,' I nod. Thank God my cheeks are blotchy red from the cold because I'm pretty sure I can feel the heat rising up my neck and spreading across my face, which is ridiculous, and I tell myself off.

'I, um...' Stellan shifts uncomfortably on the bale. 'I heard you were getting married. I assumed you were... still married?'

'How would you know I was getting married?' *He's Googled me!* The sheepish grin on his face tells me I'm right. We both laugh at our ridiculous awkwardness.

'I looked you up online, years ago,' he says quietly, his head down, still smiling.

This is crazy, I think. 'Look, Stellan, I was dumped, OK? Just before the wedding and after a decade long engagement, as it happens. So, there. No husband. Just me and Nari getting away from the humiliation of a singleton's Christmas in England. Now you know. But don't feel sorry for me. I don't. Not any more, I don't.'

As I'm saying this I realise this is the first time this has occurred to me. I've thrown myself a six month long pity party and revelled in the misery, and here I am at minus twenty degrees, miles inside the Arctic Circle, surrounded by gorgeous mutts, feeling… all right actually, and genuinely, definitely not sorry for myself! *Hah!*

'Asshole,' says Stellan.

'I'm sorry, what?'

'He's an asshole.'

'Cole? Certifiably, yes.'

'What happened?'

I gulp. I remember Stellan being straightforward. He doesn't dress up his questions, and likes to get to the point, but *wow*, it's disarming when you're used to English prevarication.

Sod it, I may as well tell him the whole story. In my new frame of mind it might do me good to say it aloud, once and for all, to someone I barely know any more, and who I'll never see again after this afternoon.

I prepare myself by taking a long drink from my steaming mug, thinking what a shame it is that we're unlikely to meet again, and how I know we haven't exactly hit it off, but it would be nice to keep in touch, when Stellan interrupts my thoughts.

'You don't have to tell me if it hurts too much.'

'I'll tell you. It's not Cole leaving that hurts, not any more. It's what happened afterwards. I don't think I'll ever recover.'

'*Jesus!* All right, I'm listening.'

–

It started the day Cole disappeared. I was in the most beautiful wedding shop you've ever seen, in Chester. I was standing in front of the mirror in my dress, all seed pearls and satin, and the seamstress was crouching at my feet, cutting the hem freehand – and me and Mum and Nari were just watching her shears working, amazed at how chilled she seemed despite having only one chance to cut it correctly, and I was trying so hard to stand still, when my mobile rang. Nari answered then passed it to me.

It was Cole. He was at the airport. He'd changed his mind. The wedding was off.

I couldn't take it in at first. I'd been staying at Mum and Dad's for a few days so I could do a practice run at the hairdresser's, sort out the champagne at the cash and carry, and do a thousand other wedding related jobs. Cole was supposed to have that whole week off work so he could collect the wedding cake and pick up his suit and see to the last minute arrangements at the reception venue, but instead he'd put his name down for some standby shifts. He'd been offered the chance of long-haul work, and he'd taken it.

He said he wasn't coming back for the wedding, he was sorry, he'd never forgive himself, blah, blah, blah. And that was it. The poor seamstress was still only halfway through cutting my hem and I was shaking uncontrollably and sobbing my heart out.

When a wedding's cancelled, it's not like in the films where, once there's been an appropriate amount of crying, they cut straight to the getting-on-with-her-life montage and she soon learns what a lucky escape she's had. In real life there's actually a bunch of admin to do. It's a bit like when somebody passes away; you want to lie on the floor and just cry forever but there's relentlessly grim paperwork to be done and a thousand arrangements to be made. I knew I'd have all this stuff to sort out, and fast, including deciding what to do with my lovely dress, which I'd never walk down the aisle in but I'd still have to pay for.

In spite of all this, even when I was panicked and distraught, there was one little bit of comfort waiting for me at home: Barney.

Cole had simply flown off that morning, leaving him alone at our house. That's what I thought anyway. I couldn't get that wedding dress off quickly enough. I threw my clothes on and we all rushed out to pick him up, me howling in Mum's back seat all the way to Manchester.

Barney was never happy being left alone for too long; he'd get lonely and bored and chew things, furniture mainly. He'd been like that since the day I found him, or rather, the day we found each other.

I'd spotted him in a rescue centre advert in the local paper. The vet thought he might be about ten weeks old, but nobody could be certain. I knew instantly that he was *my* dog. I'd been so lonely after moving to the Love Shack. I'd just finished my teaching degree and was struggling to find full time work and Cole was *always* flying – that, I'd quickly realised, was the major downside of being engaged to a glamorous, handsome airline pilot; that and his falling in love with air hostesses. Somehow Barney's big brown eyes behind the kennel bars had been irresistible and I brought him home that weekend.

When Cole got back from his run of Malaysian stopovers there was this rolling, tumbling, sofa chewing ball of fluff piddling on his pristine white carpets. Loving Barney hadn't come as easily to Cole as it had for me but the little guy grew on him after a while, and we gave him a lovely life; walking holidays in Cornwall and sausages for tea every now and then, and Frisbee-chasing and...

Well, anyway, when we got to the house Barney wasn't there. There was a 'For Sale' sign outside and Cole had had the locks changed. All my stuff was in boxes in the garage. So his sudden change of heart about the wedding hadn't been so sudden after all. And for years I'd dopily handed over my wages and never questioned why Cole was so resistant to the idea of a joint mortgage. He'd orchestrated the perfect, consequence-free coward's escape.

I rang Cole's mum and, of course, the old bat wouldn't pick up. We went to her house and she wouldn't answer the door, even though I could hear Barney barking from the kitchen extension at the sound of the doorbell.

I was frantic, but there was nothing else to do but go back to Mum and Dad's and wait. I rang her a zillion times a day for three days, until eventually she answered. She said that Cole had given her instructions to look after Barney and that was what she was doing, now that he was from a 'broken home'. She said Barney was perfectly happy and I was to leave them in peace until me and Cole sorted it all out when he got back.

I begged her to let me come and collect him but she was having none of it. I knew I couldn't bring Barney to Mum and Dad's anyway because of Dad's allergies, and Nari's flat was a no-pet rental, and I couldn't even *get into* my own house, so I gave in and asked Patricia to at least let me pop round and visit him and – this is what still kills me – she said she didn't want me 'toing and froing', especially knowing the state I was in, in case it confused or frightened poor Barney.

I know I should have put up a fight, and I suppose I could have called the police and reported her for dognapping or something – although it's not *technically* theft if it's your son's dog and he's left him in your care, is it? And there was part of me that knew she was right. I *was* in a terrible state, and I couldn't exactly care for Barney, I had nowhere to take him. Some of the other teachers at school, the ones I count as friends, would have taken him, I realise now, but at the time I couldn't bring myself to impose on their precious school holidays with their own families and pets. So I'd swallowed down the bitterness and my longing to scratch his big fuzzy noggin, and I waited, thinking Cole would have to come back and face the music sometime soon.

There was some small comfort in Patricia looking after him though. Like so many impossible old battleaxes, Patricia loves dogs better than any other creatures on earth – well, apart from Cole, her golden boy, of course. Everybody knew that Barney would be well cared for, spoiled rotten even, and it was only supposed to be a short-term arrangement. That very day I started looking for a rental property with a landlord who'd let me keep a pet – harder than you'd think on my wages.

Anyway, I still had what was supposed to be my wedding day to get through, and me and Nari had decided to spend that weekend in the hotel where the reception was supposed to be, so I couldn't really get much done in those first few heartbroken days. I simply resigned myself to the fact that Barney was Patricia's houseguest for a while and I'd just have to pine for him until Cole got home and

I could confront the bastard. But eight days later, and still with no sign of Cole, Barney got ill.

It must have been a broken heart that did it, that, and all the sudden changes in his routine, and him not understanding how much I wanted him... Oh, here come the tears again! I can't think about it without sobbing. Every single time it floors me like a kick in the stomach.

It was a seizure, apparently, while he was out for his walk with Patricia. It was very sudden and very severe.

I didn't even get to say goodbye. Patricia didn't call for two days and by then his body had been taken away by the vet, and it was all just too late.

I'll never forgive Cole, or his mother, but mostly I can't forgive myself for just surrendering like that, for giving Barney up, but I really *did* think he'd be coming back to live with me once I'd sorted out the mess Cole had left us in.

'You couldn't have known that was going to happen. You are *not* to blame.'

Stellan's voice reaches me through the grief just as I feel him shifting onto the bale beside me and wrapping me in his arms.

By now I'm a snotty, red-eyed mess and I can't stop the tears.

'I'm sorry, Stellan,' I say with an unattractive snort that has him reaching into his pocket for a pack of tissues. 'I've barely spoken about Barney since he died. Something about being here with all these huskies just...'

'You never get over losing your best friend,' Stellan says.

His voice is low and close to my ear and I feel overwhelmed by tiredness at its lullaby cadence. I could sleep here in his arms with the sounds of the dogs snuffling and

133

playing all around us, but I check myself. Haven't I only just resolved to hold back, to play it cool until Boxing Day when I fly home? I don't need any more complicated feelings to contend with.

'Stellan,' I say, extricating myself from his arms. 'I should be getting back now.'

'Not until your tears are dry,' he says, leaning into the enclosure and reaching for one of Kanerva's sleeping pups. 'Here, a hug from little Toivo will help.' He smiles as he gently places the fluffy, warm bundle on my lap.

And he's right, it does help. I spend a long time just stroking Toivo's lovely fur and whispering to him as he snores contentedly while Stellan sees to the dogs' next feed and starts locking up the shed and turning off some lights.

When he's ready to leave he comes over and sits by my side again, close enough so that the thick layers of our snowsuits over our thighs almost touch, and he hands me a key.

'Here, this is for you. You're right, I will have a lot of work to do over Christmas, so I won't always be around, but listen, there's usually someone here at the sheds, often it's me, but just in case, this key means you can visit the pups for a hug any time you need one, OK?'

'That's so nice of you, thank you.' I'm grinning into his face now and feeling all kinds of warm fuzzies in my heart that I haven't felt for years.

I see him pull his body a little further away from me as he surveys my face, and I have no idea what he's thinking.

'Will you let me take you out on the resort again tomorrow? Just us?' he says, suddenly.

I fluster a little over my reply, but I hope it comes out sounding unfazed and casual.

'Don't let Toivo hear you talking like that,' I say, covering the puppy's ears. 'He'll feel left out.'

Stellan looks down at the sleeping pup on my lap and smiles.

'But I thought you had a lot of work to do on the resort?' I add, immediately rewarding myself with an imaginary kick for being such a self-sabotaging spoilsport.

He nods, and seems lost in thought for a moment. 'No. The staff could probably run this place like clockwork, if I ever gave them the chance. They should manage without me for a while. I do have a special job for Christmas Day that I can't get out of though.' He lifts Toivo from my lap and returns him to Kanerva, all the while smiling secretively.

I raise an eyebrow, but I don't pursue it. He's letting me know we've only got tomorrow together and that's it, so I'm going to say 'yes' and make the most of his precious free time before my holiday ends.

'All right then,' I say, trying not to betray the little buzz of happiness that I feel at the thought of Christmas Eve with Stellan, which is contending with my annoyance at myself for capitulating so easily on my resolve to steer clear of him. 'I'll spend the morning with you, on one condition,' I say, and I hope it comes across as nicely standoffish.

'What's that?' he asks.

'That you drop your defences a little?' I watch as he frowns at this, and I press on. 'We used to know each other pretty well, and I feel like we've gone back to the beginning again.'

'Is that so bad? Getting to know each other again?'

I absorb the intense earnestness of his expression and think that, of course, he's right. It's been so long since we knew each other, and we've both changed. Me more than him, probably, if looks are anything to go by. His shoulders are broader maybe, and it's hard to tell with these snowsuits, but he seems more muscled and substantial somehow, and even though he's got his beanie rammed down over his hair once again, I noticed earlier that he was blonder. But he's still the same serious, calm, steady Stellan, with the same brief sparks of warmth and humour that I loved about him.

'Of course, that's no bad thing,' I say. 'I'd love to get to know more about you and your life now. And of course things have changed, but… please don't put up a wall. Let me in a bit. We're not kids any more.'

Stellan nods slowly, his smile laced with self-recrimination. I'm guessing he's heard this from other people too.

'There's an old joke about Finns, you know. It goes… you can be sure you're talking with a Finnish introvert if he looks at his shoes when he speaks, and you'll know you've met a Finnish *extrovert* because he's looking at *your* shoes when he speaks.' Despite his insistence about his introverted nature, he laughs and looks straight into my eyes. 'But you're right, I'm thirty-six now, I've changed a lot, even if I'm reserved at first.'

'Reserved? You were positively grumpy yesterday, not to mention during lunch today.'

'I know, and I'm sorry. I won't hold back any more.'

'Good, OK,' I say with a decisive nod.

'Allow me to walk you back to your cabin. Nari will be waiting. And I'll come find you tomorrow morning at eleven?'

'What are we going to be doing?'

'Just wear your snow gear, I'll think of something special.'

Chapter Thirteen

'So, are you going to tell me how things went with Niilo this morning on the husky run, now we're out of earshot of the resort staff?' I ask, as Nari clambers onto the toboggan at the top of the floodlit slope. She'd been reluctant to spill the beans over our early dinner at the hotel restaurant with the serving staff, Niilo's friends and colleagues, flitting to and fro.

'See you at the bottom!' she yells with a grin before shuffling herself to the edge of the slope and disappearing into the darkness with a delighted scream.

'Oh, for goodness' sake.' It was hard enough work dragging this plastic death wish device from the bottom of the slope all the way up here, now I've got to dodge the pre-schoolers on even smaller – and more lethal, in my opinion – versions of my toboggan, merrily launching themselves head-first downhill without a care for the other people criss-crossing the run below.

'Here goes nothing,' I say as I sit down, hearing the flimsy plastic creak beneath me. I'd cross myself, but I'm not sure I'd be doing it right, and honestly, does Jesus even do holy protection for otherwise sensible adults willingly flinging themselves down a slippery slope on something only marginally better engineered than a canteen tea tray?

Just as I'm bum shuffling my way to the edge, two teenagers bustle past me, throw down their toboggans and recklessly hurl their bodies upon them as they're already in motion. I'll just have to wait until they've cleared my landing zone; the last thing I want is to have a crash, but instead of stopping, I find the momentum of the toboggan on the hard ice is carrying me over the precipice and suddenly I'm hurtling downhill after them.

It's at this point Nari streaks past me again, screaming '*Yee-haw!*' She's red-cheeked and howling with laughter and holding the toboggan ropes in one hand while lasso-spinning her scarf above her head with the other, like an *après ski* cowgirl.

I sensibly lean back, keeping my boots on the ice as I slide, trying to slow myself down, and I watch as a toddler stuffed rigidly into a padded snowsuit overtakes me at speed, giggling wildly.

I see Nari down at the bottom, lit by floodlights, crashing her toboggan into the great fluffy snowdrift intended to help lunatics make emergency stops. She immediately gets to her feet, dusts the snow from her knees, and turns to look back up the slope towards me. She's smirking and jabbing a mittened index finger at an invisible watch on her wrist. She can mock all she wants, I think, as I sail downhill at my own stately pace.

'Do we even have insurance for this sort of thing?' I ask as I come to a leisurely halt and Nari helps to haul me up.

'Of course, all taken care of,' she grins.

'Stephen again?'

'Yep. See you in a sec.'

'Woah, woah, where are you racing off to?' I say, catching Nari's arm.

'Back to the top.'

'What? You said we ought to *try* tobogganing. I've tried it, now let's find a bar while the going's good and we've got all our limbs intact.'

'One more go. Come on. You might even want to put your feet *inside* the toboggan this time.'

Nari's hard to say no to, so I relent, and we make our way up the treacherously frozen steps which, to my mind, are as lethal as the slope itself. Kids jostle and weave past us on their way up, laughing and screaming with delight. I don't know where they get their energy from. My thigh muscles are burning with the exertion, made even worse by the weight of the snowsuit and boots.

'So, tell me then,' I puff. 'What did Niilo talk about all day? I could hear you two chattering all the way along the trail.' We're at the top again, and my lungs are close to bursting.

'Oh, all sorts. He's really interesting, you know.' She lays her toboggan down near the edge, and I do the same. 'He's full of facts about Finland, and he's polite and he's attractive…' We sit side by side and face the slope. 'And, do you know, I discovered he's got an *absolutely enormous…*'

The rest of her sentence is lost in the rushing air as she zooms off down the hill without any warning, and I'm surprised to find I'm hurrying to catch her, pushing myself over the edge.

'What?' I shout towards her back which is rapidly disappearing ahead of me. I follow behind, only this time around I'm going much, *much* faster. 'An absolutely enormous *what*?'

It's at this point that I hit the first of the moguls: great mounds of hard snow peppering this, far steeper, side of the run; the kind of thing you see skiers negotiating on the winter Olympics. Except I'm not a rugged Olympian on the telly; I'm a history teacher on a tray, and I'm terrified. My screams fill the air and my eyeballs are popping so far out of my head they're close to freezing.

I hit the bottom of the run in seconds, having been bumped and jolted and almost thrown clean off this hideous contraption. Nari's standing over me as I come to an inelegant stop and struggle to straighten my bobble hat and catch my breath.

"Enormous what?' I gasp.

'Herd of reindeer.'

I watch her walking away, her laughter clouding the air.

–

Nari buys me a cup of tea at the booth by the exit from the slopes, by way of an apology, and we make our way back towards Saariselkä town centre, a good ten minutes' walk away. The early evening is completely dark apart from the streetlights and the alluring glow of store windows and restaurant signs in the distance. Occasionally, a car crawls past on the icy road. Nari and I cling together so we don't slip on the shining ice coating the well-trodden pavements.

'I don't know, we just talked. It was nice. And surprisingly easy,' Nari is saying. 'Niilo told me all about his life before he moved to the resort. He said he was a *verrde*, I think that's what he called it, a kind of helper on reindeer migrations. He told me he used to travel with his family's own herds when he was tiny. They let herder families have special holidays from school to travel with their animals to the calving and pasture areas. But when he left school he became a helper with other people's herds. That's how he made his living for years, he said. He's crossed Finnish Lapland many times on foot and skidoo. Imagine that! But then he came back here, where his family once lived, and he got work with Stellan and settled down. He said Stellan helped him out at a time when he really didn't know what to do with his life, and he had no reindeer herd of his own. It was quite sweet really, the way he spoke about him. Maybe I've got your grumpy Finn all wrong? What do you reckon?'

I shrug off this diversion. 'We're talking about you, Nari. What else did Niilo tell you?'

'He told me some stuff about Sámi culture and said I could use some of it in the blog if I wanted, so that was nice. And he asked me lots of questions.'

'About the blog?'

'No, not really, about my life. He wanted to know about my travel books, so I told him where he could find them online, and he seemed fascinated by all the places I've been. I told him about the baby turtles hatching on the beaches at Isla Los Brasiles, and that Machu Picchu eco-tourism holiday I did – remember the one with the litter picking along the trails? And when I told him about the hot air balloon ride over the Valley of the Kings he looked amazed, as though I was describing a trip to Mars! He wasn't like other blokes though, always wondering aloud why I want to travel alone, asking me if it isn't too risky. He just seemed to understand.'

'But you're going to see him again this trip, aren't you?' I can't help delving, I need to know.

'I said I'd have to talk with you first, see if you didn't mind. He asked me to meet him tomorrow after his reindeer safari trips for the tourists, three o'clock, he said. But I wouldn't dream of leaving you alone if you don't have plans.'

I think about my arrangement with Stellan and wince. I hadn't even considered what it might mean to Nari to spend the day alone, I'd just agreed to go. I'm a terrible friend.

'It's OK, I do have plans, and even if I didn't, I'd want you to go and see Niilo. How often do you actually like a guy?'

'I didn't say I *like* him, like him,' she protests. 'He's just good company, that's all. And it's a work thing, really. There's a few things I want to check out for the blog, and maybe we can have some fun along the way. I want to sample all the Lappish alcohol and get to grips with the nightlife, if there is any. Anyway, what plans have you made?'

'Umm,' I murmur, unsure how to describe it. We've come to a stop at the very edge of the busy strip of hotels and restaurants at the town centre. We need to think about catching our bus back to the resort at some point. It's getting late, almost eight o'clock, and most places seem to be closing up for the evening.

'Is it a date?' Nari says, nudging me, almost making me spill the last of the tea from my paper cup.

'No. Not a date. Just old friends. I think he feels awkward about me being here and feels obliged to show

143

me his resort. He's picking me up in the morning. I imagine I'll be back by the time you set off with Niilo.'

'O-kay,' Nari says, with long drawn out vowels that tell me she thinks this is bull.

'*What?* You saw how he was today, all rude and belligerent. Hardly the behaviour of someone who fancies me, is it? We're friends, if that.'

I stop Nari's eyebrow raising in its tracks by throwing a question back at her.

'So, are you going to write about your date with Niilo on your blog?'

'I hadn't really considered that. I'm saying, *no*. That would be totally off-brand these days. It's been years since I combined my dating stories with my travel blogging.'

I think about the comments I often see popping up on Nari's blog posts. I've got my notifications set to alert me to any new posts and followers' comments appearing on her elegant website. Her old posts are all on there, dating back years. Some of Nari's followers from those days still remember Nari's hilarious dating antics that first drew them to her site, they often say how they would love to see a return to the old dating blog, or a combination of the two (romance and travel) again.

'No, whatever happens with Niilo, I'll be keeping it strictly off public record, thanks very much,' she says.

'So *something's* going to happen?' I say with a teasing laugh, wishing my lovely friend could at last have a bit of love in her life, and not just between the pages of the novels she reads. Nari's about to tell me off, when we both hear a sublime sound, and we turn to one another, eyes wide.

'Is someone singing?' Nari says.

We look all around searching for the source of the soaring voice resonating in the air and the deep melodious piano sounds that seem to be rumbling through the ground beneath our feet.

'It's coming from over there,' I say. 'Through those trees.'

–

The church stands alone by the roadside, concealed by great Christmas trees and white-trunked birches. The timber building has a high roof pointing heavenward with a white cross on top, and looks as though it has stood on this spot for centuries in spite of its modern architecture.

Nari photographs the handwritten sign on the door using her phone, does some kind of technical jiggery-pokery, and magically translates the words.

'It says it's open and all are welcome, apparently. There's a rehearsal for a new year's concert going on. Shall we?'

She's already got her hand on the glass and is pushing her way inside. The heavy door creaks as I pass through it and we come to a stop in the wide vestibule. I'm hit by the comforting array of smells; wood polish mingling with recently struck matches and candle wax, and there's something sweet baking somewhere, and the roasted, savoury smell of coffee.

An elderly man greets us and points towards the next set of doors. Neither of us know exactly what he said, but we get the gist that we're to go inside and investigate where the music is coming from, which we gladly do.

Nobody notices us as we sneak into the high-ceilinged chapel just as the music swells to a climax. We pull our hats off and grab two of the very few unoccupied chairs which are set out in rows, and we become part of the congregation.

A bearded man in jeans and a baggy cream jumper with a golden woollen cross on the front is standing on a raised stage in front of the pulpit. He's wearing a Madonna-style headset and microphone which is sending his calm, steady voice over the church's speakers as he leads the rehearsal. I'm guessing he's the priest – or he's just really into statement knitwear. He twinkles his eyes at us to signal that we're welcome and we settle in to listen to the singing.

The elderly man who met us at the door shuffles in holding a violin and makes his way onto the stage, where he is joined by a little girl, who can only be about ten years old. The knitted vicar helps her arrange her sheet music on the rack above the piano keys. As she sits down to play, some unseen person dims the lights. The room darkens and a spotlight shines onto the stage. The fairy lights from the Christmas tree by the pulpit glow out in the half light.

There is silence in the audience as the vicar says a few words to the child and she nods before spreading her fingers over the keys and beginning to play. The vicar takes a guitar from behind the piano and sits on a chair by the Christmas tree, waiting for his cue to join in.

I close my eyes as the room fills with a beautiful melody. I hear the violin and guitar strings join in after a few moments as the introduction swells, and I'm aware suddenly of the sounds of people rising to their feet around us. My eyes flick open and I find I'm the only person still sitting; even Nari has sprung up and is looking around, a little alarmed that we're expected to sing any moment now.

The congregation opens its voice and they sing in festive accord. Whatever it is they're singing, it's beautiful. There's nothing Nari and I can do but sway gently to the music and try to hum along – singing is difficult when you don't speak the language. The young couple next to Nari notice we're clueless and pass us one of the songbooks, but looking at the Finnish words on the page, we're still just as lost.

The sounds rise and fall and I look over the heads of the singing crowd at the huge windows at the back of the stage. There's no stained glass in this church, instead there's something far prettier; towering clear glass with a view beyond of the snowy churchyard with a cluster of Christmas trees resplendent in strands of shining white lights.

I smile at Nari and think how, for the first time since we arrived, I can truly feel my Christmas spirits revived. Here amongst the strangers making music, I'm somehow at home and completely, utterly peaceful; something I haven't felt for many months.

The tall candles lining the walls flicker, and I find myself staring at their dancing light reflected in the windows, and I try to sing along without knowing the words. It doesn't matter, I just want to sing.

After three more songs, and quite a lot of sitting down and standing up again, an exuberant round of applause signals it's the end of the rehearsal, and I feel myself waking as if I'd slept and dreamt the whole thing.

Nari and I are gathering our scarves and gloves, ready to head out into the dark night, when the violin man stops us at the door and spreads his arms wide as if to contain us. He smiles and says, '*Olkaa hyvä ja jääkää kahville.*'

Nari's shaking her head, polite but confused, and reaching for her translation app, when I realise he's directing us towards another room off to the side of the stage which everyone seems to be slowly filing into.

'Coffee and food, please stay,' he adds, in perfect English.

And so we follow him, finding a long table set out with cups and Tupperware and tins full of all kinds of homemade baked treats. And that's where we spend the rest of our evening, making conversation, sometimes aided by clever technology, with our new friends. Nari likes to at least try to speak the local languages, but I'm relieved the whole party speaks English clear as a bell; in fact, they all seem to be fluent, despite their frequent apologies for their (perfect) English. I tell them their language skills put me with my ability to say precisely zero words in Finnish (well, I do know *sauna*) to shame.

I'm eating a gorgeous nutty cake with butter cream icing when I ask the woolly clergyman – who turns out to be sweetly gentle and exquisitely quietly spoken without his microphone and speaker system – about one of the songs I'd heard. It had sounded as though they were singing my name, Sylvie. 'Did I imagine that?'

He walks off, coming back a moment later with a leather-bound songbook, and he shows me some lyrics.

'*Sylvian joululaulu?*' I say, stumbling over the pronunciation and making everyone within earshot smile, humouring the dopey English woman.

'It's a Christmas song, very famous in Finland, very important.'

'It was lovely, what is it about?'

'Oh, this is not so lovely. A song about night-singing birds, trapped and then cruelly blinded and kept in cages, so their singing in the darkness will attract other birds, who are also then captured.'

'Oh!'

'Yes, I know,' the vicar smiles. 'Very Finnish.'

'And it's a Christmas song?'

'Yes, a very old one. But it's about loving Finland too, and the winter and longing to be at home, safe and comfortable.'

'That's beautiful,' I say, as he presses the book into my free hand – the other is still clasping a plate piled with delicious cakes and cookies.

'Our gift to you.'

'Oh, I can't take this, it belongs to the church.'

'I insist. Return it on your next visit, if you like, some other winter.'

And so, Nari and I leave the church late that night, only just in time to hop on the last bus to Frozen Falls resort, with my new songbook souvenir, our bellies full of festive baking, our heads buzzing with music and the happy chatter of the congregation. And that's how it begins to come back to me, my love for Christmas. At last. I'd known, deep down, Cole and his heartbreaking hadn't stripped it away completely.

All the way back to our cabins I tell Nari how much I adore this time of year and everything associated with it, and how I'm finally utterly convinced we made the right decision to come to beautiful, surprising, welcoming Finnish Lapland.

Chapter Fourteen

Hello from gorgeous Lapland.

Our second day here has been a whirlwind of snowy adventure. There were husky dogs (adorable), elk stew (delicious), blood pancakes (yes, I said *blood* pancakes) and cured reindeer meat (tastes exactly as you'd expect it to: like something you'd buy for your poodle in a pet shop) sliced off in big hunks for me to chew by a new friend in a traditional *lavvu* tent.

Tonight, my friend S and I dined early at the resort restaurant again. The atmosphere's cosy and bustling, and its fine as far as food goes. There is a lot of meat, I mean *loads*, and some root veg and gorgeous bread. But it's expensive to transport fresh produce up here, so we're making do with the odd apple and preserved summer fruit (jam, pickles, chutney, frozen berry smoothies). I'm already becoming a bit of a stranger to greens this holiday, but the scarcity of fresh stuff makes it all the more special somehow. Imagine getting excited over a side of fresh broccoli, but that's what happened!

So, what about the overall experience so far? I'm realising that even if you get everything you came for (snow, elves, huskies, winter sports) the average tourist doesn't really get to know Finnish Lapland and its people, culture or history. Luckily, we've found two guides steeped in the history of this place – our guides to something more 'authentic'. Though, even without their help, I think we stumbled into a true local community space tonight, and we were welcomed with open hearts.

If you can visit the little chapel near Saariselkä, you must. I sang every carol; nobody seemed to mind that I didn't understand any of the words, and I couldn't pronounce them either. It was perfect, unforgettable, and beautiful. And I got to do it with my best friend; a rare treat for me, the lone traveller.

So, here's something to chew on. Did you know that Finnish Lapland is in large part Sápmi – the ancestral lands of the Sámi (or Saami) people, sometimes described as the only indigenous people of Europe? Sápmi lands stretch right across the northern Scandinavian countries.

There are thousands of people who identify as Sámi living in Finland and hundreds of thousands living all over the globe. Part of the history of the Sámi people is depressingly familiar: displacement, developments on traditional territories, and the suppression of traditions, languages and cultural practices. But here in Inari, and all across the Sápmi, there's continuance too, and cultural investment, and celebration and a flourishing worldwide sense of Sámi belonging. All of this, according to my new friend, N.

He's going to tell me more tomorrow.

I want to get to know the man, find out what it's like living and working in Lapland and, if he's happy to share, learn more about his family traditions. Until tomorrow, sleep tight, Nari Bell

#BigCosyBed #GalaxyChocolate #NoAurora #Disappointing #LaplandNights #NewFriends #WhyITravel

Chapter Fifteen

Waking up on Christmas Eve in a snowbound cabin by a Lapland forest is, let me tell you, the most Christmassy thing I'm ever likely to experience, and a world away from last Christmas when I woke up next to Cole at the Love Shack, preparing for a tense day at Patricia's. *Ugh*, I don't even want to think about that now. Not when the world is still totally dark at nine a.m. and I am contentedly sitting up in bed – I've braved a night in the glass room and found I'm not afraid to sleep in there any more.

I'm batting away intrusive memories of Cole and Christmases past and watching the snow falling from the black sky and wondering if I can be bothered clambering into my snowsuit to drag myself to breakfast at the hotel restaurant when Nari bangs on my cabin door. She's in her pyjamas and snow boots with a furry blanket clasped around her.

'Come and see what's just arrived in my kitchen!' she yells as soon as I open the door, and I watch as she runs off and up the steps of her cabin next to mine.

Grabbing keys, pulling on snow boots and wrapping a white woollen throw around me, I chase after her, making deep footprints in the crunching snow.

I find Nari unpacking a big picnic basket at the kitchen island, grinning from ear to ear.

'What's all this?'

'Stephen's PA emailed last night telling me to expect a surprise delivery today. Just look at all this stuff.'

There are two beautiful hand carved wooden Lappish bowls and matching deep wooden spoons like ladles, a bag of almonds tied with a red ribbon, a tall glass bottle of freshly squeezed orange juice, a box of apple pastries dusted with snowy icing sugar, a thermos of espresso, a jar of runny cream, something that looks like fruity, nutty muesli and lots of other little boxes and packets, all beautifully wrapped and extremely tempting.

'There's a note,' Nari says as she unfolds the piece of paper.

> *A taste of the best of Lapland. Enjoy your break-*
> *fast, x*

That's all the encouragement we need and within half an hour we're full of sweet treats and enjoying the caffeine buzz. 'Good old Stephen, what a thoughtful gift,' I say, stretching out on the sofa in front of Nari's blazing fire-place.

I notice she's made an effort and decorated her Christmas tree. I think of the bare spruce in my cabin next door and the basket beside it, still filled with pretty baubles. What with dog-sledding and dining out at the resort restaurant, then the toboggans and carolling, I just haven't found the time, and I'll be heading out again soon.

Nari's already getting absorbed in writing her blog and looks settled on the big armchair so I don't feel too bad about abandoning her this morning.

'You staying here all day?' I ask.

'Yup, until three, then I'm taking Niilo out for a night on the tiles – well, an afternoon on the gritted streets.'

'Well, you guys have fun. Don't cut your date short on my account, OK? I'll be totally fine having dinner by myself in my cabin, and I might have an early night.'

'Here's hoping you do.' Nari's waggling her eyebrows and doing her leery grin again.

'I don't know what you're suggesting. I'm only taking a look around the resort with Stellan this morning, nothing else. It's you who's going on the hot date.'

She just laughs at this and shakes her head, which is annoying because, as much as I'd like to be preparing for a romantic date, the most I can expect from Stellan is a (hopefully) friendly and relaxed meetup this morning, just two old acquaintances spending a few hours together.

Fifty minutes later, I'm waiting on the steps of my cabin, in the resort-issue black snowsuit and so many layers there's no way the cold can get through today. I've managed to blow dry and straighten my hair into submission and – don't read anything into this – I've borrowed Nari's pretty white snood and red lipstick (the lipstick was her idea), and I'm feeling pretty glam actually, which is miraculous given the extremes of hot and cold, damp and dry here. But where is Stellan? It's almost eleven and he was never, ever late, back in the day.

I can see Nari through her cabin window, still bundled on the armchair looking cosy and typing enthusiastically. I know she's more excited about spending time with Niilo than she's letting on. How could she not be? He's adorable. He has a magic quality all his own, something elemental, he makes you feel as though anything can happen when you're with him. I'm hoping he pulls out all the stops and they have an ultra-romantic date. Meanwhile I'll have caught up with Stellan and will be relaxing on my own in my cabin. I might try to Facetime Mum and Dad in New York, or I'll take a long bath and read a magazine. It'll be nice to have some quiet me-time. I'm not sure why I sigh as I look up at the dark sky.

It hasn't really gotten light today, everything is a gorgeous lowering blue, and the sky is obscured by heavy snow clouds and swirling flurries of flakes. I've seen snowstorms in England before, but they're nothing like this dark brooding wildness. Even the bad weather in this place feels strange and wonderful. I cock my head and peer through the snowflakes. I'm pretty sure I can hear a jingling, tinkling sound carried on the wind. It puts me in mind of the bells on the airport elves' hats, and for some reason, I find myself thinking about my schoolkids back home and how excited they'll be today – even though a belief in Father Christmas is just something they humour their mothers' wistfulness with.

I smile at the thought of my four little nephews too. They span the ages of five to nine. The eldest, Rupert, will most likely for the last time, be hanging a stocking with his little brothers tonight, consumed with excitement and believing they'll be magically filled with toys and treats by morning. They'll all be searching the skies looking for a sign that Santa's coming, and leaving out mince pies or milk and cookies, hoping against hope they're on the nice list.

What a shame the magic has to end, and all too soon. I have a feeling I'll never see those little boys again, not that I saw them often even when I was with Cole, but I hope they received the gifts I sent, signed just from me this year.

With all this in mind, standing under the arctic sky, I make a wish that all the children on the threshold of young adulthood have one last perfect Christmas before the magic fades, and they join us, the grownups, with all our jaded worldliness.

There's that jingling sound again. I know I'm definitely not imagining it this time. If Stellan were here I'd ask him what it is. As I'm struggling to part the thick layers between sleeve cuffs and glove to get a glimpse at my watch, and thinking that Stellan really is cutting it fine, I see it, and for a moment I can't believe my eyes.

The first thing I notice is the dancing light from two swinging lanterns, then I hear the bells growing louder, and the trotting, snorting sounds of the animals. There, dashing out of the dark forest towards me are four reindeer pulling behind them a long sled, and finally, all dressed in black, blond wisps of hair escaping from his fur-trimmed hood, is Stellan. Standing up in the sleigh, he is grasping the reins and making the silver bells sing out in the darkness. In the blink of an eye, he's pulled the animals to a halt at the foot of my cabin steps, and he's offering me a gloved hand.

'I believe!' I cry.

'What?' Stellan's eyes crinkle and he laughs a deep, delighted laugh.

'Uh, nothing.'

I clamber into the sleigh, which is a far bigger, more enclosed affair than the dog sled of yesterday and Stellan sits me down on the seat. Plonking himself beside me, he pulls a blanket over our legs.

'You ready?' he asks, still grinning, and I nod because I can't seem to get any words out right this second.

He calls out to the reindeer and jolts the reins, and we start to move off, and for a millisecond, I let myself be taken by the fancy that the reindeer's hooves are silently treading air and the sleigh is lifting off the ground. Why not, I ask you? This is a place where the sky turns to green and gold rippling liquid fluorescence at night, and where the sun doesn't rise for days in the depths of December, so why can't other unbelievable, beautiful, thrilling things happen here? Why the hell not a reindeer-led sleigh dashing across an indigo sky?

As we fly, Stellan reaches an arm around my shoulder, stopping just before his hand makes contact with my arm to ask, 'Is this all right?' When I tell him it is, he pulls me close and I lean into him, letting Christmas Eve and the warmth of this man so close to me, work their magic.

–

'*Wow!*' A big puff of white breathy steam escapes my gaping mouth as I enter the igloo and stand staring in wonder. 'This is incredible.'

Stellan hangs back a few feet behind me as I take it all in: gleaming ice sculptures of bears, wolves, arctic hares and grouse; great slabs of ice formed into tables and chairs, somehow illuminated from within by blue and green lights; and in the centre of the white, glistening room, a bar, all made from ice and stocked with colourful bottles of spirits. If anything, it's colder in here than it was outside and I daren't take off my hat or gloves.

When I look back at Stellan, he's watching me and grinning.

'You like it?' he asks.

'It's amazing. Is it part of the resort?'

The reindeer ride lasted only a few minutes so we're not that far away, but this huge ice building in the forest clearing feels impossibly remote. And we're the only ones here.

'Uh-huh. It's one of my additions to my parents' business. I have it rebuilt every November and it operates until March. The visitors enjoy it.' Stellan pulls off his gloves and makes towards the bar. 'Would you like a drink?'

'It's not even lunch time.'

'What time is it in England?

'About nine-thirty. Nice try.' I see him reveal a bottle of champagne from somewhere behind the bar and I relent. 'Well, it is Christmas Eve.'

Stellan smiles and reaches down behind the bar again, this time bringing up a tray of glass tea light holders. I watch as he takes a match to each of the little candles and dots them around the bar, and I join in, helping him place one on every table. Their flickering light makes the snowy walls and white curved ceiling high above our heads glisten as though it were studded with tiny diamonds.

I hear the champagne cork popping as I sit on the tall barstool – yet another lump of ice strewn over with blankets. Happily, I feel nothing of the icy block through my snowsuit.

'Your parents must be really proud of you,' I say.

'I hope so. They were glad to retire and leave the resort in my care.' Stellan's carefully pouring out the bubbly into tall glasses. I can smell its festive crispness from over here, the air is so clean and scentless.

'You said they were in Helsinki. How often do you see them?'

'I visit for a week in the summer, but there's a lot of maintenance and planning to do here off season, and we're always busy with walking parties once the snow clears, so my parents fly out to visit me here too.'

'To keep an eye on their empire?' I wink, as Stellan comes round the bar and joins me and we touch our glasses together. 'Cheers.'

'*Kippis.*' He looks me dead in the eye as he sips his drink, but he doesn't sit down.

The bubbly hits my bloodstream and instantly makes my limbs tingle and fizz. It tastes delicious and expensive. Stellan smiles as he watches me. He always did love seeing me enjoying something, especially food and drink.

'Are you hungry?' he asks, giving me the curious notion that he can read my thoughts.

He's on the move again and is back a moment later with a dish of chocolate truffles and pink cubes dusted with icing sugar. This time, he takes the seat next to mine.

'Is that Turkish Delight? Very Narnia, Stellan.'

He cocks his head, missing the reference, and watches as I lift a squishy square to my lips. I've never been a fan of Turkish Delight, it somehow puts me in mind of the inside of a granny's handbag, but this stuff is nothing but melt-in-the-mouth delicate rose deliciousness.

'I felt bad about the *salmiakki*, so I got you these to tell you I'm sorry. I said I'd make it up to you.' He doesn't take his eyes off me as he too takes a bite and nods approvingly. For a moment we just enjoy the sweetness.

'So you're a teacher, just like you always wanted to be,' he says eventually, and it's more a statement of fact than a question.

'Yep, history teacher. And the moral there is, be careful what you wish for.' I swipe away my laugh, and tell him that, seriously, it's a great job, most of the time, and I love it. He listens carefully as I tell him about the kids and the school, but I struggle to keep my thread because he's leaning an elbow on the bar and directing his full attention at me, and I notice there's icing sugar on his bottom lip and it's just so darn distracting. I try to ask a sensible question.

'So what are your plans for this place, then? Will you stay at the resort forever?'

Stellan takes his time answering. 'I always planned to get it into shape, so then I'd be more free to come and go, see the world a little, but that hasn't happened yet. I've been working here ever since...'

His voice trails off and I bite my lip to stop myself blurting out, 'Since you ran off and left me in Manchester?'

'My dad had a stroke a few months after I returned from England. I was just finishing my degree and I ended up far more involved in the business than I'd ever been. A year later I was signing papers, taking over the resort, and my parents were relocating to the south. It was very hurried, looking back.'

'And you've run the place alone ever since?'

'Yeah, with Niilo's help for the last few years. But now that the new chalets are finally built and we have plenty of visitors all year round, I've been thinking I could take some time for myself. Do you ever feel like that?

As though you're finally free of the weight of parental expectation you've been carrying?'

I don't want to tell him that Mum and Dad never really put any pressure on me, they just let me find my own way in life; that would feel like rubbing it in. It occurs to me that Stellan's path was already laid out for him as a kid, before he had any choice in the matter. He had to stay at his parents' resort. It was expected of him.

'I guess I've got to a stage in my career where I can worry less about the future,' I say. 'I can't see myself leaving teaching anytime soon, and I'm glad all that studying is over and I don't have to go on placements at random schools or scrabble for classroom experience any more. I can just build on the knowledge I have now and enjoy my work.'

Stellan nods and takes a long drink. I can see we've had very different experiences of finding our place in the world. I feel a guilty twinge. Perhaps I was wrong to be so uncharitable about the long silence between us. He's had a hard time of it too.

As I sip my champagne I find my mind flitting to Clementine, Cole's sister, always desperate to please a mother who was, in fact, impossible to please. No matter how much Clementine strived to be the best she could be, Patricia always moved the goalposts just out of reach again, and all to protect Cole from feeling his sister's success, and by extension, his own lesser achievements.

And, yes, Cole was a pilot, a brilliant achievement in anyone's book, and this would be exceptional in most families, but Clementine just had to spoil things by rising to become the *crème de la crème* of the medical world, like her late father had been, so Patricia, consciously or not, was compelled to bring her daughter down a peg or two at every opportunity available to her. Meanwhile, pampered, over-confident Cole, perhaps unknowingly, was an accomplice to his mother's unkindest impulses, gaining in maternal adoration what Clementine lost by steady degrees of humiliation and criticism over the years. It was likely that Clementine would never understand that she would never have their approval because they were jealous of her success, plain and simple. Acknowledging that would be akin to them acknowledging Cole's failure to become the medical man his father, who Cole had barely known at the time of his early death, had intended his little boy to be.

I feel as though I've made a breakthrough here. A blinding flash of clarity has illuminated the sad facts I'd only partly perceived before. Family animosity was the reason for Cole's sudden proposal at his own sister's wedding. Proposals are supposed to be inspired by love, not prompted by filial acrimony. I sigh and take another drink. How come I needed to travel a thousand miles to see the Jordan family for what they were, and what a lucky escape I had getting dumped by them?

I'm suddenly aware of Stellan still looking at me. He's turning the stem of his glass between his fingertips distractedly. It occurs to me that if Stellan's family relations were even a tenth as complicated and conflicted as poor Clementine's then he's had a devilishly hard time of it over the years – even though he's been striving to make a success of the business, his father's pride and joy, and maybe also his greatest burden.

The pressure Stellan was under all those years ago when we first met must have been intense, and yet I had absolutely no idea. No wonder he was so serious, so mature. He had the weight of the world on his shoulders. Meanwhile I was just a kid with an adoring family dreaming my way through uni.

I find myself pulling my mittens off and reaching my hand over the bar to find his. I watch as he responds to my touch and his fingers curl around my own in a warm clasp, the tips coming to rest against my palm. I find my breathing becoming hard to control, so to conceal it I ask another question.

'Would you ever sell the resort?'

'Never. Even though it's mine now, it's not really mine to sell. But I'd never expect a kid of mine to stay here and run the place. That's my dream; to leave this place so established and well run my kids can do what they want with their lives.'

I'm pretty sure my eyes pop out on stalks at this. I style it out. 'You've got kids?'

'No, but I'd like to, one day. Do you want to have children?'

The strangest sensation hits me and I feel as though I'm about to cry and I can't explain it. Why has my chest gone all tight? I take a gulp of air and my feelings seem to do the talking for me. He squeezes my hand and I find I'm speaking through the emotions that are crowding out my inhibitions.

'I suppose I do want a baby.' Oh no! Why are you saying this out loud? 'A family was all part of the plan with Cole, somewhere along the line. Sometimes I hear this little voice in my head saying *I want a baby*.' How come I'm still blurting all this out? 'It's like my ovaries are ganging up on me against my will, because you know, I never really, *really* wanted kids, but… things seem to have changed. Cole's about to become a father, and I'm just… not jealous exactly, just… sad about it.'

'You miss him?' Stellan's expression is inscrutable again. If he didn't think I was crazy before, he does now. He definitely thinks I'm here to get some revenge sex and a Scandi baby.

'Miss Cole? God, no.' Again with the blinding flashes of sudden realisation. I don't miss him *at all*. 'That relationship is stone D.E.A.D.' I spell out the word, breaking into a smile. 'It's got a police incident tent around it. But I do miss having my future mapped out. There was something reassuring about knowing what was coming next. Or, thinking I knew.'

'So that makes two of us then?'

'Two of us?'

'Neither of us know what our futures hold. We both have fresh starts ahead of us. I can let go of the reins at the resort a little more, and you have a world of possibilities at your feet.'

My mind's processing his words and drawing all kinds of wildly tenuous conclusions and, accompanied by the movements of his fingertips against the soft underside of my curled hand and his thumb now running slowly over my knuckles, I'm surprised by the flutter of hopefulness in my stomach. And I'm not going to tell you what the little voice I'm hearing is saying right now, but it's screaming and whooping and I'm pretty sure my ovaries are attempting a conga. *Shut up and behave*, I tell them. This is exactly why Stellan ran off in the first place; I scared him by hoping for too much.

As I'm telling myself off, Stellan lets go of my hand and refills our glasses. He doesn't reach for me again so I hastily pull my gloves back on. And yet, I think, he doesn't exactly *look* scared, and he's clearly keeping yesterday's promise to open up.

'Anyway,' I say, trying to recover some dignity. 'I'm not desperate to make babies. Cole's news just brought it home to me that I'm back at the start again, miles from marriage and kids and a family home. I don't even have a dog any more. Starting again from scratch is tougher than you think. But I'm fine. I'm only thirty-four and I just want to enjoy my life, wherever it takes me.'

'I'll drink to that,' says Stellan, as we touch our glasses again, but as he raises his glass to his lips, we hear the ringtone coming from his snowsuit pocket.

'Excuse me, just one second,' he says, before taking the phone outside.

I look around at the glimmering ice bar and smile to myself. There's no place I'd rather be on Christmas Eve than here. I can hear Stellan's voice outside, and something else, a snowmobile pulling up.

When Stellan returns, one of the resort staff in a Frozen Falls snowsuit comes in lugging a box of tinkling glassware. It must be time for the bar to open.

'Sorry about that, problem with the reception staff rotas. It's sorted now, and I've asked them to spread the word not to disturb us today.'

I find I'm feeling inwardly rewarded that Stellan clearly thinks today isn't over and he wants to enjoy it unimpeded by work.

'Thanks for showing me around your resort. It's beautiful,' I say.

'I'm glad you're happy,' he beams back. 'The bar's about to get really busy. Are you ready to move on? I have to check on the dogs, but then we can get some lunch?'

'OK. Hey, I have a fridge full of food back at my cabin, thanks to Nari's...' I stop myself, just in time, before I mention Stephen.

Stellan seemed so wary of Nari's interest in Niilo yesterday, I don't want him thinking there's some other guy on the scene, especially some flashy millionaire. But I suppose she does seem to like Stephen too, and they *are* going to spend New Year together in London. I resolve to butt right out of Nari and Niilo's date today. I just hope they have fun. Stellan doesn't need to know anything else that might encourage him to worry about his friend.

'So, um... do you want to come back to my cabin and I'll make something for you?'

'You're going to cook?' Stellan's already laughing, which is a bit rich considering he hasn't seen me cook anything in fifteen years. How does he know I haven't moved on from my Pot Noodle and eggy bread days? I could be a Michelin-starred chef by now. Obviously I'm not, though I have added Spanish omelette and spag bol to my repertoire. Again, all things Stellan doesn't need to know.

'There's cheese and some bread and salad stuff. Pretty sure I spotted a jar of olives too. I can hardly poison you with that, can I?'

Stellan laughs as he finds a silver bottle stopper behind the bar and seals the neck of the still half full champagne, before reaching behind the bar and producing another unopened bottle. 'And we have champagne and candy. Sounds perfect to me. Let's go.'

Before we climb into the sleigh we stop to pet the reindeer who have been waiting patiently and chomping the handfuls of lichen that Stellan had scattered by their feet earlier.

'Approach them real slowly,' Stellan says in a low voice.

Their antlers are huge, like I've only seen in kids' Christmas films, and they move their heads with such swift jerks I don't really fancy getting too close to them. But, with Stellan guiding me and making murmuring sounds to them under his breath, we ease closer and reach out to pat their broad haunches. They're nervous and skittish so we only touch them briefly. One of them turns its mournful eyes towards me and I step back to avoid the lethal-looking blade that's protruding straight out from the centre of its head like a unicorn horn.

Stellan smiles. 'You're right to stay back. Reindeer can be unpredictable and can give you a nasty scratch.'

'Now you tell me.' But I don't feel unsafe, not with Stellan beside me.

'Her eyes are a beautiful colour,' I say.

'Do you know they change colour? From this bluey-black in the middle of winter to a kind of golden-green in summer, very much like the colour of your eyes.'

'Did you just compare me to a reindeer?' I say, and we both crumple into laughter, helped along by the buzz of the champagne and sweets.

I always thought my irises were a sort of sludgy colour, but golden-green sounds nice to me. 'Whatever. I'm taking it as a compliment,' I say.

But suddenly, we're not laughing. There's something familiar happening between us, and we both fall silent as our eyes lock.

'Sylvie,' he says, and I recognise that deep tone that sends my mind reeling. 'I want to kiss you. Is that all right?'

I tell him in a strangely high-pitched voice that, yes, I suppose it is all right.

He exhales sharply, looking at me through narrowed eyes, before coming closer still. His lips brush mine for the briefest second. The sensation of his mouth and the sound of his breathing send an instant thrill of recognition to every nerve in my body as they pass on the message. *This guy? He's back? But we loved this guy!*

Chapter Sixteen

Hi again! I thought it was time I treated you to another festive blog post.

It's strangely quiet at my cabin today and I find I have a little spare time, so I'll tell you about the place I'm staying.

Frozen Falls knows luxury accommodation. I have a huge soft bed, there's underfloor heating in every room, and one of those fabulous wet rooms with the massive showerheads that I just love about Scandi countries. The resort provides a huge pile of firewood, so it's kind of a DIY situation when it comes to lighting up your own grate, and there's even a Christmas tree and a big basket of decorations, so you can really make yourself at home. But the highlight of the cabins for me is the bedroom under the stars. Still no aurora though. But I'm keeping my eyes open.

Looking out at the trees and the dark and the snow you feel a million miles from the big cities. I almost forget they exist. We're so remote, I get an overwhelming sense of expectation that anything can happen way out here. In fact, I'm heading out soon, ready for another adventure.

The touristy veneer is cosy and inviting but I'm ready to discover what else Lapland has to offer. I just know its keeping its best secrets hidden. Frozen Falls is quietly reserved, well organised, clean, and generous, but what lies beneath all that? I'm going to find out. I'm going to ask my new friend and guide today if he'll show me the places only locals know.

Surely, not everything about this place is cookie-cutter pretty and wholesomely homey. I don't mind getting grit on my boots and frostbite on my fingers if it means I experience something real, something only Inari has to offer, and it doesn't have to be perfect, it just has to be authentic.

#offthebeatentrack   #locallife   #NariCultureDetective
#Lapland

Chapter Seventeen

It's only been half an hour since I waved Stellan off in the sleigh, watching from the steps of my cabin as the reindeer's white powder puff tails wiggled away into the grey noon light. He'll be heading back here soon, once he's seen to a few jobs around the resort, and I've got to finish making lunch and there's this clothes-strewn cabin to straighten before he gets here. So, as much as I'd like to flop down in front of the fire and stare out of the window at the snow falling, I can't afford to daydream.

I've stripped off my snowsuit, and I don't need my extra layers, so they're gone too, and I've done my best to assemble something approaching a tempting meal from the contents of the fridge. It's all looking rather nice laid out on a big wooden board on the kitchen island, if I say so myself.

I put the bread in the oven to warm through and dash to the bedroom to brush my hair and reapply Nari's lipstick (like she told me to, if I got the opportunity). As I slick the deep red colour over my lips I can still feel the tingling sensation from Stellan's kiss. A kiss that lasted only a second before we clambered, dazed and smiling, into the sleigh for the ride back to the resort. I wonder if he'll kiss me again. He always was so… moreish. I'd better tidy myself up a bit more.

I manage to send the fire roaring and crackling in the hearth and it is so warm in this cabin I don't even need my fluffy slipper boots – I don't fancy Stellan seeing me in those – and it's beginning to dawn on me that, on this trip at least, he's only really seen me in my outdoor polar gear over big jumpers and a million layers. Back in the day I never gave a thought to my clothes, I just threw on my DMs and whichever Topshop clobber were to hand and assumed I looked reasonably cute. Is that what Stellan's expecting now? When he gets here he's going to see me in just my soft black trousers and this hot pink jumper – another of Nari's suggestions; she said it would 'pop' with my red hair and lipstick, but I feel a bit ridiculous and overdone.

Frankly, I'm freaking out as I peer at my reflection and think how Stellan doesn't seem to have aged much at all. His skin is still smooth and pale like unfired porcelain. I'm putting his fresh-face down to all this exercise and healthy arctic living, and he's been clean-shaven apart from that first time I saw him again, when Nari and I thought he was a burglar trying to kill us. And his mouth is still infuriatingly youthful and pink.

I think about his eyes as he pulled away from our kiss, heavy-lidded and dazed, and how I'd been struck by a shyness I haven't felt in years. 'How am I doing at opening up a little?' he'd said, his gaze still lingering on my mouth.

'Hmm,' I'd replied, slyly. 'Not bad, I suppose.'

It had felt pretty easy and fun kissing in the snow outside the ice bar. But now I'm beginning to wonder what he was thinking. A pity snog? A bit of nostalgic nuzzling? He can't fancy me now, not after all this time, and not with what I've been through lately. I've aged while he just hasn't. I sigh and pinch my cheeks. At some point around my thirty-second birthday my formerly smooth-as-a-baby's-bottom face took on the exact texture of flock wallpaper and I'm aware that Stellan probably thinks I'm a bit saggy of tummy and, God forbid, fluffy around the jowls.

Well there's nothing I can do about it anyway and, *oh shit*, that's him banging at the door!

Any concerns I had about how Stellan would react to seeing me in my normal clothes with my hair uncovered disappear as I pull open the door to discover Toivo, Kanerva's littlest puppy, held aloft at face height by a grinning Stellan.

'Somebody wanted to see his favourite English lady again.'

'And what did Toivo want to do?' I hear an unnecessarily goofy laugh coming from somewhere and realise it's me. 'Sorry! Come in.' Lifting Toivo into my arms and holding him close, I enjoy the sensation of his fluffy ears tucked under my chin. 'Thank you for bringing dis liddle guy.' I carry Toivo off towards the fridge. 'Let's see if I can find you something to eat, huh?'

Stellan stops by the door, immediately taking off his hat and peeling his snowsuit down. I'm glad I've got Toivo to distract me, because when I glance towards Stellan again, having offered the pup a morsel of the mysterious potted meat that was included with the welcome goodies, Stellan's standing in my kitchen in dark trousers and a deep blue jumper – the Nordic, patterned kind you seriously wouldn't expect a guy to look this good in. His hair's all mussed up and bed-headish and I'm surprised I manage to contain the impulse to leap on top of him there and

173

then. Impossible with a dog in my arms. Again, thank you, Toivo. I take a moment to remind myself I'm going to play it cool and just enjoy my last afternoon with Stellan.

'This looks great. I'm so hungry,' he says. 'Usually I eat lunch in the kitchen at the dog sheds or out on the trail with the tourists, and it's never anything as fancy as this, believe me.'

'It sounds as though you need to treat yourself once in a while,' I say, taking the bread from the oven before handing him a plate and a glass of champagne. I'm doing my best look-at-me-being-the-perfect-hostess-slash-domestic-goddess impression, even though all I've really done is tip the contents of jars and packets onto a board.

'I think you're right. You know, I can't remember the last time I took a day off work in the busy season, let alone two days in a row,' he says, as he tears a hunk of bread from the loaf and loads his plate with cheese and olives.

'Really?' I lower Toivo to the ground and set to work on filling a bowl with water for him.

'I never had a good reason to before,' Stellan says with a smile that's immediately followed by something that looks like self-consciousness.

'In that case, I'm honoured. Come on, let's sit by the fire,' I say, helping him out.

I pile my plate with the Lappish deli treats and we settle ourselves on the floor by the wide hearth, leaning against the sofa. Toivo tumbles around on the rug by our feet as we eat and I keep the champagne topped up in our glasses.

Stellan asks me what I'd usually be doing on Christmas Eve and I opt to tell him about the alternate years me and Cole would spend with my family, which leads on to me talking about Mum and Dad's New York holiday. I grab my phone, showing him the pictures they've been posting to Facebook for the last few days – they arrive in a sudden flurry of pinging notifications whenever I set foot within reach of my cabin's Wi-Fi. Stellan watches as I 'love' every one of them.

'This is them in Central Park, and that's my dad with what looks like a huge slice of pepperoni pizza and a daft grin, and there they are Christmas shopping at Bloomingdales.'

'They look happy.'

'They are. They're so cute together. Since they retired they just rattle around the house following each other about, making endless cups of tea. Mum reads stories from the newspaper to Dad and he has a grumble about politics or whatever's bothering him that day. And they cook together a lot. It's nice.'

Stellan's lips are smiling but there's a dark look in his eyes. 'Yeah, my parents never really had that kind of relationship. Dad's always been kind of… distant. He worked most of the time when he was here, and when he wasn't working he was worrying about work. Then his health forced him into early retirement and now he disappears on these long walks alone around Helsinki.'

I can see talking about his father is causing Stellan some pain, but I let him say it aloud, wondering if he's ever voiced this stuff before.

'I always thought my mother seemed lonely but I could never talk to her about it. She's probably still lonely, even now,' he says, brushing some imaginary fluff from his sleeve. 'But my sister lives in Helsinki; she sees my parents a lot and helps out.' I witness the little flicker of guilt cross his face. He gulps his drink.

'You can't be everywhere at once,' I tell him. 'Besides, you're giving your all to this place, aren't you? And that's for them, right?'

He nods, but doesn't answer, and is suddenly distracted by the buzz from his mobile on the floor beside him.

'You should probably get that,' I say, and am immediately rewarded by the sight of him reaching for his phone and turning it off without so much as looking at the screen.

'The staff can manage without me for one day.'

He sounds breezy and resolute but I appreciate the effort that took. He carries on eating and I let myself be distracted by Toivo begging for some cheese, which I slip him. I'm realising now how lonely Stellan's been, working here for years, trying to make his parents proud. There's been a toll to pay for inheriting the resort.

'Did you ever, um... have a girlfriend here, or... whatever?' I tail off, not sure I should push him on this. But he knows all about Cole, so fair's fair.

He hesitates at first, and when the words finally come, they're slow and careful. 'A few. The longest was Karin. She worked here the year after Dad had the stroke.'

He raises his eyes to mine with a hint of caution. Is he wondering if I really want to hear this stuff? I do, and kind of don't, at the same time. He sees me (fake) smiling my encouragement and presses on.

'Karin was a ski instructor. She stayed around when spring came, and she helped out in the hotel, because of me, but... I don't know, I was busy running this place. I guess I wasn't as present as I could have been. She went home to Stockholm.' He gives a punctuating nod of his head, before adding, 'Quite rightly.'

'Ah, well, it couldn't have been very serious if she left you here, could it? Maybe it was for the best.' I've said it out loud before I realise how glib and crass it sounds. Stellan noticeably blanches and I want to shrink into a ball and roll under the sofa. 'I don't mean she didn't *like* you. I mean, she is only human, she probably thought you were some kind of Norse god made flesh...' *Shut up, Sylve!* 'What I meant was...'

'It's OK.' Stellan laughs, letting me off the hook. 'I didn't look after her feelings so she left. And, you're right, it wasn't so serious... not compared to us.'

He's looking right at me and I feel myself freeze. I want to say, 'But you left me.' Instead I'm left floundering, feeling my heart skipping beats all over the place and wondering how it's possible this guy can give me this sudden jolt of hope and happiness at the same time as I'm remembering the sad, sinking emptiness of being dumped by him.

'Sylvie?' he's saying.

I don't know where to look or what to do, but it's suddenly very warm here in front of the fire and I could do with some cold arctic air to clear my head.

'Sylvie? Are you all right?'

I look at his face, all concern and what I'm hoping is regret, and I just know I'm going to say it. I can't not. The words are already spilling out and I feel fat, stupid tears accompanying them.

'Stellan, why did you leave me?' God, this is hideous and *not at all* what I had planned for our chilled out, one-off lunch date. I put my glass down, flattening my palms against the floor to stop it seesawing beneath me. 'It's not like I neglected you, or because I was working too hard, was it? I was there for you, one hundred per cent.'

'You were there for me, you *were*!' Stellan's suddenly kneeling in front of me, his plate of food abandoned beside him. His hands grab mine. 'I didn't leave because there was something wrong with you, or with us. I had to leave.'

'Without telling me first?' Oh no, I'm about to full on sob in his face, which is inching closer to mine. I feel his fingers sink into my hair, holding me as he focuses those light eyes on mine.

'Do you remember how it was… at the end? We were always together, and we were getting closer and closer?' he says.

I nod, but can't speak yet. I think about those last few days, searing flashbacks to us in bed, kissing with flying sparks, and the feel of his skin against mine. 'Why would you run away from that? It was perfect. *We* were perfect.'

'We were. Those were the happiest days of my life. I wanted to stay so badly. I could have stayed there my whole life, kissing you.'

The strange tender pain of a teenage broken heart grips me again, as if I'm falling into a time warp. I feel the physical ache in my chest just as I did back then, except I'm not nineteen-year-old me, there is no hurriedly written note on my pillow, and Stellan's not on a flight home. He's right here in front of me, and I can't think of any better way to numb the hurt than to pull him towards me and kiss him, so I do, and he lets me. For a few moments there's just us and the magical unnamed thing that connects us.

'Wait, wait.' Stellan pulls away just as I'm tipping our weight so he'll tumble on top of me onto the rug. 'I can't think when you're kissing me. I can hardly breathe! I have to tell you what happened. I can't kiss you like this.'

Now he wants to talk? If ever there was a time for silence, *this* is it. His eyes are heavy and drowsy and I can see the fight in him to break away. He has the look of a scared sinner at the confessional, and he's got red lipstick smeared over his mouth. I hand him a napkin and we both set to work wiping the greasy red stains from our faces.

He shuffles closer to the fireside, pulling me by the hand so I move over too, and he passes me my champagne glass again. I watch him take a deep breath that expands his chest and he exhales in a sudden heavy blow, getting ready to speak.

'Do you remember that day I came back to your dorm, and you'd just had some exam results, and found out you'd failed?'

'Rub it in, Stellan.' To be honest though, I barely recollect it, and it hadn't troubled me at the time, not when I had Stellan in my life.

'You said you didn't care about the results, do you remember? You just seemed so happy to spend your time with me, and then we ended up kissing as usual and we slept together that afternoon for the second time, and it was kind of incredible. And we talked about getting some dinner, remember? We got dressed and went out for takeaway. When we got back you told me that you...' He seems to be struggling to catch his breath now. 'You told me you loved me. You came right out and said it in that grim little student kitchen. And it hit me. I just knew, instantly. I was bad for you. I was the reason you were failing uni, I was a distraction.'

'I didn't care, I *wanted* you to distract me!'

'And you also wanted to be a teacher. That was one of the first things you ever told me, remember? The night we met? You said you loved researching Scandinavian history? You said that's what made you want to be a teacher.'

I shrug. 'I guess I did.' It's half a lifetime ago since I had burning ambition like that and it didn't last long. It's hard to recapture that frame of mind.

'I was thinking of your parents and how disappointed they'd be if they knew some guy who was only going to be around for a semester had turned up and made you flunk your exams. I worried about the impact their disappointment would have on you...'

It's at this point I interrupt. 'I told you this morning my parents were never like that.'

'You did, but I had no idea of that fact back then. I thought *everybody* was struggling with the same kind of pressures I was under, or something like it anyway. But, regardless of what your family would think of us, I couldn't live my life knowing I'd spoiled your chance at getting the degree you needed to be a teacher. And you were only nineteen, just a kid really. So I left before I wrecked your future.'

'But you broke my heart. I was crazy about you.'

'I know.' He takes my hand. 'And I knew if you kept looking at me the way you looked at me that last time I saw you, back in your dorm, I'd never have the strength to leave and let you be everything you wanted to be.'

'Couldn't you have talked to *me* about it? Let *me* decide what was best for me?'

'No. You'd have begged me to stay, and I would have. And eventually you'd have resented me forever.' I see him hesitate, before adding guiltily, 'The way Mum resented

180

my father.' He looks down at our still clasped hands. 'I called Dad that night and we spoke about it, and he said he'd pay for a flight the next morning if I could just get to the airport. So I did.'

This is when he loosens his grip on my fingers and his hands fall to his sides.

'But you missed your exams,' I say.

'I sat them here instead – and totally failed them, by the way. I wasn't the only one not studying.' He smiles wryly, but it quickly fades. 'I spent all that winter doing resits. I always planned to go back to England to see you in the summer. I hoped you'd have forgiven me by then. But then Dad had the stroke that February and that was the end of all my plans. But I didn't simply forget about you. I found you online a few years later and it said you were teaching... and you were engaged, so then I knew, or I thought I knew, I'd done the right thing.'

Stellan's looking at me with pleading earnestness and I'm trying to process all these feelings. I'm not angry, exactly. I'm shocked, a little indignant that he thought he knew what was best for me, and I'm embarrassed too. He's basically just confirmed my worst fears; that he ran off because I was too full on. I pushed him away because I didn't know how to just enjoy him and still be myself. I was too young to handle it.

Looking down at Toivo playing by my side – I can't face Stellan – I say, 'You're right, I *was* besotted with you. When you came on the scene I wasn't thinking about the future or anything else. I just wanted to be with you. Nothing else seemed to matter.'

'But you were happy, right? Afterwards, I mean? Don't you think it's wonderful that you're successful in your profession? *You* made that happen by yourself. Nobody handed *you* a readymade career. I made the right decision to get out of your way, didn't I? In spite of Cole?'

I look at him and try to speak but instead I mouth exasperated half words. His look of pride and pain physically hurts me. 'Yes,' I manage. Even though I don't quite believe it. He winces noticeably. He doesn't believe me either. Pulling Toivo onto his lap, he delicately scrunches his fingers on the pup's ears.

'I really thought it was for the best, for you.'

I want to save him from the feelings that seem to be shutting down our connection when it was only just getting started again. He's noticeably shrinking away from me.

'Maybe it *was* for the best… in the long run,' I say, hurriedly. 'I *did* stop studying and I'd probably have had to retake the entire year if you'd stayed at uni for the last few weeks of that semester. And we *did* spend all our time making out and never revising.' It's all beginning to make sense, I realise. 'And I guess I even stopped seeing all my uni friends and, to me, that's much worse than skipping some, OK, lots of, lectures and flunking some tests. After you left, I tried to get back into the little gang I'd been in since first year in halls, but I'd excluded myself for so long, they'd all moved on. It was too late to catch up, and they never really trusted me after that.'

It stings a bit to think of them again after all this time; we were such a close little gang before Stellan arrived, but they probably thought I'd ditch them again as soon as another fit bloke came along. I hadn't given them a second thought at the time, and now I don't even remember all of their names.

And suddenly my mind flits to Nari and how we'd met that Christmas in the uni canteen at the painfully naff students' Christmas lunch, and we'd got chatting – about Stellan and my broken heart, as it happens – and pretty much that day we became firm friends. I'd got back on track with my studies by the time I met Nari; studying was as good a way as any to distract myself from the pain. I aced the resits and got my first 'A's on my essays that January, but I'd cried myself to sleep every night for weeks.

Nari and I moved into our own flat together in Castlewych after graduation, and my parents pretty much adopted her as one of their own. We had a blast all through my teacher training and while she set up her blogging career. None of that would have happened if I'd stayed cosseted away in the love bubble with Stellan.

And eventually along came Cole. *He'd* never have happened if Stellan had stuck around. I'm glad I knew him, even after all the trouble he caused me at the end, but I think I'm making peace with it all now – apart from Barney, of course. We really did have some good times in the beginning, and it was exciting moving in with him and finding my feet as a *bona fide* grown up. And, God knows, Cole taught me a few things about settling for something that isn't quite love in all its dazzling, terrifying brilliance, so it wasn't all a complete waste. I can see that now.

'Am I going to regret what I did to you for my entire life?' Stellan asks.

'No. Don't. I don't want you to. You were probably right to step back. But, Stellan, you should have talked to me.'

He nods. 'I'm sorry. Talking was never my strong point.'

He looks so forlorn, even with Toivo climbing his chest and putting tiny paws on his face, nudging his nose with his. I smile in spite of myself. Why are we doing this to each other? Another thing that the break-up with Cole has taught me is that it's never a good idea to dwell too much on things that can't be changed.

'Look, let's forget about it. It's ancient history,' I say, standing up and balling my hands into fists on my hips. 'Listen up, Stellan Virtanen, it's Christmas Eve, you've taken your second day off work this millennia, and I damn well want to celebrate.' As I speak, my fake resolve and jollity begin to take on a more authentic hue, and I see Stellan's eyes brighten as he looks up at me. 'So what say we down this bubbly and decorate this tree?'

And that's what we do, and it's fun, actually. No, better than fun; it's perfect.

I make a real show of finding it difficult to balance on the coffee table edge to reach the tallest branches so Stellan has to hold my hips to steady me and he lets his fingertips slide up over my waistband until they press against my skin, and then I really do feel unsteady on my feet.

'We don't want any Christmas emergencies,' he says, holding me firmly. 'The nearest hospital's an hour away by helicopter and in this snow they wouldn't be able to rescue you. I'd have to take you all the way there on the back of a reindeer.'

And so we manage to laugh after the tension, and I turn to admiring the cute, rustic-looking decorations, and Toivo gets hopelessly tangled in the string of white fairy lights, nearly managing to pull the whole tree over in his tumbling, bounding panic to escape.

When we are nearly done, Stellan puts the straw star on the highest branch and the whole scene inside the cabin begins to resemble the kitschy picture on a tin of Christmas biscuits. Just as I'm telling Stellan this, he reaches into the basket that had held the decorations and pulls out one last item, not a bauble at all, but a large jar with a handwritten label attached to a ribbon tied around its lid.

'What's that?' I ask, as he helps me down from my ledge on the coffee table and places the jar in my hands.

'*This* is cookie mixture. Frozen Falls' little surprise for our guests. Want to bake some cookies?'

I screw up my nose. 'I want to *eat* some cookies.'

Stellan laughs and takes the jar from me.

'How long will it take?' I say as I hop up onto the kitchen counter top, watching him rolling up his sleeves.

'Not long, and we have the whole evening ahead to just enjoy each other's company, really chilled, yes?'

I find myself blushing at this, but as I watch him setting to work with eggs cracking and wooden spoon stirring, I wonder how such innocuous words can sound so full of promise.

Soon, the little chocolate chip speckled blobs are lined up on a tray and heading into the oven. The snow is falling outside the window and I'm beginning to realise it's probably been completely dark out there for hours already; I haven't been paying any attention to the world outside.

Our plates are discarded by the fireside. We'd made short work of the cheese and bread, and drank all the champagne. Little Toivo is basking in the warmth from the hearth as he lies fast asleep, curled up beneath the branches of our twinkling tree.

'Ten minutes and they'll be ready,' Stellan says, turning away from the oven and looking across at me. 'What shall we do while we wait?'

I lose no time in telling him I have a good idea as I lower myself down from the counter, place my hands on his chest and slowly walk him backwards until he's pinned and grinning against the refrigerator door.

'My hands are covered in cookie mixture,' he protests, all the while looking at my mouth.

I raise myself up onto tiptoes, leaning my weight against him, and he lowers his lips to mine.

We kiss away the shortest ten minutes in the history of the world, and all the time Stellan's hands hang helplessly by his sides.

Chapter Eighteen

The bar is a dive, but Nari had asked to see the Saariselkä nightlife and at only three-thirty in the afternoon there was little else open. It is, of course, already dark outside and they are the only customers in the Shamrocks in the Snow beer shack. Nari takes her seat at the bar and peers at the drinks menu under the harsh spotlights.

'I guess it's Guinness and peanuts?' she says with an amused shrug.

Niilo reminds her he's the designated driver on their date and asks instead for water. The look on Nari's face gives him a drowning feeling, but wanting to reassure her they'll have fun tonight, he searches for something to say.

'You looked busy when I called for you at the resort. Have you been working all day?' he asks eventually.

'Uh-huh. I edited some of my photos and posted a couple more blog posts. What about you? Did the reindeer safaris go OK?'

'Yes, thank you.'

Niilo can't understand why he's finding communicating with Nari so difficult today when the words and laughter had flowed so readily the day before. It had been easier with Stellan and Sylvie there, somehow. He couldn't remember the last time he'd been alone like this with someone, or when he'd last felt this awkward. He's relieved to see the barman approach, surprised to find customers in his empty pub and offering his apologies.

Nari can't guess at the nerves and tension wracking Niilo as she orders their drinks. The barman works the beer tap and Nari turns to Niilo with a placid smile. 'Is this what you do for fun, then?'

'What? This? No.' Niilo laughs. 'I don't really come to bars. You could say my work is also my hobby. I look after the herd, see to the tourists, grab a sauna, drink beers with Stellan, then I sleep.'

'And that's it? Your routine? Your life?'

A panic that feels like heat building in his chest grips Niilo.

'I work hard, I try to lighten Stellan's burden, I try to keep my mind occupied. There's little else to tell about myself. My life's nothing like your world full of adventure and new experiences.' Realising there is one more thing he could divulge, Niilo suddenly smiles. 'I write songs too,' he offers with sudden shyness.

'You're a musician, I knew it! I could tell. What sort of songs do you write?'

'*Joik*, mainly.'

'*Joiks?* I read about those researching this trip. Traditional songs. Sámi songs, right?'

'Yeah. I like to adapt old tunes and I write my own lyrics. Each *joik* tells the story of something's spirit, or *someone's.*'

'I'd love to hear one.'

'I'd love to sing you one.'

A moment's silence follows as Nari shifts expectantly in her chair, turning her body fully towards her companion.

'What? You want me to sing *now*? Oh no, I'd have to prepare first.'

'Oh, OK,' she says, flustered.

Their drinks arrive, bringing a moment of much-needed respite, and Nari immediately takes a long draught of her Guinness. As he sips his water, Niilo succumbs again to the creeping despair. This date is not off to a good start.

'How do you think the others are getting on?' Nari asks, dabbing her mouth with a napkin.

'Stellan and Sylvie? I think they'll be enjoying themselves. He was so excited about seeing her this morning. I really shouldn't say this, but I called in at his cabin for breakfast and he spent a lot of time in front of his mirror scrunching stuff in his hair.'

Nari grins, bringing her hands together in an excited clap. 'I sent Sylvie off wearing my red lipstick. She looked so cute! Oh, I hope they like each other again.'

'I know Stellan has suffered without her.'

'What do you mean?'

Worried he's said too much, Niilo attempts to shrug away the question, but seeing the curiosity on Nari's face, he relents.

'I remember what he was like when I first met him, constantly nursing a dark heart. In those days we used to drive the tourists back to the airport ourselves in the transfer coaches. One time he told me he had to fight with himself to resist the urge to just jump on the Manchester flight.'

'But he never did.'

'No. He threw himself into working here. We both did. Nari, please don't tell anyone this. I gave Stellan my word I wouldn't speak of it. I don't usually break my promises.'

'Sylvie's my best friend. I tell her everything. Don't you think she deserves to know this? She really liked Stellan, and I think she likes him now.'

'He must be the one to tell her, *if* he still feels this way.'

Deep in thought, Nari nods. She'd seen her friend devastated by Cole, the last thing she wanted to do was encourage Sylvie to think Stellan was still interested in her, only for him to be cold and distant, like she'd seen him yesterday.

'You're right, I don't want her getting her hopes up. Besides we're leaving in two days.'

Hurriedly reaching for their drinks, a little frisson of tension passes between the two again. As she sips, Nari thinks about her flight to Manchester on Boxing Day, and her date with Stephen at New Year. Her thoughts lead to sudden strained, panicked feelings that she can't account for, and she grasps for a new subject.

'Did *you* ever want to just hop on a plane and get away? What's stopping you and Stellan doing a lads' tour of Europe?'

'Lads?' Niilo laughs, thinking this a strange term. 'No, we're working men. We work.' He shrugs as though this explained everything.

'And I'm a working woman. But I make time for myself too, and I want to see every inch of the planet before I die. I've got big plans.'

Niilo nods encouragingly, hoping to deflect what he assumed was Nari's disappointment in his slow, settled life. 'Tell me about what you do back home.'

'Well… I read, I cook, I watch Netflix with Sylvie, and I take her to cocktail bars. What else do we do? When I'm not travelling, we go to her parents' house for Sunday lunch and we take it in turns to make dessert, it's a sort of cooking contest. I'm the reigning pudding-making champion, you can't beat my chocolate and walnut brownies – so that's a whole thing we do.'

'Sounds good.' Niilo leans his elbow on the bar, his cheek resting on his fist.

'You want me to go on? Umm… I like going to spa hotels. They're the best kind of working holiday, actually. For a start, they're usually freebies, and I get a good night's sleep, have lots of luscious treatments, eat beautiful food, then I write it all up and post it to my blog. Sometimes I take Sylvie with me, if they're in England, that is.'

'You two are good friends.'

'The best. Like you and Stellan. I see how you two are with each other. It's adorable.'

Niilo laughs. 'He's a stubborn ass, but I love him, yes. He's all my family now.' Seeing Nari's expression change to one of sympathy, Niilo inwardly scolds himself for bringing the atmosphere down, just as it had been picking up.

'What happened?' she asks, putting her drink on the bar.

Reluctantly at first, and after clearing his throat, stalling for time, Niilo answers. 'Nothing dramatic. My parents were both what you might call elderly for working people. Their time came. Father first, when I was sixteen, and then my mother when I was twenty. And that was it. If my love for them had been enough to keep them alive, they'd never have died. But nature does its work, when it is time.'

'Doesn't it just,' Nari exclaims in response, leaning closer to Niilo. 'I lost my dad when I was twenty-one. God, I was devastated. I'd just graduated from uni, and me and Sylvie had moved in together in a place called Castlewych. I still live there, actually. It's lovely, close enough to Manchester for the clubs, but quiet enough to feel cosy. Anyway, Mum was miserable without Dad and she started longing to be with her parents in Seoul. She just didn't want to stay there any more. She wanted me to go with her, but I had a life of my own by then.'

'You were born in Manchester?'

'Oh no, after years of living out of suitcases, Mum, Dad and me moved to England when I was little. Dad worked for a tech firm that was based in Manchester. Eventually that's where we settled, and I met Sylvie at Manchester uni.'

'You must miss your mother?'

'Uh-huh, but I visit her every spring. She lives with my grandmother now – the FaceTime queen! Every Saturday without fail, there's Grandma, asking if I'm eating properly and whether I've got a boyfriend yet.'

The ripples of gentle laughter warmed them both. This felt better, thought Niilo. The frayed threads of the grief that made up the fabric of their separate lives seemed to be somehow entwining and binding them together.

Out of this new atmosphere came talk of Nari's plans for the coming year. Niilo listened as she described spring in Seoul, then summer in the Hebrides, Paris and Mombasa, before an autumn journey on the Trans Siberian Express from Moscow to St Petersburg. All the while her eyes sparkled and she gazed somewhere beyond him into her imagination, into her future. Suddenly, she snapped out of her daze. 'And you? Where are you heading off to?'

'Me?' Niilo started. 'Nowhere. I can't leave Stellan and the resort.'

She nods, and a stillness settles as their conversation falters to a stop.

'Listen, do you want to get out of here?' Nari looks around her at the strange mixture of taxidermy animal heads on plaques, American football memorabilia and leprechauns. 'I'm not going to get much information for my blog in this place. No offense, but it sucks. Can you give me the insider's scoop? Take me somewhere nobody knows?'

'There is one place I thought of. I'm willing to bet a tourist hasn't ever stepped inside the doors. But we should eat in town first, before the drive. It's a few kilometres outside of Saariselkä.'

'I'm intrigued. Let's go!'

Saariselkä is bustling with tourists. There are festive lights in the shapes of white stars and snowflakes on every lamppost and the hotels are gearing up for special Christmas meals for the tourists.

'People eat early in Lapland?' said Nari, detecting the delicious kitchen aromas swirling on the cold air as they cross the wide main street.

'We do everything early in winter. I ate lunch at eleven today, and I'm usually asleep by ten, if the herd are behaving themselves. It's harder when there are babies to look after,' said Niilo holding his hand out to Nari, watching her step over the snow piled up along the gutter.

She too reaches her hand out to meet his but they don't quite make contact, a little of the awkwardness of the Shamrocks bar returns, and then the moment for touching is past. They walk on, hands now shoved into pockets.

'I guess the dark drives people indoors in the evening. I get it. But I'm a night owl, I stay awake reading until the early hours of the morning. We'd never get on, you and I.' Nari bumps an elbow into his arm to punctuate her gentle gibe.

Niilo's laugh is hollow, betraying the uneasiness troubling him. They stroll side by side in silence, their breath turning to white vapour and clouding their vision.

'Nowhere's really open for dinner tonight, except the hotels. Christmas Eve here is basically as important as your Christmas Day in England. Most of the shops and restaurants are closed and the workers are at home with their families. We could try the burger place? It's always open,' says Niilo, stopping to cast his eyes along the street opposite.

'Burgers it is.'

An hour later they are on the road, Niilo driving slowly and steadily as the headlights of his truck illuminate the snow flurrying ahead of them. It hadn't been a great meal and he'd noticed that Nari had been pointedly quiet as she lifted the bun lid to inspect the veggie patty nestling beside underdone French fries. Her notebook had stayed unopened on the table between them.

'I'm guessing that place won't make it onto your blog either?' says Niilo, his eyes set firmly on the road ahead.

'Hmm, I review most places I eat when I'm travelling. Maybe I'll compliment the décor. Although you wouldn't have thought Marilyn Monroe posters, Tiki surfer knick-knacks and mounted moose heads would go together, would you? I'll tell my readers this place is the perfect mash-up between a wood-panelled, Scandi hunting cabin and a cool, chrome sixties' diner. Accentuate the positive.'

Niilo misses Nari's wink thrown casually towards him with a grin. 'I wish the nice places had been open tonight. You deserve the best we can offer.'

'It was fine. My milkshake was good.'

After a moment's silent concentration on the drive, Niilo steers the truck off the road and into a dark car park. 'Here is it.'

Nari peers expectantly into the blackness. 'I don't see anything. We're in the middle of nowhere.'

'I hope it's still open, I haven't been here for years. Come on.'

Using Nari's phone to light their way they pass the recycling bins and piles of snow-covered broken-down cardboard boxes before climbing the clanking metal steps of what looks to Nari like a warehouse. A few cars and trucks are parked down below, and skis and snowshoes piled by the outer door. As Niilo pulls it open for Nari they instantly hear the sounds of music and voices coming from behind another door all the way across a workshop floor. The smell of sawdust and tree sap hangs in the air of the uninhabited, dimly lit room.

'What *is* this place?' Nari whispers as they pick their way past dusty work benches scattered with tools.

'Would you believe me if I told you it was a toy factory?'

'I'd believe anything you told me,' Nari said, wide-eyed and smiling as she tried to make out the objects on the shelves lining the room: wooden cars, nutcracker dolls, whistles and sailboats. 'I'm not about to have an audience with Father Christmas, am I? You should have warned me, I'd have dressed up a bit more,' she laughs, as they reach the double doors, glimmering light spilling through the gap in between.

'If anybody asks, tell them you work at Frozen Falls,' said Niilo.

'OK. What do I do there?'

'Whatever you want,' he replied, trying the door handles and finding them unyielding.

'All right then, I'll be the resident reindeer whisperer.'

'That job's already taken,' he says with a smile, before attempting to force the stiff doors with his shoulder. They burst open with the impact and Nari is hit by a loud wave of Scandinavian symphonic metal coming from a tower of speakers on the far side of the room.

Precariously rigged coloured lights spin and dazzle from the rafters and strands of fairy lights cross-cross the ceiling illuminating a crowded dance floor populated by moving figures. People in their twenties and kids in their late teens are jumping and swaying, arms aloft and hair swinging. A makeshift bar area is doing a roaring trade in bottled beer. Struggling to make herself heard, Nari leans close to Niilo's ear.

'A… clubhouse?'

Niilo raises his voice over the soaring guitars. 'It's where the European kids who work at all the surrounding resorts come after their shifts; ski and chalet workers, tour guides, that sort of thing. And it's just how I remember it.'

'Is it always heavy metal?' Nari roars back, just as the song ends and her question is answered by the sudden shift to upbeat Euro pop. The crowd scream and whoop and dance along as before.

'It's like a student union on a Saturday night. I'll bet we're the oldest people in here.'

Suddenly, Nari falters and turns to look at Niilo's placid expression in the swimming blue and green lights. 'Although... exactly how old are you, if you don't mind me asking?'

A wary smile spreads over Niilo's face, before he leans close to her ear and loudly informs her he's twenty-nine.

'You've got to be kidding me? I'm thirty-five!'

'Sorry?' he shouts, pointing to his ear and shrugging.

'Never mind.' Nari turns towards the bar, wincing.

Nothing Niilo did brought him closer towards rescuing the date he'd had such high hopes for and which had fallen so flat. He sipped Coke Zero and watched Nari down a shot of cheap Finnish vodka, and he smiled and made a show of willingness, hopping from his bar stool, when she indicated with a jab of her thumb towards the bouncing crowd that she wanted to dance.

He had to swallow down the mortified shyness he felt as he swayed ineptly in front of her, feeling more sober than he had in his entire life. Nari hadn't seemed to notice his awkward moves and she danced, eyes closed and with a fixed smile, her hair whipping from side to side across her shoulders.

After a few numbers though, Nari shouted that she didn't recognise any of the songs and that she felt like someone's grandma in this place, so they made their way back to the bar, dodging the kissing couples.

It was impossible to hold anything resembling a conversation and, after a while, Niilo observed Nari's pose of contented poise and excitement fade. She was the one who suggested they leave.

'I'm sorry. You said you wanted nightlife and I thought you'd enjoy it, or at least… find it interesting enough to write about,' Niilo said as the heavy doors slammed shut behind them, leaving them peering into the darkness of the car park and hurriedly pulling on hats and gloves. Nari protested that, on the contrary, it had been fantastic, but they both knew the evening was over.

The only respite from the awkward silence of their drive back to Frozen Falls is the soothing sounds of a Finnish talk show on the truck's crackling radio. Overburdened by disappointment and shock, Niilo barely hears it. He's absorbed in the task of trying to comprehend what just happened. Where had their crystal clear connection gone? Why could he not reach Nari today, make her laugh, get her to open up, as he had done the day before? Was it possible his instincts really had been wrong? Why would they fail him now, when so much seemed to be at stake, when he was driving the most incredible, wonderful, interesting person he had ever met back to her cabin and most probably wouldn't see her again after tonight?

He ruminated as he drove, while Nari, resting her head against the taut seatbelt strap, let her tired eyes close. She drifted off to sleep, not knowing the torment in Niilo's heart.

–

His voice was low and soft as he woke her. 'We're home.'

Home. How desolate and studded with thorns that word felt as it formed in his mouth. *My home, not yours*, it said. *You'll* be leaving soon.

He watched Nari groggily coming round and snapping suddenly upright as she realised she'd been sleeping soundly.

Niilo ran round to pull her car door open and she thanked him for a lovely afternoon and made her way to the cabin door, fumbling for keys in her pocket, bleary-eyed. 'Come in for a drink, now you're not the taxi driver.'

He'd been ready to accept as she worked the cabin door open, but there on the floor, just inside, stood an elaborate display of long-stemmed, blood-red roses. Nari gasped and gaped at them as Niilo watched her expression change and her mind at work.

'What on earth?' she exclaimed, still standing on the snowy doorstep.

Some of the blooms were partly dipped in gold lacquer, others were bejewelled with sparkling stones like black diamonds held on pins that pierced through the centre of their tender buds. The whole arrangement was contained in a wide gilded vase and tied with an elaborate black velvet bow.

'I don't get it,' Nari said as she stepped inside and reached for the card. 'Stephen?' She glanced hurriedly at Niilo and added, 'He's a friend of mine. He's in Singapore.'

None of this was of comfort to Niilo who was now looking beyond the bouquet towards the dining table where there lay a large, shallow dish of enormous hothouse strawberries, shining, red and fat. Their dish too was adorned with a garish bow.

'How did anyone find roses or strawberries like that at this time of year in the arctic? It's impossible.' The words had escaped his lips before he could stop them.

'Typical Stephen,' she said, flustered. 'His PA said she was sending something over from him, but I thought that arrived this morning.'

'This morning?'

'Yes, breakfast stuff. I mean, it was the most beautiful gift basket, local delicacies and carved bowls and spoons…'

'Those… those were from me.'

Nari exhaled sharply with a look Niilo couldn't read. Was she angry? She seemed mortified. Had he over-stepped the mark, sending her gifts? He couldn't tell, but he knew he wanted to get away.

They both looked back at the lavish flowers before Niilo quietly excused himself with a sharp nod, wishing Nari a good evening and a happy Christmas. As he turned over the truck engine he watched her wave distractedly from the cabin door before turning her head to look again at Stephen's gifts.

Those roses, he thought, grown in some perfumed, sun-baked Moroccan valley and transported at speed over land and sea, were just what Nari deserved: rich gifts, glamorous and sweet, befitting her temperament. They would remind her of her travels and make her think of adventures to come. The perfect gifts for Nari.

How paltry his little basket must have seemed beside them. Niilo had no mind to compete with this Stephen guy. His was not the soul of a jealous or possessive man. He had been sent another sign, he told himself, and this time it had come in the form of a lavishly expensive warning.

Stephen's gifts told him that Nari deserved better than a man tied to his homeland, a man who could only offer the simple things he had carved with his knife on long, Lappish winter nights, a man who had never even left Scandinavia.

He understood in that moment that he was not suited to Nari – not because of his modest income or his few possessions, but because Nari, when she found love, would love an adventurer, not a homebody.

Something within him said she didn't love this Stephen, but she needed someone like him to sweep her off her feet. After all, she was entirely self-sufficient, she could go wherever she pleased of her own volition. She had seen the world, learned new languages, tasted every food – and her journey was still only just beginning. Whoever joined her on it would have to be just as free and adventurous. It would be preposterous to expect her to tie herself to a tiny Lappish town and a grounded, tethered man like himself.

With the truck headlights blazing, he turned onto the wilderness road towards his own small cabin and the enclosure where his herd was sheltered. He comforted himself with the thought that it was still early in the evening and he could send his staff home to enjoy the festivities with their families. The men had been kind to cover for him on his date, but he was home again and it was, after all, Christmas Eve. He would feed the animals, spread fresh bedding straw, and tend to the young ones late into the night, just as he should, and just as he always did.

Chapter Nineteen

Everything seems to have the special lustre that Christmas morning brings. Snow has fallen heavily overnight and, unusually, the paths haven't been cleared this morning as Nari and I walk from the cabins to breakfast. The whole landscape seems fresh and new. All of yesterday's icy, impacted footprints and gritty tyre tracks are overlaid with a pristine white blanket. There is lightness and laughter everywhere, with the exception of me and Nari; we're both a little subdued today.

'So, how did it go yesterday, with Stellan?' Nari asks, peering at my face for traces of... I don't know what, wanton shagged-out-ness?

'Well,' I hesitate. 'I told him I wanted a baby, I demanded to know why he dumped me, and I cried.'

'Good work,' Nari says with a nod, pulling a 'fair-do's' sort of expression.

'Thanks.'

'Why did you tell him you wanted a baby? You don't, do you?'

'Because that's the sort of thing I do, apparently. I scare men away with oversharing and desperation.'

She just laughs and shakes her head. 'So, was it as good as the Noughties, then? Did you go retro and make out to NSYNC? Did he stay over? Ooh, did he make you breakfast in bed?'

This is when I falter, feeling like a fool as I tell her how it all ended so abruptly last night. 'Well, there was some kissing involved, yes… and it was beginning to feel like it did back then.' Better, I think actually, way better. 'But,' I huff a ragged sigh. 'But we were making out and waiting for some Christmas cookies that were baking in the oven—'

'Hold the phone! You came all the way to Lapland looking for the man you had the best sex of your life with, and you baked cookies?'

'Yes, and it was nice,' I protest, but she's right, it did all turn into a bit of an anticlimax – excuse the pun.

'Well, things were turning interesting when there was this banging at the door. It was one of the resort staff. He barked something at Stellan – in Finnish, so I had no idea what was going on – and Stellan said he had to go. He grabbed Toivo and left in the guy's truck. And I was left to eat six Christmas cookies all by myself in a strange country on Christmas Eve.' OK, it was twelve cookies, and they were amazing – you'd have done the same, given the circumstances. 'By six o'clock I was in bed, alone, watching telly in Finnish because I couldn't get the stupid remote control thingy to work.'

'Sylvie! Why didn't you knock on my door? I was back home and on my own by half nine.'

'You're kidding? I thought you had the perfect date planned with Niilo?'

Nari shrugs and looks down towards her feet as we shuffle through the snow. 'I thought we were talking about *your* date.'

I give her a hard stare.

'Oh, all right! It just didn't seem to work out, somehow. Niilo looked *so* good in a white shirt and black jeans, and he was polite and asked me lots of questions and he *really* listened to the answers – and you know how rare that is – but we just didn't click this time. I don't know what went wrong.'

I watch her as she thinks for a moment and notice her look of sudden embarrassment.

'What is it?' I ask.

She sighs. 'It *might* have been my fault… a little bit, if I'm honest. I insisted we go searching for Lappish club land – kind of a long shot, I know. He really tried his best, but it was all a bit dire. He was like a fish out of water and I just felt totally stupid and spoiled for asking the impossible. And did you know he's only twenty-nine? *Twenty. Nine.* I usually love discovering rando clubs but, next to Niilo, who had the good sense to know the place was rubbish, I just felt ancient and ridiculous. And then…'

'Oh God, there's *more*?'

'Strap in, Sylve, there *is* more! When he dropped me off at the cabin, he saw Stephen had sent me this hideous, gaudy bouquet of flowers – who knows how, he must have had them choppered in or something – and there were these massive strawberries too. Niilo took one look at them and bolted.'

'Strawberries and roses? These Lapland men are easily spooked.'

Nari gives me an 'ain't that the truth' kind of look, and I suddenly feel as though it's only charitable to share the horrid embarrassment of my date in all its cringey awfulness.

'OK, well this'll make you feel better,' I say. 'Last night Stellan told me the reason he dumped me when we were students was because he thought he was spoiling my chances of a successful career. And the more I thought about it after he'd left, the more I felt like I really must have been a nightmare girlfriend. Was I really so mad about him that I scared him off?'

Nari's diplomatic silence isn't lost on me.

'Even if I was, it's a bit of an overreaction, isn't it? *Oh no, this girl's so into me, I must leave her immediately so she can rediscover herself!* You and I both know I never had any burning desire to graduate top of my class or to win a Teacher of the Year award or anything. And so what if I'd flunked my degree first time around? I'd have managed somehow, even if I was all screwed up with love and high on Stellan Virtanen pheromones. I'd have been happy taking a job waxing Piers Morgan's back, sack and crack if I still got to go home to Stellan every night.'

Nari pulls a revolted, dubious face at this. 'You say that now, but that's because you've got a job you love and a nice flat and enough money to pay for all the things you need *and* some of the things you fancy. Doesn't a small part of you think maybe he did the right thing after all, the mature thing, even if he went about it the wrong way?'

I let this sink in, and grudgingly admit she might be right.

'Well, maybe a teensy part of me, but he could at least have stuck around for a while to see if it all worked itself out. I never got the chance to find out how it could have been between us, long term.'

As we arrive at the restaurant and strip off our snow-suits, hanging them on hooks by the door, a little pang rises in my chest as it occurs to me that we might still have split up, but for much sadder reasons, like trying and failing to make a go of things long-distance. How would I have visited him at Frozen Falls when I was a skint teenager? How would he have made time for me and got away from the resort after his dad fell ill? We'd have fizzled out to nothing. Maybe.

Inside the restaurant, there are squat red candles burning on every table, and Christmas carols playing over the speakers. We're arriving late to breakfast but there's still plenty of food at the buffet. The restaurant staff are all wearing the traditional clothing of their home countries, and I'm aware of a multitude of languages being spoken all around me and realising for the first time how this community of Frozen Falls workers are actually a little world in microcosm, all brought together by the need to work and the wonder of the snowy season in the frozen North.

The few children staying at the resort seem to have abandoned their breakfasts and are driving remote-controlled cars and playing with bright plastic figures on the floor by their parents' tables.

As we settle at the breakfast table, Nari stares dreamily into the air above my head. 'I think it's romantic; enduring heartbreak so the woman you love can be free – like when Prince William ditched Kate because he didn't want her to be attacked in the press for the rest of her life like his mum was.'

'That's not how I remember it,' I say. 'I thought she was known as Waity Katie, hanging around hoping for a proposal while he sowed his royal wild oats?'

I quickly realise Nari's got her selective hearing switched on. She's off again.

'And see what happened to them? A few years later, he *still* couldn't forget her, try as he might, and the next thing you know, they're blinged up, sauntering down the aisle of St. Paul's, and passing on male pattern baldness to new generations of Windsors. *Aww*, it's charming really, when you think about it.'

I decide not to comment on this, but I cast Nari an unconvinced look, which she patently ignores. Pleased with herself, she accepts a coffee from one of the serving staff then wanders off to forage for chocolate croissants at the buffet. I'm still brooding.

After a while spent thinking, and with Nari commenting all the while on the delicious pastries, I say, 'Stellan wouldn't fully admit it, but he's always been seeking his father's approval. Between you and me, his dad sounds like an old stick in the mud, pressing Stellan to take over the family business, and Stellan thought *my* parents were cut from the same cloth so, in his mind, he was saving me from the shame of blowing my degree and letting them down.'

'Bit patriarchal, isn't it? There are worse things in life than letting your dad down, especially if what your dad wants for you is to become some millionaire ski resort entrepreneur when you'd actually be happy with a bog standard career.' She's got some wind in her sails now. 'In fact, all these resort blokes have a touch of the sexist twats about them, don't you think?'

'Not really,' I say, but she's not listening.

'Come to think of it, Sylve. I don't know why you're not more indignant about Stellan. He says he left because

207

you were *too into him*, at the expense of your studies and your friends and your family, but you could look at it from another point of view. You showed him genuine emotion, he freaked out and bolted. It's him that's got a commitment problem, not you with an over investment problem.'

All I can do is grimace. This thought had briefly occurred to me last night alone in the cabin as I went over and over it all, but when it boiled down to it, I knew I was to blame. However, there's no time to tell Nari this, she's really got the bit between her teeth now.

'These Scandi men! Do you think Niilo did a runner last night because of Stephen's flowers? He saw them and thought, *but I've staked my claim to this woman, she's mine*, and got all territorial and possessive like I owe him my hand in marriage just because he shelled out for a dodgy burger and a few vodkas? Actually, that's not true, we went Dutch, but *still*!'

'Did he *seem* angry or jealous?'

'Not exactly, he was just a bit… sad-looking.'

I watch Nari as she takes a long glug of coffee and I can tell she's not as outraged as she's pretending to be. 'Nari… are you all right?' She sighs and shrugs, and I see the problem instantly. 'You're sad about it too, aren't you?'

There are tears in her eyes when she answers. 'You know, I felt so comfortable with him, I actually followed him into a scary-ass toy factory at night! I mean, that's the stuff of bad horror movies right there, but I trusted him implicitly. I even fell asleep in his truck last night, and I'm sure I was drooling all over the place. And, did you know it was Niilo that sent the breakfast basket yesterday? Isn't that so like him, so… real? And all the time I thought

Stephen had sent it and got it so right. It didn't even cross my mind that it might be from Niilo, and, stupidly, I told him that, in as many words. That's when he left. He thinks I'm spoiled and ungrateful.' After another deep breath and a long sigh – not like Nari at all – she says, 'Oh well. You win some; you catastrophically fuck up some.' And there she is, putting a brave face on it.

'Tell me about Stellan,' she says, waving away thoughts of Niilo. 'At least spill *some* of the deets. What was it like – before he scarpered into the night, obviously?'

'Thanks for the reminder,' I say, grimly. 'It was fine. We talked and we decorated the tree and it was good just getting to know him now we're older.'

'But you didn't get lucky.' Nari jabs at the crumbs on her plate with her finger, obviously disappointed I don't have any gossip to report.

'I doubt it would have happened last night anyway. You don't know Stellan like I do, he always wanted to take things slow and just, you know, make it special when it did happen.'

Nari's staring blankly at me. 'But we're leaving tomorrow morning. Are you even seeing him today?'

'I don't know,' I admit, and my heart sinks. 'He said he was working today, some special job he had to do. So, I'm guessing… no.' *Ow*, that hurts.

'Well, listen, it's Christmas morning, in case you're forgetting, and we've got the whole day ahead of us. We can chill out, take a walk, sit by the fire, have a nap, read a book… maybe we'll see the northern lights later.' I can tell Nari's trying her best to cheer me up, but her heart doesn't seem to be in it either.

'I hadn't forgotten. In fact…'

Her face lights up as I pull the silver gift bag from under the restaurant table.

'Aww, thanks, Sylvie. I got you something too.' She reaches for what turns out to be a Christmas stocking. It's stuffed with pots and tubes of expensive skincare brands, and there's chocolates too and a couple of romantic novels with pretty, Christmassy covers. Nari always was an expert gift-buyer. She gives me a Christmas card too – a pink, glittery one with a ballerina on the front.

'For a special little girl at Christmas time.'

She's laughing as I read.

'Open it up!'

Inside, the printed message continues, 'Hoping Father Christmas gives you everything you wished for this year.' She does this every time. For my thirtieth birthday I got a card with Minnie Mouse and a badge that said '3 today' on it. I'm giving her my usual sardonic thanks when the gift certificate slips from the card onto my lap.

'Luxury Pamper Treatments at Frozen Falls Spa? Oh, Nari, that's amazing, thank you! Is this what we're doing this morning?' I deliver a big kiss right onto her cheek.

'Uh-huh, I scored a freebie for myself and thought you'd enjoy a bit of festive exfoliation too. The spa's only open for a few hours but your treatments are booked in for ten. I'm going to hit the sauna and the counter current exercise pool.'

'You're *not*? One of those little pools where you swim like mad and the water keeps pushing you back to the same spot?'

'Yup! I could do with working off some stress after last night.'

'You wouldn't catch me in one of those. If I'm swimming I want to be moving through the water.'

'On your way to the bar at the other side.'

'Obviously. Swim with purpose,' I say, grandly.

This is more like it, just me and Nari and our familiar chatty nonsense, exactly what we came here for, and it's soothing my ragged emotions after last night's strange and sudden disappointment and the sleepless night that followed Stellan's departure.

I won't tell Nari about how I lay awake digesting the horrible knowledge that I'd scared Stellan away all those years ago, and brooding on the embarrassment of him running off into the night after I'd opened up to him yesterday, when we'd been kissing and it had all felt so promising. I really thought he'd come back but he hasn't even called. I can't believe that's how our lovely day ended and I won't see him again because he's busy today and we're leaving early tomorrow morning. I've blown it again.

I try to pack away these thoughts and concentrate on Nari opening my gift, which I'm still not sure about: it's a gold leather passport cover with her name embossed on the front and a matching luggage label from her favourite handbag designer. I've been worrying they're a bit clichéd for a travel writer – not to mention that they cost me a week's pay – but her delighted reaction makes that meaningless now.

Nari sits down again after hugging me and she's looking at her presents when I see her face turn deathly pale and her eyes bulge. 'Oh no!' she cries, looking me in the eyes, horror-struck. 'Oh God, no!'

'What is it? You're scaring me?'

'I completely forgot!' She's talking now with her head in her hands, her hair falling onto the table.

'Forgot what?'

'I wrote it yesterday, the blog, and I scheduled it to go live early this morning. Oh no!'

'OK, what's the problem?'

'I *might* have mentioned Niilo and our date, a little bit.'

'What did you say? It can't be that bad, surely?'

'It's too late to delete it now, people will have seen it, won't they?'

'Well I haven't. I've run out of data. What's the problem?'

'I might have made a few hints that I liked him, totally off brand and weird, I know! And...' I watch her raise her head, her eyes big and apologetic. 'And...'

'What?'

'I might have made a little, innocent reference to you seeing Stellan.'

'You didn't!'

She nods and scrunches up her eyes as it comes back to her. I can see she's remembering the actual words and it's obviously mortifying.

'Nari, you pillock! What's gotten into you on this trip?'

'I don't know, it's Niilo's fault. I was doing fine before he turned up, being all rugged and worthy, and much younger than me, and super hot.'

'Look, I doubt Stellan or Niilo have time to faff about reading blogs, do you? They probably haven't seen it. And what does it matter anyway? We're leaving tomorrow and it's not like we're seeing them again. Can't you just delete it now? Are you worried that Stephen will see it?'

'People will have read it. I scheduled it for seven a.m British time, and I forgot all about it, what with everything going on last night. I've spent years building my following, distancing myself from the old dating blog – not that I'm ashamed of it, not *at all* – but I worked so hard to be taken seriously in the travel industry and now I'm known as this single-girl adventurer.' Her shoulders droop. 'And no, Stephen won't have seen it. He's never read my blog.'

I watch Nari checking her phone and scrolling through the comments.

'Can I at least see what you wrote?' I say, reaching for the phone.

'It's nothing, really. Probably best you don't bother.'

She's biting her bottom lip now, and I see the colour returning to her face.

'I'm sorry, Sylve. Everything felt so different yesterday, remember? How could I know our dates were going to go tits up?'

There's a wicked gleam in her eyes now, and I know I've already forgiven her, whatever it was she said on that blog about me and Stellan. Like everything else that happened yesterday, it doesn't really matter. Nari turns the phone to me.

'*Woah!* Seventy two notifications, and on Christmas day too,' I say.

'That's the most comments one of my posts has ever had. Look, this follower's really into it, and so is this one.'

Nari shows me their messages and I scroll through, reading some aloud.

'*Tell me more about this herder, Nari Bell! You're taking me back to the old days of your dating blog!*'

'*Maybe she's met her match?*'

'*OMG, I NEED to know what happened!!!*'

'Well, Nari, whatever you wrote, you've caused quite a bit of excitement,' I say, handing her phone back.

Nari's shaking her head, half amused, half mortified, and she swipes the screen to power off, too distracted to notice him arriving. He's stolen into the restaurant in silence and comes to a standstill behind her shoulder, his chest rising and falling heavily.

I see the grave, determined look on Niilo's face. He's waiting for Nari to turn around.

When she follows my widened eyes and finally clocks him, her face breaks into a huge grin. So much for being angry and feeling judged by this guy; she's positively beaming. Niilo remains serious and, I realise, he's nervous too. His hands are shaking.

'Good morning, Nari, Sylvie.' He makes two sharp nods with his head. 'Happy Christmas.'

Nari doesn't reply. She's staring at him in his traditional high-collared, royal blue tunic with a cluster of plaited pewter decorations at his throat and a colourful quilted belt studded with round silver buttons at his waist. The impressive get-up is crowned with a tall blue hat also decorated with bright embroidery. I'm fairly sure there are love hearts forming in Nari's eyes like in a cartoon.

'I'm just gonna grab more coffee,' I say.

'They bring it to the table, remember?' Nari says over her shoulder to me, never tearing her eyes from Niilo.

Nevertheless, I slip away to the breakfast buffet just a few feet away and pretend I'm busy behind the juice machine, and I watch what happens.

I see Niilo crouch by Nari's knees and she leans close to him. They speak in low tones to one another so I can't overhear – very inconsiderate – but I see Nari's expression change. She looks as embarrassed and apologetic as Niilo does and she's making a crossing action with her palms outspread in front of her, waving away what is clearly Niilo's attempt at an earnest apology.

Then, as I watch, he asks her something which makes her look… well, *bashful*! Bashful and Nari aren't a natural combination, so this isn't something I've seen much of before. Whatever he's asking, she nods in assent. Niilo takes Nari's hand in his, upturning it and smoothing his fingertips over her palm. All the while they're looking into the other's faces. He gently turns her hand over again, dips his head, and presses a kiss against her skin. Then, smiling shyly, he stands and walks off across the restaurant. I make my dash from behind the juice glasses back to the table to get the salacious details.

'What was that?'

'I'm not sure.' Nari seems dazed, but she's still smiling as she watches him make his way around the tables towards the low stage at the other side of the room. 'I said I was sorry for wanting to go clubbing on what's basically Christmas day in Lapland, and he said he was sorry for being quiet, and then…'

'I saw!'

Nari shuffles her chair back under the table, settling herself again and wrapping her hands around her elbows in a hug as she watches Niilo ascending the stairs onto the stage.

'Has he seen your blog post?' I ask.

'He didn't mention it if he has,' she replies in a whisper, her eyes trained on Niilo, who has come to a halt in front of a keyboard lit by a spotlight.

That's when I notice all the restaurant staff have lined up along the walls and are grinning and winking at one another. They've clearly hatched a plan with Niilo and something special's about to happen.

'He says he's going to sing something. For me,' says Nari, still staring dead ahead.

The piped carols coming over the restaurant speakers cut out, and there's the faint crackle of a microphone switching on. Niilo's voice, a little shaky, rings out over the room.

'*Huomenta ja hyvää joulua.* My name is Niilo Oskal.'

Some of the staff whoop and cheer at this. He has the attention of everyone in the place.

'I look after the reindeer here at Frozen Falls resort. My family are Sámi people and have lived in the lands to the south of this area for generations. They taught me how to sing traditional *joik* songs. I would like to sing one now, a new song. It is called "Nari's Joik".'

He adjusts the microphone in front of his mouth and looks down at the keyboard before him. I hear Nari exhale sharply, but we both sit in silence, awestruck, as he stretches long fingers over the keys, and then he closes his eyes and opens his mouth to sing.

His voice, when it reaches us, is soft and tender, repeating the first word of his song: *Nari*.

As he incants her name, his fingers touch the keys and lend a melodious swell which builds as his voice grows stronger and he breaks into longer lines of poetry. The words sound a little like Finnish, but somehow more ancient and with greater complexity and power. And he's looking only at Nari, as if they're the only two people here.

Their gaze feels so intimate I shift my chair a little distance away, leaving Nari in a space of her own where only she and Niilo exist.

The music is like nothing I've ever heard before, and is sung in languages I'll never understand, but I do understand the look on their faces and the electric feeling in the room, which is palpable.

I've never actually seen two people fall in love before, right in front of me. I imagine it's what seeing a baby being born is like: the perfect combination of wonderful, splendid nature in all its terrifying glory and magical, unfathomable love in all its intangible, inexplicable wonder. Niilo is singing his love for my friend, and I watch helplessly, my own heart swelling with happiness for her as she falls. I can see the tears shining in their locked eyes.

Niilo's song ends with a sweet sustained note, and suddenly, Nari's on her feet and I bet she isn't even aware of that fact yet. She's leading the applause as the room wakes from Niilo's enchantment.

I look down at the spa gift token still in my hand as Nari breaks her gaze away from Niilo and turns to me, wiping her eyes with her sleeve. We're both thinking the same thing.

'Sylve?' she says, with a shaking voice.

'Off you go,' I say, and I admit a tear or two might have spoiled my own mascara at this point. 'Have fun.'

She kisses me hard on my cheek, and she's gone, and I'm left smiling sadly like a mother of the bride waving off her daughter at the end of the wedding reception.

I watch as they meet in the middle of the room and take each other's hand and race for the doors and out into the snow. Through the frosted pane I see Niilo fastening Nari's helmet straps under her chin before they leap onto a snowmobile with a loud, revving engine and disappear into the white world beyond the resort.

And suddenly, I'm very aware that I'm alone and still standing by the breakfast table. I have a sudden urge to check my pockets, feeling as though I've misplaced something, but nothing is amiss.

I look around the room, which is slowly emptying. The staff are chatting amongst themselves as they clear away dishes and strip table cloths into big laundry baskets.

'Right,' I say aloud to myself, catching my breath. Christmas day. Alone. In Lapland. Of course. What should I do now? I stand there for a while, like a satnav rerouting after an unexpected diversion.

I suddenly think of the key to the dog sheds back at my cabin. Although I doubt I'll see Stellan today, there is someone who I know will be pleased to see me later. I gather up the remnants of breakfast in a napkin and put it in my bag. Toivo will enjoy these, I tell myself.

Then, looking at Nari's Christmas gifts lying on the table, I try, with a bit of effort, to smile, shake my hair back and straighten my shoulders. My best friend is off having a romantic adventure with a beautiful, talented, surprising man, and if she's happy, I'm happy.

I run my fingers over the jackets of the books she gave me. They're festively foiled and glittering. I have something nice to read *and* I have something nice to do today. That's not too bad. Surely, I can be content on my own for one day? I catch one of the staff as they bustle past with a tray of coffee cups.

'Can you point me in the direction of the spa, please?'

Chapter Twenty

Niilo stands astride the snowmobile, clasping the throttle tightly, powering through the landscape, as Nari, her hands gripping his waist, laughs and screams. Once out of sight of the resort and on the wilderness track, Niilo throws his head back and howls a deep call into the grey light of the late morning sky.

The vehicle's suspension absorbs the impact of each snowy mound and curve as Niilo pushes it to its absolute limit, sending birds scattering from the few scrubby trees and bushes they pass by before crossing the vast frozen lake and taking a turn southward onto a narrow forest track that Nari has never seen before.

Under the cover of the thick evergreen branches burdened with snow the headlights shine out, making the fine flakes in the air shine like glitter in a snowglobe.

Niilo takes the opportunity offered by a straight stretch of track to look around at Nari. Their faces are obscured by their black ski masks and helmets but each knows the other is smiling. The pair voice elated shrieks as they speed over a snowy mound and are, for a few exhilarating moments, airborne.

As the track widens, Niilo slows the pace and sits down on the wide seat. Nari pulls herself close to his back and wraps her thighs tightly around him, causing Niilo's heart to pound even harder as a breathless, light-headed sensation washes through him. Gasping for air, he briefly reaches his gloved hand for hers and presses it reassuringly against his chest.

Nari closes her eyes, loving the sensation of this man being in control. When she opens them again, she gasps, though Niilo cannot hear her over the engine noise. There, running alongside them, just a few feet inside the treeline on both sides of the track, are a pack of wolves, their sleek necks bobbing and stretching as they run, their shaggy backs undulating with the speed of the chase. Niilo knows they are there but keeps his eyes fixed on the track ahead, and he and Nari race on through the wilderness making wild howling cries into the air before the creatures suddenly turn and disappear into the dark wood.

–

The cabin at the edge of the forest is almost entirely snow-bound. Niilo parks the snowmobile beside what, in the summer months, would be recognisable as a herb garden. Clambering off the machine, he helps Nari step down into deep, untrodden white drifts.

'Where are we?' she asks, lifting the helmet from her head and pulling the ski mask down so it hangs around her neck.

'This was my grandparents' home. It's mine now,' Niilo replies as he searches in the snow near a tarpaulin-covered log pile for a wide shovel. 'Give me a minute and we'll be inside.'

Making her way over to the log pile, Nari finds a second shovel and joins him on the path. 'You dig, I dig. OK?'

Niilo accepts with a nod and they clear their way to the low wooden door which bears the evidence, blackened and withered, of a contorted summer rose stretched over a lattice frame surrounding the entrance.

'It's going to be cold inside, I haven't been here for months. There's no time to get away from the resort during winter and check on the place. But I'll light a fire and get you warm again. And I brought food too.'

'You've thought of everything then?'

'Uh-huh.' Niilo grins, bringing an ornate key from inside the chest pocket of his gákti jacket and opening the door with ease. It swings inwards and Nari steps over the threshold.

'Sorry, it's very basic, and it's not decorated for Christmas day.'

'I don't need decorations,' Nari says with a warm smile, as Niilo runs a hand along the wall by the door, feeling for the fuse box.

The lights flare inside the room and Nari takes in the low-ceilinged kitchen with its scrubbed wooden table, pitted and slashed from decades of use. The grey cabinets and work surfaces around the room are uncluttered, clean, and dating back to the nineteen-eighties at least. Nari is relieved to spot a modern electric stove and a few new-looking radiators which she hears burbling and clanking into life.

'Go through there, into the lounge. I'll get the fire-wood,' says Niilo, leaving again by the main door.

Nari makes her way into the little den with its low sofa in front of a tall chimney, a wide hearth, and solitary standard lamp topped with a crooked yellow shade which she straightens as she passes by. The walls are papered in orange and green diamond patterns, the likes of which she hasn't seen since her earliest childhood. But everything is neat and homely and she knew it would become cosy once the fire was lit.

She watches Niilo returning and kneeling by the grate, first piling on the small pieces of kindling, then scrunched yellowing newspaper and something that looks like dried bundles of lichen. He forms them all into a little pyre. It takes two matches to start the flames licking up the chimney.

After a satisfied moment watching the fire grow, Niilo bundles on the logs. The flames soon build to a bright heat.

'One moment,' Niilo says as he leaves the room again.

Waiting expectantly, Nari watches him through the low window as he opens a hatch at the back of the snow-mobile and pulls out bundled blankets and a grocery bag.

When he returns he's careful to close the doors behind him. Crouching by the fire again, he unpacks the bag onto the hearth.

Nari lifts some of the packages and squints at their labels. 'I don't recognise any of this food packaging, but if we're going to cook, I want to help you.'

'OK, open this.' He hands her a tall bottle. 'Cloudberry liqueur. Have you tried it?'

'Nope, but I've heard it's deathly strong,' she says with a smile, taking the bottle from him.

'That's why we're drinking it with coffee.'

'Just coffee?' Nari pulls a face as she cracks the lid and takes a quick sniff at the boozy vapours emanating from the bottle.

'And vodka, cream and ice.' Niilo waggles his eyebrows, making Nari laugh.

'Oh, you're a cocktail waiter too?'

'You'd be surprised, the things I can do. You get resourceful, living out here on your own.' Niilo pours ground espresso into a silver coffee pot along with water from a plastic bottle and, tightening the lid, he places the pot close to the flames to heat up. Nari simply watches him, her eyes sleepily fond and heavy-lidded.

'So do you want to tell me about the song you sang this morning? It was beautiful.'

'I wrote it last night, for you. I couldn't sleep, and I find I can think most clearly on the occasional winter nights when I'm awake.' As he spoke, Niilo took a cloth and wiped out the inside of a shining cooking pot by the fireside which had the look of a witch's cauldron before setting about pouring powdery milled oats, sugar and a carton of milk into it.

'Me too. What were you thinking about?'

'That I shouldn't be such an ass,' he said with a dry laugh. 'And I should make your visit to Lapland the best it can possibly be.'

'So you wrote me a song.'

'A *joik*, yes. It was the song of your spirit. It wasn't hard to write, it just… happened.'

'It was beautiful, what were the lyrics?'

'Maybe they weren't so much lyrics as… a kind of list?'

'A list?'

'Of things that you are, things about you that I like, or things you make me think.' Looking away hurriedly, he busied himself rummaging in the bag for a jar of nutmeg.

'Are you turning red? OK, OK, I won't push you. Just show me them written down one day?'

'I will. I promise.' Niilo nods, sprinkling a pinch of the nutmeg into the pot and passing a long-handled wooden spoon to Nari who crouches by the pot over the hearth and stirs.

The cosiness of their simple domesticated scene isn't lost on either of them, and Niilo finds he can't help smiling contentedly as he reaches for the coffee pot and pours the steaming black liquid into two tall plastic beakers.

'These need to go outside on the windowsill for a minute, then we drink.'

As Niilo briefly opens the low window, a sudden blast of cold air helps Nari realise it has become warm enough in the little room to strip out of their snowsuits.

While the coffee cools on the snowy ledge, and without looking towards each other, they remove their outer layers with a curious shyness.

Niilo is hooking the suits on the back of the den door when Nari gives in to temptation and turns to watch him in his wonderful blue clothing, ornate, elegant and timeless. Finding herself in danger of staring and in need of distraction, she lets her gaze flit towards the glass cabinet behind the sofa. 'What's in there?'

'Family stuff. Come, take a look.'

Unlocking the cabinet doors, Niilo carefully lifts out a large flat object with painted figures all over it. Nari comes to stand near him.

'This is my great grandfather's drum.'

'It's beautiful. It looks so fragile.' Nari isn't sure why her voice has shrunk to a near whisper.

Mirroring her stillness, his voice lowers to a murmur too. 'It's made from reindeer skin. Grandpa made it himself, and painted these animals on it.'

'They're bears?' Nari asks, peering closely with a delighted smile.

'Some of the old people of the Sápmi believed in a kind of animism – that everything in nature has a spirit. We believed you could speak to our ancestors through the natural world. My family were particularly associated with the spirits of bears, I think, although I don't really know much more about them. Their stories got lost when my parents died. Maybe I should have listened better when I was a kid.'

Eyeing Niilo cautiously, Nari can feel some of his loss and regret.

'Singing songs was one way of passing on family histories. When a new person was welcomed into my family, they received their *joik*. It told them of their place in the family, and in the universe.'

'And you wrote a *joik* for me.'

Niilo returns her gaze. 'I did.' He immediately looks back at the drum, a little ruffled. 'There's so much I don't remember about my family, and so much that wasn't written down that must have been contained in songs and stories that I'll never hear.'

'I'm sorry,' Nari says, for want of better words.

'But I still have the summer and winter cabins.' He looks around with a faint smile. 'And I have this drum, of course. It should probably be in a museum, but I don't feel it belongs there.'

'No, it's yours.'

226

'And I have these too. My father's knife and belt, and these are the boots my grandmother made for me when my mother was pregnant.' He reaches into the cupboard before handing her the tiny reindeer hide shoes.

'They're beautiful. But... no photographs?' Nari glances around the room. 'I haven't seen a single picture.'

'I don't have many here. My cousin has some family albums, I think,' Niilo said with a sorry shrug, noticing that Nari was gently cradling the tiny shoes to her chest.

In the silence that followed, Nari let her eyes look over the beautiful fabric of Niilo's outfit with its skirted jacket, shining buttons and golden thread embroidery again. Something moved her to reach her hand to his belt, gently running her fingertips over the sheathed knife that hung there.

Niilo glanced down at her hand, his breathing suddenly ragged. Was she going to touch him? He didn't think he could bear it, and he didn't think he could survive without it. But Nari, sensing his panic, and suddenly confused and not wanting to show it, let her fingers fall away, pointing instead to the bundle of small sticks in the chest pocket of his *gákti*.

'And those, what are those for?' she asks, a little flustered and with the air of someone expecting another story.

'These? They're sticks. For the fire.' This was said bluntly and accompanied by a level stare, and then, in a sudden, awkward movement, Niilo took the shoes from her hands and locked them away with the drum and his other precious treasures. Nari noted the change in mood and the sharp turn of the cabinet's little key.

'Oh!' She tried to laugh off her mistake.

'I'm a man, not a wizard.'

227

'What? I'm sorry, I—'

'I'm tired of visitors to the resort seeing me as some kind of Shamanic He-man, a kind of exotic make-believe man… a conquest. They see nothing but a fancy costume and it sparks some kind of fantasy in their heads, but they haven't got a clue who I am.'

'OK, I said I was sorry.' Nari paced over to the hearth and looked down into its flames. 'But if you think you've got the monopoly on people misreading you, then you don't, OK?' She looked up in time to see Niilo's throat move as he swallowed and cast his eyes to the floor.

This couldn't be happening again, he thought. Not this strained awkwardness, not after the exhilaration of their ride out to the cabin, not after he'd sung for her and seen the tears in her eyes.

'No, I'm the one who is sorry,' he said, taking a few steps towards her. 'I shouldn't have said what I said. Not to you. Will you forgive me?'

'It's all right. I get it.'

'No, I didn't mean to accuse you of… I got nervous. I thought you were reaching for me, and I don't know why, I panicked. I got it wrong.'

She *had* wanted to reach for him, to slip her arms around him and let him hold her, but the panic in his eyes had startled her too.

Attempting a smile and a shrug, she reaches for the bottle of liqueur. 'Come on, mix me that cocktail you promised me.'

The pair settle on the sofa, and Niilo uses his knife to work open the can of cream before pouring the sweet straw-coloured liqueur and vodka into the chilled coffee, the rhythms of their hearts steadying again.

'I'm sorry… again. I don't want to hurt you. I'm not suspicious of you, I know you're not here for the wrong reasons.'

Nari raises her hand and stills him, and his eyes smile. Their brief storm has blown over.

'*Geonbae*,' she says, holding her tumbler to his.

'*Kippis!*'

Nari joins him in a cautious sip, her eyes widening over the rim of the cup.

'Good *grief*! That's delicious, but it's strong. Can I have some more cream in mine?' Nari's voice is hoarse and she coughs hard to clear the burning sensation in her throat as Niilo dilutes her drink a little. She is careful to keep a little distance between them on the sofa, remembering how startled he had been a moment ago.

'Tell me more about your family. They were herders?' she asks, hoping he'll open up.

'Yes, going back for a few generations.'

'Is that what you wanted to do as a kid?'

'It was all I knew. I helped with my family herd, but I was too young to take over when my father died and so my father's brother received the family herd, and I hear it's much smaller and belongs to his daughter now.'

'But you have your own herd here.'

'Yes. For tourists. It's not the same thing.'

'How many do you have?'

'It's not very polite to ask this question, and far worse to give an answer. That's like me asking you how much cash you have in your bank account. Although, since I'm not technically a herder, I guess I can tell you. I have only forty-eight. At one time, my family farmed thousands of animals. But my Frozen Falls reindeer are still marked with

229

my family cut on their ears; the bear's paw. I learned to cut the marks when I was just a child. My grandmother taught me.'

'You said you used to go on migrations with other family's herds, do you miss it?'

'I do, but it was hard, dangerous work.'

'Is that how you got this?' She raises her index finger to his cheek hesitantly and with the lightest touch presses her fingertip to the white scar beneath his eye. Niilo follows the movement of her hand as it gets closer and holds his breath, closing his eyes as she makes contact in a sudden burst of sensation, first warmth and then the tingling pain of the scar.

'Did that hurt?'

'No.' He exhales and opens his eyes. 'No, it doesn't hurt. I just...' His words tail off into a frustrated shrug.

Nari looks down at her hands, now both safely clutching her cup, her shoulders rounding as she recoils.

Swallowing hard, Niilo races for words. 'Do you think Sylvie will be all right alone at the resort?'

'*Umm*,' Nari's brain works, trying to catch up with the sudden shift. 'She'll be fine, I think. She's at the resort spa.'

'I've always wondered why people pay to go there. Are those beauty treatments really so good?'

'Yes, of course they are. Haven't you ever had a massage?'

'Sure; in the sauna there's the birch branches. They get your circulation going; it's restorative after days on the trails.'

'I doubt Sylvie's going to let anyone bash her about with a bundle of twigs. No, I booked her a facial, mani-cure, back massage, and a body wrap. She'll be in Scandi spa heaven.' Nari watches him sip his drink and consider her words. He doesn't even wince as the alcohol burns its way down his throat. He seemed bemused. 'You should try it sometime, go in for a facial or something?'

'I'm always busy with the herd, or out with the tourists. There's no time to lie around doing nothing while I pay someone to rub oil on my face.' Niilo softened this with a laugh.

'But you must get tired? And you need to stay healthy.' She lets Niilo think this over for a moment, taking a drink.

'I guess,' he says.

'And everybody needs to be touched,' she adds quickly, looking away but aware of Niilo's throat moving as he swallows.

He doesn't speak but when she glances at him the curious look in his eyes emboldens her to go on. 'Have you ever felt like it's been ages since anyone put their hands on you? Adults don't really touch, do they? I mean, we might hug a friend or something, but that's always so brief – economical, even – and you queue up with people, and get squashed together in elevators, or some manspreader might press his thigh on yours on the train, but none of that is touch. What I mean is, when did anyone last make an actual concerted effort to reach out to you and just connect with you? That's part of the spa ritual, I think. And it's comforting. To be touched.'

Niilo locks eyes with his guest, a look of incredulity on his face which broadens into a smile. 'I have thought the same thing many times. Nari, I must explain. I think so often about the people living in the south, crowded in the cities and packed into houses with friends and family and loved ones of all sorts, and I can't imagine what it must be like to be close to people like that.'

Nari looks into his eyes, wordlessly tipping her head by way of encouragement to keep him talking.

'Out on the trails some mornings, its minus thirty degrees and the snow feels like pinpricks on your bare hands, and the air's so cold your lungs are shocked by it, even if you've experienced it every winter morning on every trail you've ever done. It sends adrenalin rushing to your brain, telling you to run, to find warmth. You build a fire for the tourists with silver birch and the bark's so smooth, like satin, and the embers spark out and burn your skin. And there's just you and your fire and your *puukko* knife keeping everyone alive out there. You have to sharpen your knife every day on a stone and check with your thumb that it's sharp enough to use.'

At this, Nari reaches for Niilo's free hand and, holding it in her own, she soothes the rough, weathered skin with her fingertips in soft, slow circles. A rush of breath escapes Niilo's lips before he speaks again, this time with more difficulty.

'On mornings like that, out in the wilderness, it feels like every sensation is more intense. Heat burns hotter, the cold has to be colder than any other place on earth, and the stars are more piercing in the darkest sky.' With this he returns Nari's caress, letting his fingers tentatively trace slow lines over the back of her hand. 'Everywhere there's these intense sensations, and they're overwhelming sometimes, but what I was always waiting for was—'

'Someone to touch you.'

'Yes. And not just anyone.' Niilo raises his arm, placing it along the back of the sofa, leaving a space for Nari to slide inside.

With a smile she leans into him, resting her head on his chest.

For a long while they hold each other and watch the flames in the hearth.

Chapter Twenty-One

I've visited a lot of spas in my life – thanks to Nari – from high end luxury in towering glass city hotels to a decidedly dodgy place over a suburban takeaway with dead pot plants in the grubby windows, but this place is off the charts, jaw-dropping, simple Scandinavian chic and tasteful opulence.

I know I'm onto a winner as soon as I arrive at the spa: a futuristic snowy dome in the forest of baby pine trees in a secluded spot behind the hotel. Another one of Stellan's recent improvements to the resort, I imagine.

I'm welcomed into the reception area, white, warm and tranquil, by a blonde woman who ushers me in near silence to one of the little rooms leading off from it, each, I assume, like this one – a smaller pod with a rounded ceiling and a spa bed at its centre.

Where's the tootling whale music and panpipes, scented candles and the glassy-eyed beauty therapist saying, 'you can just pop your things on the chair'? This is soundless, pristine, Lappish luxury like I could never have imagined.

The woman leaves me to slip into a white cotton robe and I sink onto the heated bed. There's something resembling a big shiny pebble on the shelf over there making clouds of white steam and I'm so warm and, frankly, shattered, I'm feeling sleepy already. Nari will be kicking herself that she didn't come, though I doubt she's regretting her choices right this second.

The therapist returns, wheeling a little cart loaded with products in elegant packaging, and for the next two hours I'm wrapped up, smoothed, scrubbed and soothed, and it is wonderful. And I almost drift off entirely in an aromatherapy-induced haze except I find I can't switch off that last little bit of my brain, the bit where Stellan lives rent free, an emotional squatter, sending out constant reminders of how things were yesterday when we were together.

I'm trying to shut out the memories of the sweet, familiar feeling of sinking into Stellan's kiss and the safe, secure warmth of his arms around me and the sense that maybe we actually *were* meant to be reunited here at his Lapland home, and maybe we *do* have something as elemental and irresistible as the magnetic pole pulling us back together.

But, I remind myself, he isn't here. He's somewhere nearby, sure, but he's not with me. And it's Christmas day.

I've always said that if someone wants to be with you, they *will* be with you, and nothing will keep them away. Like when you bump into someone in the street you haven't seen for years and you both say, 'We really *must* meet for that drink', secure in the mutually acknowledged, but never voiced, understanding that, thank goodness, it's never actually going to happen.

Was Stellan's hurried cry of, 'I must go, I'll see you again,' as he rushed from my cabin yesterday, how this was always going to end? A repeat of the first time he disappeared out of my life without a trace? I could have sworn yesterday as we kissed in the kitchen that he'd be staying the night and that we'd be together today; that he wouldn't let anything come between us, especially when I'm only here for another, what, twenty hours?

I thought all of this over last night after he left, when I didn't get to sleep until gone four and I'd cried like a teenager and used up all my tissues. I'd stared up at the snow on the glass roof above my big empty bed and it had struck me; maybe I am guilty of getting over invested in things, of being infuriatingly intense. I know Nari said this morning she thinks it's Stellan and his commitment issues and not my over-enthusiastic investment in him that's the problem, but I'm unconvinced.

I went through it all last night, thinking about my long history of liking things passionately to the exclusion of all other interests, and how each new obsession fades in time and I move on.

There was that twelve-month period after I met Cole where, inspired by a sunny week in Madrid together, I'd shelled out for Spanish lessons and a weekend at a Flamenco dancing residential school in London, and just as I'd mastered the art of making oversized dishes of seafood paella, I totally lost interest in all things Spanish and switched my obsession to gardening our little plot at the back of the Love Shack.

It had come as a huge surprise to me to discover I had green fingers and could grow my own spuds in a bucket and train tomato plants up canes by the back door, and I'd listen to *Gardener's Question Time* every Sunday whilst deadheading hanging baskets of stripy petunias and sipping tea from a National Trust gift shop mug that told everyone I was the 'Head Gardener'. I let the whole thing go to seed after a few seasons when I realised Cole never joined me out there in what was supposed to be our own little Eden.

And, yes, there was a time in my adolescence when I balanced twin loves for the myths and legends of Scandinavia and a powerful interest in the back catalogue of Kate Bush, to the extent that I bought a pair of replica Viking amulets off eBay and, in imitation of my new musical idol, I wore a black fringed caftan and no shoes for the entire summer of 1998 to complement my *Wuthering Heights* feathered hair and general whimsical demeanour.

And then there was my Zumba phase, quickly passed over for the more intense PowerZumbaBlast: those lasted a good three months each.

Granted, some of my obsessions haven't been quite so healthy, since we're on the subject. There was the winter after Stellan left where I lived off snack boxes of raisins and hot chocolate (a whole jar of cocoa powder a day at its peak – the kettle was forever boiling), and then there was this past autumn after losing Cole, and Barney, where I watched nothing but Norwegian thrillers and true crime documentaries back to back and it all got a bit noir. And we already know about my recent shopping channel exploits. Some of those packages are still lying unopened in the bottom of my wardrobe. I haven't a clue what's in most of them.

But I *never once* followed this pattern of obsessive love through to exhaustion and disinterest with actual human beings. I won't *ever* dump you. I mean, sure, if I'm in your inner sanctum of friends, I've got your back no matter what, and if I'm your girlfriend you'll get my passionate, all-or-nothing commitment, but that's because I'm nice, not nuts. At least, that's what I thought until this week. Stellan's got me reassessing everything, and it kept me awake all last night as the sickening realisation dawned.

Looking back to 2004 and the few short weeks we were together that autumn, I saw that I really hadn't thought of anything but Stellan and what time his lectures would be done for the day, and what we'd be doing that night, and how long we'd have together before he went to class or to see his friends. And I *did* neglect my uni pals and flunk my exams and forget to call my parents for two months solid. It all seemed kind of normal back then, and I bet I wasn't the only girl doing it. But it's no surprise I scared Stellan off.

You can put it on my gravestone: Sylvie Magnusson: *Didn't do things (she liked) by halves.*

Anyway, I'd got up this morning with crusty, tired eyes from crying and a headache from dredging up all the old memories and analysing them until I couldn't think straight, and I'd made a promise not to spoil Nari's Christmas morning by letting her see that I was actually really bloody miserable and not at all festive.

It was me who insisted we come to this resort, after all. We could have taken Stephen's other option, but oh no, I was dead set on a chance encounter with the ex I once obsessed over, and who, if I'm honest, I never really got over. Now here I am, thirty-four years old and stuck in a tragic teenage love story time warp, while Stellan's in the real world, sensible, serious and successful. No wonder he's avoiding me, laying low until I leave his resort tomorrow.

Can this therapist see there are tears trickling out the corners of my closed eyes? I try hard to relax and clear my mind and not let last night's crushing realisation that I am in fact a lifelong boiler of bunnies and overly obsessive fangirl spoil my spa experience. But the more I try to clear my mind, the more I hear it: Stellan's voice saying, 'I was bad for you. I was the reason you were failing uni, I was a distraction.'

He wasn't a distraction, he wasn't ever bad for me. I'm the bad one. I'm the obsessive. I'm the reason we can't have nice things.

I try to channel all of this horrible energy into putting on a convincing performance of looking peaceful and thoroughly enjoying myself, solely for the benefit of the therapist's feelings. Finally, she gives my shoulders one last smooth over, turns the lights even lower and cocoons me in warm blankets. I hear the door close as she leaves me alone to inhale the perfumed steam in the air, and ah, there's the whale music! Last night's sleeplessness catches up with me and I begin to sink into a strange, cosy slumber, spoiled only by my awareness of a frosty lone-liness inside me that won't thaw, no matter how faultless and appreciated my Christmas Day singleton spa gift is.

–

'Hello tiny one, I've got a little something here, just for you,' I tell the tumbling, clambering puppy.

The moment I unlocked the door to the dog sheds Toivo had wriggled his way out from beneath the pile of sleeping siblings and padded over to the edge of his little enclosure, whipping his tail from side to side. I like to think he recognised me.

I'd called out a polite, if awkward and quintessentially English, 'Yoo-hoo? Anyone home? It's only me,' in case

Stellan's staff or some other tourists were here, but no one replied, even though the lights were on and the big door at the back of the shed was open with dogs running around in all directions, coming and going as they pleased.

'I'll only stay a minute, anyway,' I told myself as I settled beside Toivo on the floor of the shed. 'Have you *grown* since yesterday?'

I feed him the croissant scraps and a piece of buttery toast that I sneaked from the buffet for him and he chews greedily as though he's never been fed in his life. When he's done eating, I lift him onto my knee and ruffle his furry neck.

'Merry Christmas, little guy. I don't suppose you're all that bothered about Christmas, are you?'

I cast a glance around me, just in case someone's come in and mistaken me for an easily distracted dognapper who's taken leave of her senses. Still nobody here, so I kiss Toivo's pink nose and tell him he's got the best schnozz in all of Lapland, and he seems pleased with that.

'So what did Father Christmas bring you, then?' I ask him, as I look into his little enclosure, spotting a handful of chew toys that weren't there on my last visit.

I reach for the closest thing to me, a toy monkey, and show it to Toivo who immediately goes into overdrive, wanting me to tug it around while he clings to it with his needle-sharp puppy teeth.

Those baby gnashers always seem so tiny and delicate looking, and I worry they'll be yanked clean out of his mouth if I'm too rough. This had unnerved me in those first few weeks of getting to know Barney too. I know those teeth aren't going anywhere, but still, I try to calm Toivo, throwing the monkey a few feet away.

To my amazement he tumbles after his toy and retrieves it, laying it by my hand again and leaning in close to me for a congratulatory pat on the head. Either he's super smart or someone's started his puppy training early. Or maybe he just wants to please me?

I seem to remember reading somewhere about huskies having a strong prey drive which they redirect into their work as sled dogs; all they want is the attention and approval of the head of the pack, who I'm guessing in Toivo's case is Stellan.

'I can relate,' I tell him.

I throw his toy for him umpteen times and each time he obediently returns it to me. After a while, and as I'm realising I should probably go before one of Stellan's staff arrives and finds me sniffing huskies, Toivo's keen eyes begin to grow droopy. He's tired out already. So, I scoop him up again and he immediately falls asleep on my lap.

'Oh, Toivo, I'm going home in the morning and I'm going to miss you so much. I didn't think I *could* love another dog after Barney, but here we are. Has anyone ever told you that they love you? Has Stellan, I wonder? Hmm? Well, *minä rakastan sinua*, little Toivo. *I* love you.' He snores almost imperceptibly and I watch his round belly moving. 'The last guy I said that to made a run for it, all the way from Manchester to Lapland. But you wouldn't do that, would you?'

I lean over his fuzzy, wrinkly head and plant a kiss between his ears, and something in me breaks, and I suddenly want to sob my heart out. Saying goodbye to this little guy is harder than I thought it would be.

I shouldn't have come here today. Why put myself through another heartrending goodbye? I've had enough of those to last a lifetime.

Just as I'm searching my snowsuit pockets for a tissue, I hear someone clear their throat behind me, and I wilt a little more, because I know who it is.

'How long have you been standing there?' I say, as I turn around to look at Stellan. My jaw drops open and I take a few bewildered moments to recover myself. '*Wow!* What are you wearing?'

I'm looking at head to toe dark red velvet, white furry cuffs, curly-toed reindeer hide boots, and a fur-trimmed hat with a pompom hanging down by Stellan's grinning face.

'I told you I had a special job to do on the resort this morning.'

'You're *Santa Claus*?'

My eyes must be as round as saucers because Stellan's like none of the moth-eaten department store Santas I ever saw as a kid. He is high-end, deluxe Mr Christmas. His tunic is embroidered with patterned Scandinavian ribbons of colourful thread and he's wearing a thick green sash around his trim waist. There isn't so much as a hint of dodgy cotton wool sideburns or an unconvincing elasti-cated beard, thank goodness. All I'm seeing is the sleek blond ends of Stellan's hair squashed down under the hat, a smoothly shaven jaw and killer cheekbones.

The effect is hypnotic, and I grin back at him because that smile he's giving me means my Christmas day is most definitely looking up. I purposefully don't give voice to any of the inappropriately smutty remarks about sitting on his lap or asking what he might have in his sack for me – even though they're queuing up on the tip of my tongue ready to be blurted out. The strain is almost too much to bear.

'So, have you been a good girl this year, Sylvie Magnusson?' he asks with a devilish wink.

'Oh, *thank God* someone said it!'

And we're off again, laughing like we did yesterday and his eyes are sparkling in the harsh strip lights above us.

'I'm sorry about last night,' he says.

'It's all right, you had work to do. I understand. Listen, you took a day and a half off from the resort for me. I'm happy with that.' I try to give a carefree shrug, but he knows I'm faking it. He comes to sit beside me and gives the sleeping Toivo a scratch on the head.

'You *don't* understand. One of the enclosure fences was pushed over by a snowdrift. Usually I'm around to clear the snow, but yesterday I wasn't.'

'I'm sorry about that. You neglected your work because of me, and I shouldn't have let you.'

'Are you kidding? I was having the time of my life yesterday. I wouldn't have left for all the world, only the fence came down and some of the dogs got loose and one of the pregnant bitches got frightened and ran off into the forest. If she'd whelped out there there's no way the puppies would have survived the night.'

I raise a hand to my mouth.

'That's why my phone was ringing yesterday after I'd told the staff not to disturb us, but they knew, in her frightened state, she'd only respond to my calls, and so one of the husky team drove over to your cabin hoping to find me there, and I just panicked and flew out the door. I'm sorry.'

'It's OK, I'd have done the same thing. Did you find her?'

'Yes, thank God, after a long search. She was hiding, terrified, under a bridge about a kilometre away. But by the time we'd got her settled again, and rounded up the others, *and* repaired the fence, I was worried it was too late for me to come back to your cabin.'

'You should have come, I was hoping you would. I saved you some cookies.'

'You did?'

'For an hour I did. Then they got eaten.'

'I thought it wouldn't be right, turning up uninvited, late at night, especially after I ran out on our date.'

'Stellan, you never need to wait for an invitation to come see me. OK?'

'OK.' He nods to himself, processing what I've said, taking the reassurance I'm offering.

But my brain's reeling and I'm speaking again before I have the awareness to stop myself. 'I thought you left because... well, because we were kissing and I was too...' I break off for a moment because Stellan's looking at me, his brow hitched and his lips quirking. Is he amused or does he think I'm insane? 'I was afraid you didn't come back last night, and you didn't call me this morning, because I was too... full on, like, you know, weirdly too into you?'

I hear a guttural exhalation of his breath and he's shaking his head in protest. 'That *definitely* was not the reason.'

Hallelujah! Rewarded and reassured, all I can do is grin daftly and hope he's thinking about picking up where we left off when we were interrupted last night.

244

'What has been going on in your head, Sylvie Magnusson?' he asks, but he's not mocking, he looks worried, guilty even.

I look down at Toivo and find my cheeks are burning. 'I don't know, I get carried away thinking about things sometimes, and I was really enjoying being with you last night, and...'

'Me too,' he cuts in, letting me breathe. 'I've been looking for you all over the resort today. I finished delivering the kids' presents hours ago. I checked here twice, thinking you'd eventually come to see this little dude. Where have you been?'

'I was at the spa, actually. Had the place all to myself. I guess it's unusual for women to spend Christmas morning alone wrapped in Finnish seaweed and volcanic clay?'

'I guess so.' He laughs a tense laugh, still a tiny bit guilt-stricken. 'I should have called you last night.'

'Yes, you should, Santa Stellan. You could have been stuck down a chimney and unable to get out for all I knew! So... what are you doing for the rest of Christmas day?'

'Nothing,' he shrugs. 'Do you have plans?'

'Well, I *was* going to get cleaned up and head back to the restaurant for the Christmas meal tonight, but I wasn't exactly relishing the idea of eating by myself, not today. Nari's not with me, you see.'

'Ah, yes. Niilo told me about his plan. The *joik*. I guess it worked?'

'You could say that. They scarpered on his snowmobile faster than you could say "ditch the gooseberry".'

'I'm glad we're alone.'

I don't say anything, but I smile and give him the time he needs to form his words. I'm not going to rush Stellan today. I know that it wasn't me that made him leave so hastily last night, but I'm still not willing to risk another of his sudden departures. Maybe I'm finally learning what it means to just enjoy being with Stellan without getting lost in him and craving more and more.

'I have a plan of my own. For us,' he says.

'You do?'

'My truck's outside.'

I pretend I'm thinking about it for a moment, and see Stellan's expression change to one of sudden panic, before I laugh aloud. Who am I trying to kid? 'Let's go,' I say.

'This is one date Toivo can't come on.' His voice is gentle. He knows this is going to be difficult.

It takes me longer than it should to lower Toivo into his pen, and I watch as he nestles sleepily against his mother who flicks her tongue over his snout before falling asleep again too. After taking a few pictures with my phone, I stand up, take Stellan's outstretched hand, and I walk away from him, for good. Goodbye, little Toivo, my Lapland husky.

I'm struck by the awareness that on arriving home tomorrow my flat's going to feel a whole lot emptier without a pup to greet me, an emptiness I thought I'd started to get over.

I swallow hard as I climb into Stellan's truck and fasten my seatbelt. There won't be *anybody* to greet me back home. But I'll have plenty time to wallow in that reali- sation back in Castlewych.

Stellan's turning the ignition key and smiling at me from behind the wheel. I'm not going to overthink any of this. Whatever happens today I'm just going to enjoy it, really chilled, like Stellan said yesterday.

As we're about to pass the resort centre, Stellan pulls the truck to a halt by the restaurant's kitchen door where a man in chefs' whites appears. Stellan steps out into the snow and takes a box from him, putting it in the back of the truck and exchanging some friendly words before hopping into the driver's seat.

'What was that?' I ask.

'There's no food where we're going, and no stores, so Rasmus made us a picnic.' Stellan's pulling us out onto the road again and throwing the chef a wave.

I resist the urge to interrogate Stellan about where exactly we're heading; he's obviously enjoying having arranged a surprise and I don't want to take that away from him, and besides, I trust him.

As we pull up at my cabin door a few moments later I admit I give him a puzzled glance. He pulls the brake lever and turns to me, putting an elbow on the passenger seat headrest, noticeably pink about the cheeks and coy looking.

'Sylvie, without any pressure or expectation, I wonder if you mind...' He stops, suddenly self-conscious. He raises his eyes with embarrassed annoyance to the fur trim of the Santa hat he's just realised he's still wearing and hurriedly pulls it from his head as a blush spreads appealingly across the lightly freckled apples of his cheeks. 'What I'm trying to say is, where I want to take you, it's a distance from here. Is that OK?'

He sees me nod with raised, intrigued brows, so he carries on.

'The thing is... do you want to sleep there, with me? Overnight, I mean.'

He's adorable when he's struggling like this; his respectful reticence somehow contrasting sharply with his broad ruggedness and the curve of his lips that seems to betray his unvoiced thoughts.

'Are you saying I should pack my jammies?'

For a split second I see the blaze in his eyes before he grins. 'Jammies are optional.'

I stifle a laugh and unbuckle my seatbelt. 'Give me a sec, then.'

Carried by some higher power other than my snow-booted feet, I dash up the steps and into my cabin, grab the thing I need and turn immediately again for the truck, stopping only to wave my pink toothbrush jubilantly in the air from the doorway. I see Stellan through the driver's window, resplendent in his festive outfit, tipping his head back in a laugh.

Chapter Twenty-Two

Merry Christmas to all my readers out there! If this blog is posted as scheduled, you should be able to see this bright and early on Christmas morning, and I should be safely tucked up in my cosy bed following a night out on the town with a new acquaintance... more of this in a moment!

Readers, if you're Scandinavian, you might be getting steamy round about now. I'm talking about the traditional Christmas day sauna.

Did you know there are approximately five million Finns and three million saunas in Finland? They take this red hot ritual seriously, people. It's a necessary part of everyday life here, and it's especially important at Christmas when the sauna has an early spring clean and a festive makeover before the family pile in together for a holiday sweat.

I asked a (very cute, very chatty) local, one of the resort workers (a handsome reindeer herder, in fact), about his sauna habits and this is what he had to tell me:

"I sauna every day; it relaxes me and helps me switch off from work for a while. And yes, we sauna naked. It's not a sexual thing. We have good body image here because nakedness is just a natural part of our day. If a Finnish friend invites you to sauna then he really likes and trusts you, and you've been extended a great honour, so make sure you bring some beers. You can talk, or not talk, you can make it hot or not too hot. As long as everybody is happy".

Now, I've sweated with the best of 'em: in a (hokey, just for tourists) steam ceremony in the California desert; in Turkish baths in Istanbul; in a serene Japanese *onsen*, so I have zero qualms about the Finnish Lapland version, but my travel companion, S, really isn't into it. The very idea of it had my BFF clutching at the zipper of her fleece and pulling it up to her chin. She said, and I quote:

"*As if!* There's not a snowflake's chance in a sauna I'd strip off in front of [**name redacted**, LOL!] and then publicly perspire. Its gross and it's weird and it's just too Scandinavian".

She might be too far gone to help. But my handsome herder got me thinking about how public communal saunas seem to be at odds with the national stereotypes about shyness and introversion. Now you know I love to crush a stereotype, but I'm hoping all this 'good body image' and healthy attitude to nudity means these Finlanders are just as uninhibited in other parts of their lives... for example, when sharing a cosy Christmas date with a new blogger friend from England, maybe?

Happy Christmas, you guys! xx Nari

#NariBellInvestigates #BFFsGoDating #Christmasin-Lapland #HotHerder #SmokinHot #Sauna #Christ-masDay

Chapter Twenty-Three

The journey out to wherever we are going is one of those wildly happy moments you only get in the excitement of getting to know someone new – or in my case, getting to know them again – when your jokes all land perfectly and they catch every offhand reference you throw. Nothing's miscommunicated, nothing's amiss, and you're convinced no two people in the whole world could possibly have the intense connection you're sharing right this minute.

We drive on a main road for some time in the grey light of the early afternoon. As far as my eye can see there's nothing but tall forests of pine trees covered in snow and the occasional truck making its way in the opposite direction.

'Want to see how the resort got its name?' Stellan asks.

'Frozen Falls? I've been wondering about that.'

A moment later, we turn off the road and Stellan pulls the truck to a halt in what is unrecognisable as a layby. The snow is piled high in drifts and I can't see any way out of here. That's when Stellan reaches behind his seat and hands me some weird metal rectangular-frame things and says, 'Snowshoes, they fit over your boots.'

'We're *walking*?'

'Sure are,' he says, as he steps out the truck, shrugs on his thick black jacket, and packs the things Rasmus the chef gave him into an already heavy-looking backpack.

–

The pace is embarrassingly slow as I struggle to stay upright and to stop laughing. With every step I take my feet sink into the powdery snow right up to my calves, despite the snowshoes, and I have to haul myself out again, and the whole time Stellan's effortlessly walking backwards and heaving me by the arms. He's sinking too but doesn't seem to be having the same amount of difficulty I am; mind you, he has half a foot's height advantage over me, not to mention his muscled thighs powering him along.

It feels colder out here than back at the resort as we enter a gully with steep rocks on either side of us, unusual in the flat landscape. My nostrils prickle and I can feel my airways constricting in the arctic chill.

'How much further?'

'Everything in life worth having requires some effort and patience,' he says. 'It's just through this ravine then a climb to the top of the reach. Keep going, you're doing great.'

I make a concerted effort to keep my legs moving and just as I'm approaching the limits of my endurance I realise we've arrived at the top. Looking behind me I see the truck only a few metres below us, but I feel like I've conquered Everest. And that's when I face forwards again and notice it down below us, like a sunken gothic cathedral of melted candle wax sheltered inside a small, rugged gorge cutting through the forest.

'*These* are the frozen falls.' Stellan's beaming proudly as though he's carved them himself.

'*Wow!*' That's all I can manage under the circumstances as I take in the magnificent sight of what must, in the warmer months, be a mighty waterfall, now magically suspended in thick layers of icicles, some transparent like crystal, some opaque and icy blue, others shining and golden as though lit from inside.

'They're nothing like as big as the Korouoma falls but they're more remote so you don't get as many tourists here. I'd be surprised if anyone's been here for weeks.'

I don't know anything about this other, rival waterfall, but there's no way it can be prettier than the sight I'm beholding right now. 'Can we get down there?' I ask in wonder, not quite able to trust my eyes. Maybe I'll be able to believe what I'm seeing if I can actually reach out and touch it.

'Follow me.' Stellan deftly leads me down into what feels like the chancel of a frozen church. There's a perceptible change in the crunching sounds of the snow under our feet and I become aware that below us and the thick layer of powder is a deep pool of frozen water.

'In the summer, I swim right here,' says Stellan.

I think instantly of all the things I would give to see that sight. 'It must be stunning,' I say. 'The waterfall, I mean.'

'Oh, it is. My mother used to bring me and my sister here when we were kids. We'd have a cook out, and we'd dive into the water from that ledge over there.'

He's pointing to a snowy outcrop jutting from what I'm assuming must be craggy rock when it isn't encased in glittering ice. The ledge is nearly twice Stellan's height; I have no idea how he summoned up the courage to plunge from that precipice into the water below as a child.

'Is the water warm in the summer?'

'It's *so* cold. But it's clear enough that you can see the pebbles at the bottom.'

He's got a hazy look in his eyes remembering his childhood summers and daredevil antics, and I'm happy for him. It means he had some joyful moments with his family as a kid, even though it doesn't sound like his dad was present during those trips to the waterfall. I won't ask him about that; I wouldn't cause him pain right now for anything in the world.

'So… are we going to have a picnic?' I say, aware that my stomach is rumbling under my many thermal layers. The fruit plate and herbal tea back at the spa really didn't cut it as fuel for a wintry trek through deep snow and Lappish forests.

'Here, have this.'

He hands me a chocolate bar in a pink floral wrapper, and I melt a bit because I see his smile as he gives his gift. He's delighted to make me happy. I thank him and gleefully take my thick outer gloves off and tear at the wrapper with my teeth.

Stellan swings the backpack off his shoulders and sets it on the snow. 'That should keep you alive until I cook lunch.'

'Should do, but I was nearly a goner for a moment there!' I snap a piece of chocolate from the bar, reach over and pop it into Stellan's mouth, which he opens for me before snapping his teeth shut, pretending to bite at my fingers, and we both laugh again.

How is this so easy? How can two people have this kind of connection and be expected to live two thousand kilometres apart?

There I go again. *Less of that!* I chastise myself as I munch the creamy hazelnut milk chocolate. Life is sweet right this second. What more can I ask for?

'You can sit over there, look.' Stellan stops unpacking items from the bag, which I see contains a small gas camping stove – not a fiddly little thing like Dad would pack for my childhood trips to Anglesey; this is a sturdy army-issue looking contraption. I wonder how the hell he managed to carry that on his back, and turn conspicuously swoony at the thought of his strength.

I realise he's still pointing behind me to a wide fissure in the great folding curtain of ice cascading from the frozen waterfall, and I clamber into it, sitting down on what, I decide to fantasise, is a broad icy throne.

Stellan laughs as I settle myself with a satisfied smile.

'Comfy?'

'Yep. What are you cooking?'

'Ever had *muikku*?'

'Never heard of it,' I say, as I watch him rest a frying pan over a flaming gas bottle.

He sorts ingredients in zip lock bags, putting on what he clearly thinks is a good American accent and pretending to present a cookery segment on a TV show. Looking up at me in mock earnestness, he says, 'First we add the *muikku* to the seasoned flour.'

That's when I realise *muikku* are tiny silver fish, like whitebait.

'I prepared these at home earlier,' Stellan's saying confidently.

'You did?'

'Well, Rasmus did. Hey, is this your show, or mine? No heckling from the audience please. Then you shake the bag. Heat a little oil and butter in the pan and, *whoa!*' Stellan jumps as the pan sizzles, splattering hot oil. 'Always be careful not to get snow in your oil,' he says with a lopsided grin.

After a few moments, during which Stellan wryly declines my offers of assistance, I smell the glorious aroma of warming garlic on the impossibly clean air and the savoury scent of the floury fish hitting the oil. My stomach somersaults in response. Stellan shakes the pan, the fish are already turning crisp, and we both fall contentedly silent.

He comes to join me on my gleaming icy throne inside the waterfall where we eat our meal straight from the hot pan, each of us taking turns to make stabs at the *muikku* with our forks. One for me; one for him, until every morsel is gone.

There isn't a sound or movement anywhere in the forest; no breeze, no birdsong, not a snowflake falling, and the sky is turning a wonderful blush pink as the watery sun makes its way below the horizon again. This, I think to myself, is Stellan's world; healthful, outdoorsy, elemental.

I suddenly feel overwhelmed with gratitude for whatever force it was that reunited us and let me share this moment with him. And I don't mind that it will soon pass. All that matters right now is me and Stellan sitting beneath the waterfall.

–

After our lunch by the frozen falls, and after Stellan has shouldered the heavy backpack again, I find myself unexpectedly dismayed that he isn't leading me back the way we came towards the truck. Instead, we follow a steep and thickly snowdrifted route between the trees in the opposite direction.

'A hike?' I say, my heart sinking. I'd been enjoying the satisfied, pleasantly well fed feeling and thinking I'd soon be back on the road in the comfort of Stellan's passenger seat, heading onwards to the next part of his whirlwind mystery tour, but now we're going to slog uphill in waist-deep snow? *No thanks!*

I never was one for a Christmas day walk. Back home, no sooner had the three of us demolished enough roast turkey and sprouts to feed a family of fifteen, than Dad would hustle us into coats and out the front door for the obligatory muddy trudge to the duck pond and back, when all Mum and I wanted to do was flop on the sofa and stuff Quality Street into our faces in front of *Mary Poppins*.

'No hike. This is the way to my parents' lake house,' says Stellan.

A lake house? Now that *does* sound festive. Ahead of us, far across the open whiteness, I make out a spire with a black cross atop a white church. Stellan and I struggle on through the snow arm and arm towards it, beneath a waning moon so slim it is barely visible.

'The house is a little beyond the chapel there.'

'It's so pretty here. Basically you were raised in a Christmas card?' I hear his low laugh but I'm concentrating on dragging my snowshoes out of the white powder that's trying to sink me like quicksand, so I can't look over to catch the accompanying grin. 'This area is stunning. Who owns it? Is it your family's?'

257

'No, not at all.'

'So we're trespassing?'

'It belongs to everybody.'

I squint in confusion, and he must notice it, because he explains, 'It's called Everyman's Rights; the freedom to go where you please, and for free. I've never understood the rest of the world's obsession with parcelling off patches of land that are yours by right. I remember seeing grubby yards and overgrown gardens full of trash in Manchester and thinking how strange it was to fence yourself in and keep others out in this way. And there are English gardens and estates you have to pay to walk in. So weird! Maybe it's because we have *so much* space here and the population is so sparse, people don't feel the need to enclose their little worlds and prohibit people's movement over them.'

Wow! That's pretty much the most he's said without stopping since we met up again, and it's about how crap and hemmed in England is! I feel a flicker of resentment at him for criticising my lovely Manchester, but more than that, I feel sad. I'm sad that he'll never feel inclined to come to England and visit me. He had his fill of our parochial habits long ago, on a four-month exchange trip that he couldn't wait to terminate early.

It strikes me, as I walk along, that I'm now breathless and tired, and not just from the exertion of the walk.

'I do miss the chippy though,' I hear him saying hurriedly. 'And the outdoor football games, and the English ale, and the birds in the trees all winter, and that pizza place near halls, and...'

And the girls? Or one girl in particular? Just say it, and all will be forgiven. But he doesn't.

'And those things... those... sweet flan things from the bakery. With the coconut on top? You eat them with custard?'

'Manchester tart? I'll be sure to mail some over in the New Year, if you send me more of those hazelnut chocolate bars.'

'*Deal!*' He stops suddenly, unlooping his arm from mine to offer me a handshake through thick gloves.

We smile and I begin to forget why I was wounded a moment ago, recalling my resolution to enjoy this fleeting escapade for what it is.

I watch him break his eyes from mine. It seems so causal the way he can do it, when I'd be content just standing here and gazing at him all afternoon.

'It's there.' He's pointing now to a large white cabin, just visible through the trees to the east of the church. Both buildings sit on the frozen shores of a lake.

'Good! Can I make us both a hot chocolate?' I offer.

'I was actually thinking of another way to warm you up,' he says, and we lock eyes again.

–

I peer at the towel, then back at Stellan, my incredulity written all over my face, and he's got the cheek to just laugh.

'A sauna?'

'Yes.'

'Do you mean that shed thing by the jetty?'

'Uh-huh.'

I look from the snow-covered hut back towards the lake house which I only got the briefest glimpse inside. It was luxurious and modern, and there was a massive white

259

sofa in front of a fireplace where I'd happily have flopped down and put my feet up for a bit. I had a quick peek inside the downstairs bathroom too; maybe I could just have a nice hot bubble bath? I follow Stellan's line of sight towards the wooden sweatbox and it holds *zero* appeal.

'You want me to strip out of these perfectly comfy thermal leggings to sit in a cramped, overheated, airless room and just… perspire?'

'That's the idea. It's good for you.'

I remind myself that I came to Lapland to experience all that it has to offer, and I think of Nari raving about the cultural importance of saunas here. If I want to understand Stellan properly, I suppose I ought to at least try this cornerstone of life in Finnish Lapland.

I begrudgingly take the towel and make my way towards the jetty, following Stellan's broad strides.

He turns the handle and the sauna's outer door opens. 'It wasn't locked?' I ask as we step inside.

'No, it's communal, anyone in the area can use it. In the spring there are hot tubs too. The neighbours all come over, we cook sausages on the sauna coals and drink beers. It's cool.'

Stellan must have already come out to the sauna to start heating the coals while I was nipping to the loo back at the lake house because I can see the glass in the sauna room is already steamed up.

'You have neighbours? But there isn't another house for miles around,' I say.

'There are houses secreted all over this forest. We just live out of sight of each other. We're kind of private.'

'Except when you're roasting your chestnuts in the sauna together?'

Enjoying the sound of Stellan's laughter and hoping he'll laugh again – and partly because I'm jabbering on to hide my nerves – I tell him about Piero, my elderly Italian neighbour in the flat below mine. I've met him three times now by the bins and we've chatted about the weather and how I can never keep track of when the recycling collection day is, and we've even had a cup of tea in his little kitchen, but in that entire time, it never once occurred to me to ask him if he'd like to strip out of his cable-knit cardi and hop in a steamy room with me and Marjorie, the retired bank clerk from 3A.

Stellan's still laughing when it strikes me that he's already out of his jacket and boots and is standing barefoot by the big baskets I'm clearly supposed to be putting my clothing in. Oh God, is he undressing? Right in front of me? *He is!* I don't know where to look.

'Is this OK, Sylvie? Honestly?' he's saying to me, though I can barely hear him over my heartbeat somehow pounding out a rhythm on my eardrums.

How do I answer that? If Stellan's planning on stripping down to his birthday suit then I am definitely A-OK with the idea. It's just reciprocating that's going to be a problem. Thank Thor I ran a razor over my legs again this morning, but still, moving straight from two fully clothed kisses yesterday to non-sexual full frontal lounging around feels decidedly odd, and I know I'm blushing bright pink.

'We can go back to the house, don't worry. It was just an idea.' He's scrunched up the bottom of his T-shirt ready to peel it off – and I caught a tiny glimpse of belly button and firm muscle – but now he's standing there unmoving, looking at me, cautious and concerned. I'm not sure where to put my eyes, but I hear myself speaking.

'No, I want to. You go first.'

He grins and in an instant the T-shirt is chucked into the basket and... just *wow*!

'So you've spent fifteen years doing bench presses then?' I've said it before I can stop myself, and all I can do to recover is take a sudden interest in the straps of my snow boots. He laughs again and although I'm not looking, I can tell he's setting to work on his bottom layers.

Failing to keep my cool, I turn my back to him entirely and make quick work of my snowsuit and boots, jumper and thermal leggings, thinking if I do it swiftly it'll be less hideous. But as I turn back, checking to see if he's watching me struggling with nervous fingers to get this damned bra unfastened, he's gone.

I notice the coals' glow through the steamy glass of the swinging sauna door and let out a relieved breath. And I do still have my towel. So, kicking my underwear into the basket and hiding my horrid beige long johns in the big pocket of my snowsuit, I quickly wrap the towel around me, wishing it was slightly less skimpy, and I reach for the sauna door handle.

There's further comfort when I hear the hiss of beer bottle tops being opened and I see Stellan through the steam in the dim light, smiling reassuringly. There's a towel around his waist.

I know my voice is shaking when I ask, 'I thought Finns sauna naked?'

'We do, but not if our guests aren't into it.'

'Oh! Of course.'

So I settle myself next to him, not too close, and I try to acclimatise. It's not the heat I'm aware of first, it's the strange dryness of the air. I try to slake it away with a big glug of the beer Stellan's handed me, and we both stare into the coals.

'Have you enjoyed your trip to Lapland?' he asks.

'I have.' It hits me how much I don't want to leave in the morning. 'I feel as though I've only just touched the surface of the place. I haven't even seen the Northern lights.'

'You might be lucky tonight, in fact I'd say there was an eighty-eight per cent chance of seeing some solar wind activity.'

'Eighty-eight per cent? Really? That's quite precise, isn't it?'

Stellan laughs and drinks from the bottle before saying, 'There's an app that gives me the cloud cover and solar wind data direct from NASA. I need it to help manage the tourists' expectations. Most times Niilo and I take groups out for the aurora experiences we don't see much, just faint lights in the sky, but if I tell them their chances of success before we set out, it stops angry demands for refunds. Sometimes.'

'Are we really that troublesome, us tourists?'

'Some are more trouble than others.' He turns to face me with a sly wink, and he gets a snuffly laugh in return because I guess I asked for that.

The heat's making my nose run, and I'm just so glad I didn't wear any make-up today or I'd be in full Alice Cooper melting mascara mode by now. I huff out a breath.

'Too hot?' he says.

I shake my head. He doesn't look convinced but I want him to keep talking, now he's on a roll. 'You grew up under the aurora. How lucky is that! Does the novelty wear off?'

'Never. And it's never the same twice. I'll always look to the skies at night; even if I only catch a glimpse, it's always incredible.'

I shake my head slowly, wondering at the childhood Stellan must have had out here, and I realise I've relaxed into his company. Instead of feeling gross, sweaty, and next to naked, I just feel safe and happy, and, without even noticing, we must have shifted our bodies around so we're facing each other.

As I sip my beer and we chat, I allow myself quick glances along his glistening shoulders and over his throat and collar bones. I daren't attempt to look over his stomach, but I can't help thinking of the tantalising glimpse of abs I clocked earlier.

I realise it's my turn to talk but I'm struggling a bit, so I scrabble for a rushed question. 'What even *is* the aurora borealis?'

'Well, when I was a kid my teachers told us a story of the fox that stirred up a cloud of snowflakes with a flick of its tail. The snowflakes sparkled in the moonlight and that's how we get the Northern lights.'

'I like that,' I say. 'I think I read that somewhere, a long time ago.'

'Or… you can say its electrically charged particles streaming from the sun, attracted by the magnetic pull of the earth's poles. The particles meet with oxygen atoms in the earth's atmosphere and omit beautiful green light. But that's just not as romantic.'

'I don't know. It sounds magical when you say it. But I guess the fox is cuter.' I realise we're looking directly into each other's eyes and falling silent.

'See, you're not thinking about the heat now, are you?' Stellan says eventually. On the contrary, I feel like I'm burning. 'What do you think of your first Finnish sauna?' he asks.

'Great. But then again, I might feel differently if your bare arsed neighbours turned up and asked me to shift along a bit.'

'It's really not so strange, you know.'

'It is a bit. The average British person would rather die than reveal their body to their friends and family.'

'What even is the average British person?' Stellan says with a wry laugh, and I find myself nodding and shrugging. 'You can't be talking about yourself,' he adds. He's rewarded with a smile for that. 'But there is nothing to be ashamed of, Sylvie. The sauna cleanses you, body and soul. It's an important custom. You strip away your status, your worries, your sexuality, and you just relax.'

'I think I get it,' I say, but admit to myself I haven't managed to conquer my curiosity over Stellan's nakedness. Suddenly my memory replays the way he brushed his lips over mine yesterday with the tentative, respectful caution he always showed when we were younger, and I feel my top lip tingle at the recollection, like the barely perceptible chime of a tuning fork, still resonating into silence.

'Sylvie? Are you all right, do you need some air?'

'Sorry? I was miles away. I was thinking about, umm…'

'I know. Me too.'

As he says this, his voice low, I catch the wicked hitch at the corner of his mouth and a bright flash in his eyes, and I get a glimpse of the other side of the Stellan I knew when I was nineteen, the Stellan who would undress me deliberately slowly, who would kiss my entire body until I was breathless and wild, the one who'd…

'Sylvie, are you here?'

I focus on him once more and see him draw his bottom lip between his teeth as his eyes rest on my mouth. I find myself wanting to shift closer to him on the slatted bench, so I do, and I watch as Stellan reacts, reaching for my hand.

The feeling of our slippery wet fingers slowly interlacing has me exhaling a measured breath. Suddenly, and without thinking, I lift myself from the bench onto Stellan's lap, straddling his thighs, and his hands immediately spread over the small of my back, pulling me closer to him. We're face to face in the dry air and the low light when I kiss him, hard and long, and it's perfect.

But after a few blissful moments where our breathing accelerates and Stellan's hands find my face and my neck, I realise I'm seeing stars. I can hardly breathe.

He pulls his mouth from mine, and I try to focus on his face. 'We should stop,' he says. His lips are swollen and red. 'Somebody's going to pass out unless we cool down, and it might be me.' He rakes a hand through his wet hair and laughs.

I have to admit he's right and I slip back onto the bench beside him as he reaches for the bucket of water on the floor and pours it out onto the hot stones, staunching their heat instantly. The steam billows up in a white cloud then stops with a dying hiss.

'You said you hadn't even scratched the surface of Lapland?' Stellan's reaching for my hand again, and his eyebrows are quirked wickedly.

'Uh-huh?' I say, wondering where he's going with this.

'How about we take the ultimate next step in the sauna experience?'

Oh my days! What *is* he going to do?

'Come with me?' He's leading me to the door and I'm going to follow him no matter what. But instead of turning for the house, he's leading me onto the jetty. That's when I notice it: a pool cut out of the ice at the jetty's end. 'It's traditional to plunge into the water after a sauna.'

'I'm sure it is Stellan, but that's also completely insane.' My toes curl at the thought of it. 'I was born in Castlewych, you know. We're not rugged like you Scandinavians.'

'You're a Magnusson, aren't you? How about you take one for your ancestors?' He's grinning provocatively.

'You got me, *dammit*! Well, if we're really doing this, you'd better make it quick, before I change my mind.'

'*Sweet!*'

He takes me at my word and leads me through the dark and biting cold. My skin prickles and all the heat of the sauna leaves my body. He picks up his pace, starting to run. There are lights underneath the jetty illuminating the lakeside, and I see the large black mouth of the diving hole getting bigger. As we reach it I slam on the brakes and Stellan lets go of my hand, grabs the towel from his waist and throws it to the ground. I watch him launch himself into the air before plunging under the frigid water. There's barely a splash.

I stand horrified at the end of the little pier and look for him resurfacing from the black rippling ink, hugging myself against the cold and stamping my bare feet, wide-eyed and panting. I swear my heart's about to stop and I try to call his name, but can't.

Suddenly, the surface breaks and Stellan appears with a deep gasp. And in an instant he's back on the jetty.

'Your turn,' he rasps. He's shivering uncontrollably. 'Nobody enjoys the dive. It's the feeling you get afterwards that counts.'

I give myself a millisecond to weigh up my situation. I either jump in now or I stand here feeling like a spoilsport and a coward faced with a freezing, naked Stellan, and so I sit on the side of the jetty and lower the towel from around me, never more aware that I'm being watched, and I drop my body in, trying to keep my head above the water.

The cold takes my breath. I gasp and flounder my arms in the black slushy water. No air reaches my lungs. I can't move. I can't think. But strong hands drag me out of the water and back onto the jetty before I sink deeper.

'You did it!' Stellan shouts, gleefully. 'Now let's go before I lose my *kivekset* to frostbite.'

I feel the cleanest air in the world enter my lungs again, and my skin tingles with pins and needles as my circulation restarts. I'm not one hundred per cent sure what *kivekset* might be but from the way Stellan is breaking into a hunched run and protecting a very delicate part of himself with his hands, I can hazard a guess.

I realise I'm running full pelt beside Stellan, and I'm screaming like a siren from the lake.

'It's exhilarating, right? Some feelings are worth the agony,' Stellan's shouting, and we're both laughing hysterically, blood fizzing and nerves buzzing, gasping for each breath.

As we run, I stoop for a handful of snow and throw it at Stellan's broad back. The holler he makes leaves me howling, and I'm rewarded with a pelted snowball which breaks up in the air between us and falls in a sparkling shower of finest powder on my skin.

We reach the lake house door and he hauls it open, its wonderful warmth enveloping us. The house is in darkness, but we don't stop running all the way up the winding stairs and into a dim room, snug and warm. In the half-light I see him reach for a thick robe from behind the door which he drapes over my shoulders, running his hands over the material across my back, pulling me close to him. The warmth of his skin pressing hard against mine through the open robe is dizzying.

I feel the sinking softness of the bed as we hit it and, diving under the covers, we roll into each other's arms, ravenously kissing until the cold is gone.

'Wait, wait,' I hear him say, and, frankly, I want to scream because waiting is the last thing I want to do. I watch him kneel up over me, looking down at me on the bed. 'Are we doing this?'

I know what he's doing, making sure this is what I want. 'Yes, of course,' I say.

'Well, then,' he grins, 'let's do this right.'

For the first time I become aware of the high glass ceiling above us. There are stars framing Stellan's blond hair in a silver halo, and for a moment we just look at each other as he pulls me up to kneel in front of him, face to face.

Everything slows.

Stellan's fingertips slide between my neck and my hair and he lifts away the strands, exposing my skin. There's a green-blue light glimmering on his shoulders and I let my hands swim through it and over his body.

For a moment his eyes rest on mine then move down to the spot just below my ear that I know he's going to kiss first. It's so torturously slow in coming that I close my eyes and lean my head back into the cradle of his hands at my nape.

I say a little prayer to all the ancient Scandinavian gods. *Please let it be like it used to.*

Chapter Twenty-Four

After watching the flames dancing in the hearth and finishing their cloudberry cocktails, they dined on honeyed porridge by the fireside. Niilo watched in delight as Nari found the hidden almond in her creamy, steaming bowlful – the almond that meant she'd be bestowed with good fortune all year long, and she'd dug in her pocket to show Niilo the silver sixpence Sylvie had given her in the taxi as they left the airport.

'So you're going to get very lucky this Christmas, then?' Niilo said with a smile and a meaningful look passed between them.

Trying not to betray the thrill Nari's glance sent down his spine, Niilo quickly cleared the bowls. 'Should we, um, go for a walk, do some aurora chasing?'

Within moments they had clambered back into their snowsuits, and Niilo was rummaging in the cupboard below the cabinet of family treasures.

Nari cocked her head, watching him select a glass jar and a small candle. 'What do you need that for?'

'I light a candle for my parents at Christmas. I already visited their graves yesterday morning, but I need to place it in the snow. Is that OK? It's not weird, is it?'

'Not at all. Can I have one too, please?'

'Of course.'

'For Dad,' Nari adds in a quieter voice, watching as Niilo finds another set.

'Let's light them now.'

Nari watches as he brings the two candles to life, silenced by the way the light loved the angles of his face and his rounding lips as he blew out the match.

Instinctively, they reach for each other's hands and don't let go on their slow stroll into the forest, their candles lighting their path.

'It doesn't seem quite so dark tonight,' Nari said, looking skyward as they enter the treeline.

'That's the beginnings of the aurora. The sky seems lighter at first and suddenly you'll see a flash of green. Give it about an hour and we'll have a decent display, I expect.'

Leaving the cottage's lights behind, they make their way deeper into the forest, crunching through snow and snapping twigs and branches deep underfoot.

'In the early autumn my grandmothers would come out here foraging for berries. I remember they'd be gone all day, only coming back late at night with baskets full of bilberries, raspberries, lingonberries, mushrooms, anything you could wish for. And then they'd cook, and preserve things, and dry the mushrooms for the winter. I can still remember the smell of the sugar and the fruit in the big pan. Lingonberry jelly was my favourite as a kid.'

'I'd love to see this place in the warm days. It must be transformed,' Nari said.

'It is. Everything is green by June, and the white nights in the summer when the sun doesn't set, those are wonderful. Stellan and I fish on the lake and we hold midnight barbecues for the staff sometimes. Those are good times.'

'Maybe I could come back to see that?'

'Come back any time.'

A sudden gust of wind sweeps through the trees sending powdery snow from the overladen branches flurrying into the air. Nari stops dead and they drop hands to protect their candles, now guttering in the falling flakes.

Just as Nari is grinning at Niilo's face, recovering from the sudden icy blast, a sharp screech rings out, and a swift shadow moves somewhere up above them.

'What the hell was that?' said Nari with unexaggerated panic.

Niilo laughs. 'Only an eagle, I imagine.'

'An eagle? *Golden* eagles? They can snatch human babies from prams, can't they?'

'Or it might have been a wolverine.'

'Up a tree?'

His delighted laughter helps quell her fear. Niilo seems to be enjoying teaching his guest about his homeland and, more than that, he's enjoying the way she has grabbed his arm and is still applying the lightest pressure to his bicep through the thick layers. 'Possibly, they're like little bears really.'

'They're not wolves, then?'

'Nothing like a wolf, more like a big weasel.'

'Are you pulling my leg?'

'You said you would believe anything I told you,' he replied with an arched brow and a smile. 'It's all true.'

The forest has grown thick and black and they find they've come to a natural stopping point on their walk.

'Here?' asks Nari.

Niilo nods, and the pair crouch, placing the candles in the thin snow at the foot of a towering birch. Standing again, looking at the glow from the jars, they find each other's hands once more, and observe a reverent silence.

'Do you pray? Nari whispers after a peaceful moment.

'No, do you?'

'No, but Dad would have done. Scottish Catholic. He was a chorister in Glasgow as a boy, before his itchy feet carried him off around the world. He was a wanderer like me, and he met my mum while he was working in Seoul.'

'I'd love to see Scotland... and Seoul, come to think of it.'

'You see! You do have the wanderlust in you.'

Niilo reaches into his snowsuit pocket and pulls out two torches, handing one to Nari. As their lights cut through the darkness, eerily illuminating the white tree trunks and their footprints leading their way back to Niilo's family home, a piercing howl rings out in the night. Saying nothing, Nari yanks at Niilo's arm, gaping in wide-eyed horror.

'It's OK, it might just be a lynx,' Niilo shrugs, nonchalantly, before adding in a wicked whisper, 'or a hungry bear.'

'That's it, I'm done, let's go. One of the best things about travelling solo is that nobody gets to see me doing this face.' She turns to him, making him laugh joyously at her comically bared teeth and horror-struck expression. 'My Instagram feed shows me smiling, happy, confident, but never the moments when I'm behind a hotel room door terrified someone's trying to get in, or when I've got my keys between my fingers walking back to my villa at night.'

'A very different kind of wildlife you're describing there?'

'Hmm, yes. Give me bears and wolverines in a dark forest any day.'

'But you still travel. You're not that afraid.'

'I am! I'm scared *all* the time, but I'm not letting them win. You can't shut me out from half the world.'

'Won't you travel with someone, one day?'

'I never wanted to, before.'

As Nari speaks, her voice low and contemplative, they emerge from the trees into the clearing where the little cottage stands. Above it, like a hologram projected onto the firmament, flash the rippling lights of the aurora, bold and breathtaking.

Nari gasps, while Niilo grins up at them, nodding proudly, the corners of his mouth curling, as though he were thinking the phenomenon was right on time, just as he had planned.

'*Guovssahasat*,' he whispers.

Nari peels her eyes from the miraculous wonders above to look at him inquisitively, striking Niilo almost breathless by the changing colours reflected in her irises.

'A Sámi word for the Northern lights,' he manages to explain, all the while gazing, awestruck at her face.

Overwhelmed by the need in his eyes, Nari makes the small step towards him and their lips meet in a kiss that Niilo feels all the way down.

If he could have thought clearly, he'd have joined up the fragmented ideas scattering in his brain. Yes, she was kissing him hungrily, passionately, but it didn't feel like the others; the girlfriends of his youth, or those few visitors to the resort he'd let himself kiss. As he enfolded Nari

275

in his arms, he recognised a different kind of intensity, a deep, overwhelming connectedness. She was taking his hand now, and they break into a run for the cottage door.

Inside, they fumble with snowsuit zips and peel off layers, and they laugh, throwing off their boots.

He had been right all along. Nari was exactly the person he'd been waiting for. But none of these thoughts materialise clearly in his mind, only a feeling of light-headedness washing over him again and his muscles melting at her touch as their bodies meet for the first time. Niilo inhales sharply through gritted teeth at the sensation of her skin touching his and her long hair against his chest.

Nari pulls back, looking at him levelly. 'Where do you sleep?'

Wordlessly, Niilo looks to the low door leading from the kitchen. He grasps her hand and walks her from the room.

Chapter Twenty-Five

When I wake, the room at the top of Stellan's lake house is warm and silent. It takes a few moments of blinking into the darkness to work out that I'm not imagining the rippling green fluorescence above me. Through the glass I see it; the aurora borealis, lighting the sky, shimmering and changing, disappearing suddenly then recovering itself in a flash of brilliant colour. How long has it been shining above me? I try to remember if it had been there all along, the whole time Stellan and I have been wrapped up in each other in bed, too focussed on each other to notice the magic in the sky. I look around, amazed, wanting to tell Stellan, but he isn't here.

A fluttering panic fills my chest, and I scrabble around looking for clothes that, it suddenly hits me, are still at the sauna. So I haul a sheet off the bed, wrap it around me and go in search of Stellan.

He can't have left me here, can he? No. He'd never do that. But if he's sitting by the front door, full of regret and ready to take me back to the resort as soon as morning comes… No. Not after last night. It was perfect.

Perfect doesn't even do it justice, Stellan and me. It was as sublime and ecstatic and magical as the first sip of Friday night prosecco after the longest week; like fresh bedclothes on a Sunday afternoon; like Johnny Marr expertly slipping between chords; like the scratch card that reveals a million; like the unexpected concert hall encore when you think the band has left the building; like Idina Menzel's highest note on her very best day.

Long story short: It. Was. So. Good.

I float downstairs and I see him, his back to me, in a white robe, busy working in the gleaming, elegant open-plan kitchen by the immaculate white lounge where there's a crackling log fire. He's lit candles all around and the whole impression is blissful, and I can smell sweet foody scents in the air.

'Is it still Christmas Day?' I say, as I approach him, pressing a kiss between his shoulder blades and letting my hands explore his chest.

Turning with a grin and pulling me to him, he tells me it is, but only just, and asks if I'm hungry. I get a kiss on the forehead and a glimpse at the tray behind him on the counter.

'Oh wow. Another of Rasmus's surprises?'

There sits a dish of marshmallows, little gingerbread men cookies, segments of freshly peeled mandarins and black cherries on stalks beside a steamy bowl of thick, melted dark chocolate.

'Let's eat,' he says.

We wander to the hearth where I find an open bottle of red wine and glasses. And there's a fresh dry robe on the sofa for me.

I see Stellan glance towards it as he settles himself on the rug. I know he's wondering what I'm going to do. Feeling no hint of my former shyness, I let the bed sheet fall to the floor and Stellan watches me slip into the cosy dressing gown.

We eat our Christmas night meal in the flickering light, and it barely enters my head that in a matter of hours I'll be flying home to England. Instead, I dip a shiny cherry into the liquid chocolate and let it knock messily against Stellan's smiling lips.

Chapter Twenty-Six

Niilo climbs back into bed, avoiding the clothes strewn over the bedroom floor. He passes the mug of milky tea to Nari, who had been dozing under the covers.

'It's midnight, Christmas is over,' he says.

'That's a shame. I don't want it to be,' Nari replies sleepily, leaning back into his arms as they settle themselves comfortably and she sips from the mug. Niilo's fingertips brush Nari's forehead, pushing away her hair so he can kiss a soft, smooth spot.

'I forgot to give you your Christmas gift,' he says, reaching for the bundle by the bed; it's wrapped in brown paper and tied with embroidered ribbon, like the colourful decorative bands she'd seen on his *gákti* jacket.

'What? But I didn't give you anything!'

A breathy laugh escapes Niilo's smiling lips, thinking how only an hour ago he had held his breath, lifting his hips and arching his spine beneath her, their fingers interlocked and heads thrown back. A shudder ripples his nerves at the remembrance of it. 'On the contrary...' he started to say, only to be met by a gentle dig in his stomach from Nari's elbow.

'Can I open it?' Nari asks, passing him the mug before pulling at the ribbon.

Inside the paper lies a carved bear, standing tall on its grizzled legs, looking upwards as though searching the sky.

'You made this? For me?'

'Uh-huh. Out on the last trail, before you arrived.'

'Oh right, so you didn't carve it for me exactly, you didn't even know me then,' Nari says teasingly, smiling at the gift.

Niilo doesn't dare tell her how he'd known she was coming to him, but just hadn't met her then, or how he'd felt compelled to set to work on the bear that very day.

'Well, it's beautiful, thank you, Niilo. I'll treasure it.' She turns to kiss him, stretching her neck to reach the tip of his nose, making him smile. 'You should really sell these. You could make a fortune.'

'Then I would no longer enjoy making them. I believe in the beauty of one of a kind.'

They fall contentedly silent as they hold each other in the little warm bedroom beneath the patchwork quilt made one winter long ago by four pairs of hands under that very roof.

'We should sleep. I'll be getting on a plane soon.' Nari's voice is low and grave.

'And I'll be heading out on the wilderness trail again tomorrow morning with a new group. Five nights camping out.' He places the mug on the table by the bed and stretches his arms out, stifling a lawn. 'I'd rather stay here with you. The trails are getting old now. I must have spent half my life sleeping in tents and driving sleds.'

She hears him breathe a sigh. 'Don't think about it now. Think about that tomorrow. Let's just sleep.'

'Goodnight, Nari Bell.'

She wriggles down under the covers, letting Niilo mould himself to the shape of her back, warm and curved. He listens to her breathing, and says softly, 'I'll miss you.'

'Mmm, me too,' she replies dreamily, still clasping the carved bear to her heart.

As he holds her, the thoughts of the day before re-emerge and after a long time spent brooding over them, he finds himself whispering them to Nari in the darkness.

'I'll miss you terribly. But it's only right that you leave, go back to your travels and your work. You have a whole new year ahead of you where you can do anything and go anywhere. I'll be right here, rooted to the earth, my home, and my routine at the resort. You know, Stellan had a girlfriend once, Karin, and she tried to live here with him, but it was too much to ask. She got tired of always waiting for Stellan, and one day she left, went back to Stockholm, and she was right to. He was messed up for a long time after she left, but I don't think it ever occurred to him to go and see her. He was too busy here. Like me.'

He places a soft kiss on Nari's shoulder blade with a sigh. 'I knew if we met, and if we touched, I'd fall in love. I told you I used to think that nobody could be lonely and waiting like I was, before you. I used to be convinced that if the right person were to present themselves to me, if they pressed their fingers to my chest, I'd melt like snow falling on the flowing river. That person is you. I knew that if I let you touch me, I'd be scattered into particles that would burst in the sky like the aurora. I was right. And I knew it would be harder to say goodbye. And all along I knew I'd risk making you feel miserable, or guilty – or, even worse, make you feel as though I'm here judging you for being free and having a life of your own out there. I don't want to clip your wings, those are what I love about you most, Nari.'

He waits for her reply, her acknowledgement that she understands what he's saying; that he's sending her on her way tomorrow morning and it pains him, but that he wants her to live her life, full of fun and adventure, and sometimes think fondly of him.

'Nari?'

But she was asleep, breathing softly.

A wry smile spreads on his face in the darkness, and he sinks deep into thought. Perhaps it's for the best that she never knows the depths of his feelings for her. She'll leave tomorrow and be happy. She doesn't need to know how he'll pine and ache.

Just then, a blue flash of light flickers from the floor. Nari's phone. It must be Sylvie in a frantic panic, wondering why Nari hasn't returned to her cabin. Carefully, he frees his arms, leaving Nari to roll away, smiling in her sleep. He tucks the quilt around her then reaches for the phone. A quick reply to say she was safely with him would suffice, he thinks.

But instead of a panicked message from Sylvie, there's a tiny thumbnail picture of a smiling man, older than Nari, wearing dark shades, smart in a white collar and tie. Beneath the image was his message.

> *My advisors tell me I can't enter the UK until the spring. Don't ask. Tax reasons. So London's off, sorry. I've arranged a charter from Manchester airport on New Year's Eve for you. Come meet me in Grand Cayman for some fireworks, lobster and a champagne sunrise on the beach? No pressure,*

but I hope you come. My pilot is at your disposal,
Stephen, x

Niilo replaces the phone where Nari will find it, and Stephen's message, tomorrow. 'Of course,' he whispers with a nod of acceptance. 'Of course.'

He swallows down the lump in his throat, and slips beneath the covers once more. For the next few hours he can hold her as she sleeps, and then his life will return to the way it had always been, only colder.

Chapter Twenty-Seven

Lying on the rug in front of the dying fire, face to face, our robes long since chucked into a crumpled pile at our feet, we're whispering.

'I've loved being here, thank you for bringing me.'

Stellan laughs gently, amused that I'm thanking him. 'My pleasure,' he says.

'I don't want to go home.'

I think of the wet airport tarmac and the Manchester traffic; a bleak contrast to the white magic of Frozen Falls. His fingers lazily twirl the hair falling around my face, and I say, 'I've loved every second of meeting Niilo, and seeing Nari happy, and Toivo was just the highlight of the trip!'

Stellan's eyes widen. 'Oh, really?'

'You know what I mean,' I say with a low laugh. 'I love the food, and the colours in the sky, and the snow. Oh, and your ice bar, and the champagne, and the waterfall. I've loved every bit of my time here.'

I slide in closer to Stellan and he wraps his arms around me tightly, but he doesn't speak. Maybe he's going to sleep again. So I make the most of the silence and list every other perfect little detail. 'I love the comfort and the Scandinavian practicality of it all; the triple glazing, the wet rooms, and the underfloor heating, and how the beds have two single duvets instead of a big double one so nobody can hog it! And I love—'

'You say that a lot, don't you?'

'What?' I ask, lifting my eyes, even though I can't see him. I don't want to leave the cosy nook of his chest.

'You loved those cookies we made on Christmas Eve, you love the chocolate, you love everything.'

There's a little alarm bell ringing in my head. Don't say anything, just tell him you're an appreciative kind of person, laugh it off, and go to sleep. You're leaving soon and it's been so perfect. But there they are, my fingers hovering over the self-destruct button.

'Is there something wrong with that?' I hear myself saying.

'No, that's not it. It's just that's not a word we use for everyday things, or for other people really. Not often.'

'I know. You already told me that, years ago. But love's not an unusual word for me to use.' I've got a little dagger of resentment clutched in my palm, and for a moment I wonder if I'm going to use it. 'And it's not unusual for my family to say it. My parents tell me they love me all the time, and I say it back. It's white noise in our house.'

I realise that I've just confirmed exactly Stellan's point; my exclamations of love are just white noise, repetitive and meaningless. That's definitely enough. Stop now, I warn myself. But I can't help adding one last little stab. 'It's normal.' I'm as cross with myself as I was with him.

I know exactly what I've done. I've taken what he shared with me about his cold, demanding, undemon-strative dad and used it against him. I've dredged up and weaponised painful memories of his poor sick father who surely must love his son with all his heart, whether he says it or not.

Stellan moves his shoulder out from under my head. He's looking down at me as he talks, his arms still holding me, but slacker. I daren't move.

'Saying you love something or someone, using that word, it pretty much does mean you're *in love* with the thing. It's not something I'd say to my parents, or about a biscuit.'

Or a girlfriend? I don't say it, but I'm thinking it.

He's silent now, signalling he's moved on from the topic. But I'm recklessly hurtling back round for another swipe at him. It's been fifteen years and I've kept these thoughts inside and if we don't blurt it out now, we never will.

'I didn't know that… but I meant it, then, when I told you I loved you. I meant the actual *I'm in love with you, won't you love me?* kind of I love you.'

'I knew that. That's why I had to leave.'

'Oh, not this again! The white knight making his noble sacrifice to save the damsel from an extra year of student loans or, *heaven forfend*, a job in a call centre or something! It sounds very much like the commitment phobic knight got his end away then beat a hasty retreat!'

'No. I loved you.'

Silence.

My heart thumping.

A gulp moving Stellan's throat.

'You were *in love* with me? Not the biscuit kind of love?' I say.

'Yes. Of course I was in love with you.' Stellan exhales a long breath and I feel his grip around my body break as he lets his back flatten on the mattress, rolling away from me.

All the while, I'm replaying what he's just said, running diagnostics, scanning his voice for modulations and intonations and finding a definite stress on '*was*'. Undeniable. He's taking pains to ensure I understand he's referring to the past. He *was* in love with me *then*.

I hear the voice inside my head once more, wanting me to prod, poke, interrogate. *So what about now?* But I won't ask. I've said enough, and for my efforts I've been rewarded with the hideous embarrassment of memories of myself launching million megaton love-bombs at a bewildered twenty-one-year-old Stellan and sending him running for cover, an embarrassment unchanged, inalterable, even with this new information that he was in love with me.

We don't speak. I don't want him to say anything else, in case he reiterates his point that he loved me in the past tense. I heard him loud and clear and once was enough. And I *daren't* say anything.

'What now? Shouldn't we talk about this?' he says.

'Silence is golden. Let's just sleep.'

–

The morning arrives, but no light dawns.

It's only an hour or so since I managed to drift off. Now there's an uneasy anxiety spreading through me. The clock above the fire that by now has turned to dull embers tells me it's almost six o'clock and I have a ten-thirty flight to catch. If we don't leave now I'll miss it. I think of my unpacked suitcase back at the cabin. I turn to wake Stellan, but as I'm about to nudge his shoulder, I pause.

This is the last time I'll be with him like this. I let my eyes take him in, trying to memorise every detail: his pale skin and the shape of bone and sinew beneath, the taut muscles I'd been spellbound by last night, now relaxed. I look over his long pale lashes and straw-coloured brows, every freckle on his cheekbones.

I'm put in mind of what Niilo told me the day we threw crumbs for the wagtails and sparrows outside the *lavvu* – that day seems like weeks ago now, but it was only the twenty-third, four days ago. How strange. Niilo had told me that in remote and austere places each tiny crumb is precious. We ate, he said, then the dogs ate our scraps, leaving miniscule crumbs for the birds to find. And that's what I'm taking away with me. Waste not one moment. Enjoy every little crumb of pleasure that life throws at you. Be satisfied. And don't dare ask for more.

Stellan's eyes flicker open and he looks at me, blinking and sleepy. I'm hit by the paleness of his irises once more. I'd sink into their depths if I could. I'd bleed myself into his veins, embed myself forever like a tattoo under his skin, if he'd let me, but I learned long ago what happens when I feel this way. When I ask for too much, I lose everything. So, I'll be contented with what I had here.

I tell him I'm ready to leave.

Chapter Twenty-Eight

Back at my cabin I'm throwing things frantically into my case, grabbing for my passport, checking under furniture and in drawers for things I might have left behind, and feeling sure I don't have everything I arrived with.

'Anything the cleaning staff find they'll send on to you, I promise,' Stellan's saying from my cabin door. He's adopted the lowering, grave attitude he had when we first came face to face again on this very doorstep five adventure-filled days ago.

I'm pulling on my trainers, an extra jumper and my coat because I've had to surrender the lovely thick snow-suit and big boots to the resort again, and I've packed my cosy pink suit away. I'll be making my journey to the airport in the clothes I arrived in. They feel oddly light and insubstantial.

'Have you finished packing? I called a cab.' I hear Nari screech from somewhere outside.

She too has clearly spent the night away from the resort and is in a similar mad panic to my own, but Niilo's nowhere to be seen.

I pause for a second by the Christmas tree and lift one of the decorations from a branch, a simple star. 'The resort won't mind if I take just one of these, will it, Stellan?'

He's leaning against the doorframe watching me, a vague smile playing on his lips. 'I doubt it'll be missed.'

As I stand my suitcase by the door trying to peer past him to see if the taxi's here, Stellan reaches for my waist, pulling me towards him, and even though we spent the night kissing, it's so unexpected that I gasp. I catch sight of Nari screaming, 'Tickets!' and racing back inside her cabin, so I let Stellan kiss me, and I swear I can see stars and the aurora when our eyes are closed, but it's accompanied by a sad pang like hunger in my stomach.

The sharp blast of a taxi's horn brings me round.

This is it, this is all you're getting, I tell myself, so you'd better smile and make the best of it.

Neither of us has mentioned the tetchy argument we had this morning back at the lake house, and how I accused him of being a commitment-shy liar and a cowardly heartbreaker posing as a concerned, self-sacrificing hero, always maintaining he left me for my own good.

We haven't talked about how he picked at me for saying how much I love this and that, harmless, joyful exclamations of happiness.

Now, with only seconds left at Frozen Falls, I'm torn between sulking about it all, and wishing with all my heart I'd kept my big mouth shut and just let him fill me in on his understanding of what love means.

I spoiled our last night together, right at the last moment, when we should have been wrapped in blissful sleep. Maybe if I'd shut up he'd be smiling brightly again now, telling me how he'll miss me, letting me see this affecting him.

For once, I find it easy to stop myself saying the things in my heart. I can still hear Stellan's words. He loved me once, long ago. Past tense.

So, the words that I *do* utter are guarded, enfeebled and, surprisingly, accompanied by a stream of sudden tears which seem to shock Stellan into even deeper silence.

'I have to go, the taxi's here. Stellan...'

He wipes my wet cheeks with his thumbs and I plaster on a plucky smile.

'It was lovely getting to know you better. When you weren't being cold or pedantic, I really, really... liked you,' I garble. I see him smile grimly at this, and I keep talking. 'I wanted to know you from the first second we met at uni, Stellan Virtanen. I thought you were gorgeous, actually, that night at the exchange students' welcome party... when I first saw you.' The string of sounds coming from my mouth fall flat in their inadequacy. Stellan's holding me stiffly around my waist now.

'I remember,' he says. 'I thought you were amazing too. But that wasn't the first time I saw you.'

'It wasn't?'

'No. I saw you the day before, in the corridor, when you were pinning the notice about the welcome party on the board. And I thought you were beautiful. I came to that party hoping to meet you.'

I rush out a breath, wide-eyed with surprise. 'Why didn't you tell me that before?'

'There are a lot of things I should have told you.'

Exasperated and now utterly wordless, I can only look at him. Stellan seems to be retreating again and he looks glad of the interruption as Nari barges against the door from the other side, making it bump against my hip.

In the string of apologies that follow, and with Nari shouting instructions to hurry up, and the heaving of our bags into the boot of the cab, there's no time for any other kind of goodbye.

As I fasten my seatbelt, the arctic wind slams my door shut and I helplessly watch Stellan on the steps of my vacant cabin, his eyes shining and watery from the whipping gale coming in from the north. We wave through glass as the car starts, and in seconds he's out of sight.

I see nothing of the Lappish landscape in the late dawn light as we race to the airport, the tyres crunching over ice. I tell myself our reunion has been perfect, passionate and fun (until I spoiled it), and that now I'm fortified with the knowledge that he loved me once, and that's better than nothing. In fact, it's all I'm getting, so I'll try to be glad.

Chapter Twenty-Nine

'Hi honey, I'm home,' I say into the silence of a Castlewych Boxing Day afternoon as I shut the door behind me, trundling my suitcase over the small pile of Christmas cards on the mat.

My flat's freezing and, I notice for the first time as I turn the thermostat up and click every light in the place on, surprisingly bare and sparse-looking. I don't remember it being so bland and unwelcoming. I really must get some pictures up, maybe some colourful blankets and some rugs. Perhaps a proper fire with flames, and some candles?

I pour some water into the pot concealing the cut, dry stump of the Christmas tree in the lounge. Still wearing my coat, I hang the bauble I brought with me from the tree at Frozen Falls that Stellan and I decorated, and I watch as the branches instantly shed half their needles onto the living room carpet.

Vacuuming up the sharp browning spikes, I try not to let in the memories that the tree's scent conjures up in my head: snowy Lappish forests and festively decorated fireside scenes in a cosy cabin, and Stellan, warm, broad, and beautiful in his woollen jumper with his blond-white hair and pale eyes.

Air traffic control to Sylvie. Prepare for landing. You're home now, I tell myself, but I feel as though I'm still in the turbulent air. How can I be back here in my flat? I wasn't done with my holiday. I wasn't done with being in the presence of Stellan Virtanen.

I switch on the telly and turn up the volume as I empty the suitcase out, filling a laundry basket to take round to Mum and Dad's when they get back from New York in a few days, and vowing that I must get a washing machine of my own in the January sales.

I put away the milk and bread I picked up at the motorway services on the way from the airport, and I walk from room to room, not sure what else to do with myself.

Nari had to write up her notes for her blog, so she dropped me outside the flat and headed straight across town to her own place.

She'd been so quiet on the flight home, reading and re-reading her notes on her phone and looking time and again at a neatly folded piece of pale blue paper she'd been clasping all the way from the resort.

Come to think of it, she'd been unusually, weirdly quiet. I'd gradually become aware of her scrolling through pictures on her camera during the flight – she'd be picking the best ones for her blog and Instagram, I imagine – but I saw her pause and look for a long time at an image of Niilo.

I was pretending to read one of the novels she'd given me the day before, but actually I'd been staring at the same paragraph ever since take-off and none of it had sunk in, so I sneaked a peek over at the photos and smiled to see Niilo.

He was sitting serene and cross-legged by a roaring fire inset into a wall papered in a retro seventies pattern. He looked as though he was toasting bread on a long fork held up to the flames. A cosy, homely scene.

'You OK?' I'd asked, and she'd simply smiled, secretively and sadly. 'Do you want to talk about it?'

'Talk about what?'

'Niilo, of course. I thought, when he picked you up at the restaurant, when he sang you the song…'

'There's nothing to talk about, really. A holiday romance, that's all. He made that quite clear this morning when he left to go on the trail. He told me he hoped I'd live a long and happy life and that I'd get to see every inch of the planet.'

'He said that? No plans for meeting up, or…?'

'No. just a goodbye. He was in a hurry this morning, anyway, the tourists were waiting, but… yes, just a goodbye.'

'Are you happy with that? A holiday romance? You're not upset about it?'

'He was the perfect gentleman. I've got no complaints.'

'Oh, OK,' I said, dubiously. 'And you guys were safe, right?'

I'm thrown an irritated eye-roll. 'Obviously.'

In past conversations on the topic of nights spent with a cute guy, Nari would say this with a smirk and a fist bump, but this definitely isn't the time for celebrating getting lucky. She's solemnly looking at her photos again and hasn't even asked if Stellan and me used condoms, which we did, thank you very much. I shake my head at the irony of the situation. The first time in eons I have something sensational of my own to share and we're both in a daze so deep we can't even enjoy the novelty of it.

'So, what about Stephen?' I'd asked, still hoping to get Nari to open up. 'Are you seeing him in a few days?'

She interrupted my question with a brusque, 'No', and her thumbs started scrolling again.

I took a surreptitious peek over at the other shots she took, all beautifully filtered and cropped to perfection: Niilo and Stellan laughing together at the *lavvu*, and umpteen pictures of me and Nari, our faces squashed together as we grin up at the camera held aloft for silly selfies with the huskies in the background, or at the hotel restaurant, or outside our cabins in the snow.

Looking at those pictures six miles up in the sky above Scandinavia this morning, I already felt as though the whole escapade had taken on the unreality of a dream I couldn't faithfully recall.

As we'd checked in our luggage and watched for our departure gate on the boards, I'd felt strangely altered. Even when the elves appeared to say goodbye, handing out colourful certificates decorated with images of a smiling Santa to celebrate the fact that we had crossed the Arctic Circle, I felt my previous cynicism had dissolved, and the elf lady with the basket of sweets looked shocked then delighted as I'd offered her a hug, overcome with a strange feeling of loss and regret. She'd handed me a tissue when I started to cry on her shoulder.

She'll forever think of me as the mad, tragic single lady who arrived in Lapland crying and left crying too, but I'd just shrugged at myself and let the tears fall, thinking that this must be who I am now, somehow changed, somehow sentimental. I'd accepted her kindness with a smile just as the gate was unlocked and I'd walked out to the plane across the treacherously frozen tarmac.

Stellan had said he'd text when he returned to the resort after the wilderness trail with the tourists. No signal all week, he'd explained. But I have the feeling our connection is already entirely lost.

What would our virtual friendship look like? A text here, a Facebook reminiscence there? (Though I notice, he still hasn't 'friended' me.) Either way we're a thousand miles apart with no signal.

It's definitely time for a Boxing Day glass of gin, I think. If my life had a musical score this particular bit of my soundtrack, with me wandering around my flat unsure what to do with myself, would be accompanied by a morbid Morrissey wryly lamenting my choices, telling me I just haven't suffered enough to have earned my happy ending yet. I hear him whining, and he accompanies me whatever I do as my first night back in my flat slowly drags by.

I find myself flicking through the pages of the song book that the kind priest gave me at the concert rehearsal, but the Finnish words look even more indecipherable here than they did that night in the cosy, Christmassy church, so I file it away on my bookshelf with Mum's lucky silver sixpence marking the page of 'Sylvia's Christmas Song'; the carol that must mean so much to Stellan and his Finnish friends, but is, it turns out, incomprehensible to me.

I even downloaded the aurora-watching app that Stellan had mentioned at the sauna and I discover that a cloudless aurora sky is forecast for tonight. He'll be beneath it, out on the trail in the wilderness, but here in England the heavens will simply be black.

Eventually, I settle on the sofa with a pot of tea and the big box of spiced Finnish biscuits I bought for myself in the airport's little departure lounge. I pull my mermaid blanket over my legs and try to focus on the *EastEnders* Christmas episodes, crumbs falling over me.

And this is how I spend the following days, alone in my flat, staring at the screen, living off crumbs.

Chapter Thirty

'Come in, Sylvie dear!'

Dad's delightedly showing off an 'I heart New York' T-shirt with matching baseball cap, as soon as he opens the door. It looks incongruous with his Christmas robin print cardigan, beige slacks and slippers, and makes me smile instantly.

It's the thirtieth of December. Their flight only got in last night, but they're already in full 'catch-up with Christmas' mode.

'Welcome home,' I say, as I'm ushered inside and am met with a big hug from Mum in a jazzy mohair candy cane jumper.

'I could say the same to you,' Mum says. 'Come on through. Nari not with you today?'

'No, she's been laying low since we got back. She texted to tell me she's been catching up on some sleep and doing a lot of writing.'

'What a shame, her present's under the tree, and I've steamed a whopper of a Christmas pudding. Your dad's whipped up some brandy butter and it feels like a proper Christmas with all this white stuff.' Mum looks excitedly out the kitchen window.

It's been snowing big fluffy flakes for an hour or so and I resist the urge to say that this is nothing compared to where I've been. Instead, I help Mum peel the carrots and baste the little supermarket 'cook from frozen' turkey that's already turning golden in the oven and we all pretend this counterfeit Christmas is as much fun as the real, missed day would have been.

'One of Nari's posts is scheduled to go live on her blog at three. We can have a look at it together if you like. She took some great pictures,' I say.

'Did she enjoy Lapland?'

'I think she fell in love with it.'

'And did you?'

'Yes,' I say, and it comes out sounding grim and ominous.

Our belated Christmas dinner, just the three of us, is just how I knew it would be: too much food, all delicious and hearty; Dad wearing his cracker hat even on the oblig- atory duck pond walk and as we dried the dishes together; and lots of chatter and pleasantness. We exchange presents and Dad says his musical socks are the best he's ever been given, and Mum appreciates the new celebrity cookbook I give her.

I unwrap the standard Christmas pyjamas and the big selection box that I always get – thank goodness they didn't stop that tradition when I'd bemoaned it as a moody, embarrassed fourteen-year-old.

Everything is familiar and simple, the way it always is at home. It's not quite Christmas, but it's good all the same.

We demolish the big box of Roses chocolates and Dad spends a long time flicking through the *TV Times*, which they only ever buy at Christmas, the sight of which always fills me with wistful nostalgia for Christmases past.

As the day wears on I pour out the red wine and help set out the massive cheese board on the coffee table. Despite feeling too full to contemplate it now, I know in ten minutes I'll find I can manage a nibble.

'Show us Nari's blog then,' says Mum, stretching out on the sofa in her new Christmas slippers – exactly identical to the pair Dad gave her last year, but we hadn't said anything, and he was oblivious as I watched Mum surreptitiously kick the old pair under the sofa and slip into the new ones, exclaiming how comfy they were. 'Just what I needed,' she'd said.

I open the cover of Mum's tablet and search for Nari's blog.

'Here it is.' I scroll back a few posts, handing it over and watching as Mum and Dad digest the details of the husky trip, the food, Sámi culture, the sauna rituals, and the lovely cabins.

I'd already caught up with the blog posts back at my flat, but I knew Nari had one last Lapland post scheduled for the year and it was going to appear any second now.

Mum's holding the tablet an inch from her nose, struggling without her reading glasses. 'Who's that? she says.

'That's Toivo.' I try to say it like a normal, rational human would, but my throat tightens, making me sound hoarse and emotional.

'What a lovely dog,' Mum's saying, peering very closely at his sweet little face. 'Who's that holding him?'

'That's Stellan.'

If they recognise his name, Mum and Dad do a good job of hiding it. I had neglected to tell them that the owner of Frozen Falls was my ex-boyfriend from infinity ago. No point mentioning it now, I think.

That's when Mum suddenly knits her brows and crumples her lips, deep in thought. 'Stellan?' she says and looks from me to Dad. You cannot get one over on Mum, she's like a romantic Dr Watson, sniffing out every hint of each torrid, confused dating drama I ever had. '*Your* Stellan?'

Well there you go. They do remember! I suppose they did drive through the night to pick me up from my halls of residence after it dawned on me that Stellan really wasn't coming back. They'd found me out on the street in the sleeting rain clutching the note he'd left me. "Please forgive me. I'm going home. I won't be back. Sylvie, please try to forget about me", it had read, followed by the immortally hideous line, "It isn't you, it's me".

Thinking about it, they're unlikely to forget the weeks that followed when I stayed in bed, living off drinking chocolate and little snack boxes of raisins, writing letter after letter that I could never send because the Finnish postal service would be hard pushed to deliver thirty-five tear-stained envelopes addressed only to "Stellan Virtanen, somewhere near Saariselkä".

I'm saved from a Mumquisition by the pinging notification on my phone that tells me Nari's new post's gone live.

'Scroll down her blog, Mum. There's the new one now.'

I read it off my phone screen, feeling like one of the family is missing, and wishing Nari was with us now.

–

Readers, you know me well enough by now to know that I can't lie to you. I've been home from Lapland for five days and I'm supposed to be planning my adventures for the coming year. I mean, there are literally hundreds of things I should be doing: booking flights and transfers, researching hotels and restaurants, finding out where there's a hidden gem bookstore or a mama and papa's cafe making the best waffles in the world. I should be counting out strange new currencies and trying to figure out if the bashed-up little coin I'm holding is the equivalent of a dollar or fifty quid. I should be blogging my heart out with excitement about all the new people I'm going to meet; school kids and gap-year girls, local dignitaries and dodgy souvenir sellers.

And the romance novels. I should be telling you about the beach reads I've got packed and how I'll be reading stories set in the very towns and cities I'm planning on visiting. And maybe I should be reflecting on the fact that no matter how far I travel, how many hands I shake or glasses I lift with a toast in the local dialect, no matter how many empty beaches I stroll along at sunset feeling self-sufficient and independent, I might actually be starting to get a bit fed up of solo travel, and wondering why I never actually meet someone I really like while I'm away.

Except this time I did meet someone. And he's the reason for all this… whatever this is that's stopping me planning for my next dream destination. You've probably already guessed? The herder? Well, you're right. I met a guy called Niilo and we shared an incredible adventure together in Lapland.

But right now, I'm in Cheshire looking at an empty suitcase and a stack of *Lonely Planet* guides for all the places I'm supposed to be jetting off to this year, and all I can think about is where Niilo might be and wondering if he's thinking about me too. I don't know what to do. He is my new dream destination.

Signing off, Nari

#LeftmyHeartinLapland

–

The coffee pot arrives and I find I can manage another plateful of cheese and crackers, as it happens. And I end up telling Mum and Dad about Nari and Niilo, and then I tell them about Stellan, keeping it all strictly chaste, but blushing wildly as they listen to me, Mum nodding matter-of-factly, taking it all in.

My story ends with me on the verge of tears, blowing my nose, and Dad shuffling to the edge of his chair and uttering the words I've heard oh, so many times before.

'Did I ever tell you the story of how your mother and I met?'

Oh Jesus. 'Only a few thousand times, Dad.'

'Really? Surely not?' he says, looking puzzled.

Mum butts in. 'It was nineteen seventy-nine. Our final year at high school. Another world, wasn't it Malcolm?'

In my head I've already pre-empted this. Recollections of their early romance always take place in 'another world'. Next it'll be the bus stop and '*poof!*' Just listen.

'Sandra Bowler had been drooling over your father for months, hadn't she, poor girl? But I was hoping he'd ask me out, and you never did, did you, Malcolm?'

'No, I never did,' he says fondly, shaking his head at his younger self. It's adorable, but I've seen this a lot, remember.

'Your father was walking us both to the bus stop one night after school. It was the coldest winter we'd had in years and there was a terrible storm, coming down in buckets it was. When suddenly *poof*! Sandra Bowler was struck by lightning, poor girl. A zillion volts straight down the brolly handle and into her body.'

I widen my eyes because they're expecting a reaction.

Satisfied, Dad takes over. 'Well, the sight of her lying in the rain in a puddle, hair sticking up like a porcupine, was enough to have one of my pals, Jamie Field, running for her. Do you know, he knelt in that puddle by her side, he did, and clasped her hand.'

That's new. Porcupine is new. Nice detailing, Dad.

'And she came to in his arms,' says Mum. 'The pair of them left together in the ambulance. And you'll never guess?'

Just say what. 'What?'

'They were married the following summer. We gave them a rubber bath mat as a wedding present, didn't we, Malcolm?'

This story gets stupider and more far-fetched every time they tell it.

'That's lovely.' I say with a nod of finality, topping up our coffee cups.

'No, it isn't. At least it wouldn't be lovely if it weren't for what happened next,' says Mum, a bit annoyed that I'm trying to wriggle out of the familiar Happy Ever After ending to this daft romantic caper. 'You see, it took your dad weeks to ask me out after that, even though the lightning had put paid to Sandra meddling in our after school walks to the bus stop. Eventually, I said to him,

306

"Malcolm Magnussen, are you going to take me to the end of term disco, or aren't you?"'

'And I said, "I was just building up to asking."'

'And so he did ask.'

'I did.'

'That's lovely. I should probably be heading off now, it's getting late...'

But Mum's not done. 'My point is, Sylvie, love, if you don't take a chance and grab what you want with both hands and make it take you to the disco, you might end up missing out on the best things that could ever happen to you.'

I watch my parents smile at one another. Dad pats Mum's hand.

'I can't believe I'm being Mr Miyagied by my own mother.'

'Well, I don't know this Mr Miyagi, but I do know that lightning doesn't strike the same place twice, so you need to grab hold of the one you love and make sure they know it!'

Chapter Thirty-One

I trudge back to my flat in the increasingly heavy snow. Castlewych's streets seem apocalyptically deserted, but I can see the lights from the tellies flickering behind blinds as I walk along and I remember that everyone's indoors because English people don't make Unnecessary Journeys in snowy weather.

They're probably inside watching news reports about the snow instead of actually setting foot in it. I'm willing to bet that across the country right now there are at least eight meteorologists standing in front of blustery motorway gantries pointing the cameras towards slow-moving traffic below and warning of black ice and treacherous conditions. Funnily enough, I didn't see a single weather warning or snarled up road the whole time I was in easy-going, stoic, snowbound Lapland.

My ersatz Christmas day at Mum and Dad's has left me exhausted, so I head straight to bed when I get in, and the last thing I think of as I fall asleep is my parents' love story.

It was all right for them, I think, last century. They were in the same class at school, for heaven's sake. They took the same bus every day and lived on the same street. Love was bound to come for them.

But now, it's more complicated than that. We're all studying abroad, travelling overseas, chatting with people from the other side of the world at the touch of a button. And with dating technologies that can match you up to your perfect partner or let you swipe away potentially unsuitable men like you're swatting flies, we've got a whole planet of people to choose from. These days, your husband's just as likely to be in an office in Casablanca as he is to be waiting at the bus stop in Castlewych.

And as for me, the only man I've ever really loved is somewhere in the wilderness right now, and no amount of lightning strikes and longing will send him running to kneel by my side in this storm. We're worlds apart.

I've been asleep for a while when I hear it. *Ping!* A notification. I'd left my phone on in case Nari wanted to chat, but it must be the middle of the night now. Peering at my phone in the darkness, I sit up and read in bed. It's from Nari's blog. She's posted something new.

–

Readers, I'm at the airport.

Its three a.m. on New Year's Eve. Normally, when travelling, I'd be posting an Insta of my artfully foamed breakfast cappuccino posed quirkily on the cover of my in-flight novel right about now, or I'd be telling you the travel hack or the beauty tip I've just tried out, or I'd be raving about the treatment in the first class lounge or the new travel accessory I've blagged in return for a review, but, honestly, all I'm doing is pacing by the gate, like a bear in a cage.

I suspect that right this second my Uber guy's pulling away from the terminal having given me a score of one out of five and warning other drivers I'm a bit shouty, possibly insane, but this was a mercy dash, a sudden, unplanned journey.

I have only the contents of my coat pockets with me: my passport and my credit card (and my Eight Hour Cream – I'm not an animal). My flight's boarding in twelve minutes. And I'm going to find him.

Niilo Henrik Oskal, if you're reading this, somehow, out there in the arctic wilderness, I'm coming back to you #ILoveYou

–

She's actually lost her mind, I think. But then I find I'm grinning from ear to ear, beaming with pride. My best mate, who loves adventure, is in the air this very second making her way to the man she loves on the adventure of a lifetime. She's making it happen. *That* is solo travel. *That* is the ultimate risk.

What will he say? Will she even find him? I can just imagine her hotwiring a skidoo and making a death-defying journey across the icy tundra in search of him.

I wish I'd gone with her. To keep her company. Just in case.

I wish I had her guts.

I mean, it's crazy, isn't it? Dashing off to see a man who isn't expecting you and who may or may not be in love with you. A man you can't stop thinking about.

Somehow I'm out from under the covers and on my feet, and the bedside light is on.

My own suitcase is still on the floor in front of me, I've been too lethargic to actually put it away in the loft. I find I'm standing over it, eyeing it warily. Its unzipped lid gapes like a mouth calling to me.

I *could* just chuck some clean knickers in there. And I've still got some euros.

I could do a Nari.

No! Obviously not. What are you thinking, Sylve? Anyone can see Niilo and Nari are up to their ears in the first flush of love where everything's new and pristine and exciting. And she probably *will* track him down and fall into his open arms.

But Stellan and me, we're choked up with history and misapprehensions and me being, well… me, spoiling things.

Then again.

He did say he loved me, once upon a time. And it's not like we spent last week playing Scrabble and talking about the weather, is it? We really did still have all our old magic and a sprinkling of something new too, something grown up and more real.

'*Screw it!*' I shout, as I obey my impulse and tip my newly tumble-dried laundry (thanks Mum) from the basket onto the bed, and before I know it, there's fresh pyjamas and jumpers thrown into the suitcase and I'm running, yes running, to the bathroom for my pink toothbrush, and pulling clothes on.

As I zip up the case, having grabbed my coat, I look at Nari's blog on my phone again, one last read through to check I've got the guts. She and Niilo "shared an incredible adventure together in Lapland", she's written. Well, so did Stellan and I. It really was incredible, like nothing that's ever happened to me before, not since the last time I was with Stellan. And in those intervening years, fifteen whole, long years, I was just waiting for the lightning to strike again, with someone new, someone I trusted, someone I loved, but it never happened; not even with Cole, and I let him put a ring on my finger, when really, I only ever loved Stellan Virtanen.

And at last I'm sure.

I don't want to be satisfied with just the crumbs. I can't survive on morsels of memories. I don't want an austerity diet of bits of half-recollected love. *No more crumbs!* I want to have the whole Stellan cake! Every rich, sweet layer of it.

I'm texting, my fingers tapping out a staccato on the screen.

> **Nari, do you think I can buy Saariselkä flights online right now?**

What am I doing? She's in the air. She won't see it. I'll phone Mum and Dad, ask them for a lift to the airport, and I'll just buy any flights I can find online while I'm waiting, slap them on a credit card, even if I have to hop between airports to get to Lapland. I'll just buy whatever I can. How hard can it be? Nari managed it. Then again, she does have a remarkable talent for getting what she wants, and she does know *literally* every travel insider on the planet.

Hold on, I'd better get my flights booked before I ring Mum and Dad, don't want to startle them in the middle of the night, in case I can't get anything until tomorrow...

'Manchester flights, Manchester flights,' I mumble to myself as I'm searching online. It takes a while, my phone's being slow, and I find I'm sitting on my suitcase by the door, shoulders slumping, as I read.

Weather warning: All regional airport flights cancelled as further heavy snow forecast

They can't mean *all* flights. They always say that, don't they, as a precaution, but it never comes to that? I bet Heathrow's still open.

I get up to look out the hall window. Street lights illuminate the white blanket settling over everything, and getting thicker by the minute.

'That's just a sprinkling!' I shout, seeing the harassed, open-mouthed woman shouting back at me in the dark glass. 'Lapland air traffic control would laugh this off!'

But, as I Google and scroll ticket sites and then wait in a queue listening to nerve-twanging jaunty hold music as I try to get through to an EasyJet operator, and then a rip-off last minute ticket broker, it starts to sink in. They all keep giving me the same answer: No flights for at least twenty-four hours.

I'm not going anywhere.

Chapter Thirty-Two

They've all done their best to cheer me up. All the Channel 4 and BBC presenters trying to cajole me into a Happy New Year. And this bottle of red and the selection box have done their darnedest to get me into the party spirit. But its eleven o'clock at night, an hour until the bells ring out the old year, and I'm on the sofa in a morbid slump. Mum and Dad are at Auntie Brenda and Uncle Alan's for Twister and nibbles but I, with some relief, declined the invitation, saying I was having an early night.

What's so happy about a new year anyway? Another twelve months of lonely slog ahead: work, cook, tidy-up, sleep, repeat. I'm not even listening to the sweet-little-Sylvie voice at the back of my brain reminding me not to be ungrateful and that I've got Sunday lunches at my folks' place to look forward to, and I'll have Nari, if she ever comes back, and there are two hundred and thirty-eight teenagers who won't get their rocks off about Oliver chuffing Cromwell or the Bletchley Park codebreakers without me, but right now, there's not much comfort in any of that.

The telly's a bit blurry, I notice, as I empty the dregs of the bottle into the red-stained and finger-printed tumbler, and the light from my phone's giving me a headache. I've been refreshing my notifications since four o'clock this morning when I finally gave up my impulsive search for non-existent flights, hoping for some word from Nari. Did she get there? Did her flight turn back? Did it ever take off?

'This is the time of year we think about our loved ones and wish them well, wherever they may be,' says a grinning, bobble-hatted Fearne Cotton from the Thames Embankment surrounded by crowds of singing, shivering drunks waiting for fireworks.

It couldn't hurt to wish Stellan well. A little New Year message. He'll be back at the resort after the trail by now, surely? I'll send him something friendly and final, something nice to find as he gets back to his cabin after five hardworking days under canvas, as he peels away his layers, takes his aching body to the sauna… his aching, muscled, fit, smooth-skinned body…

I look at my phone screen. I've texted and sent something.

I peer with seesawing, telescoping eyesight at the kaleidoscope of dancing letters. Three texts? I've sent three increasingly boozy texts!

> **Book your flight to England
> and then get into my bed.**

Excellent. That doesn't sound desperate and leery at all.

> **Come and see me sometime.
> Soon. Please. X**

Oh God!

Right. Well, if he hasn't fully retreated into his crazy-lady-shy man cave before, he will now.

Starting the New Year as you intend to go on, Sylvie Magnusson: a sad, pathetic, loser, all alone.

I cry, for what feels like a long time, am overwhelmed with tiredness, and then nothing.

I miss the notification at first, sleeping through the soft pinging sound. But then I sit bolt upright on the sofa, staring at my phone, just as the Embankment countdown comes to an end and fireworks pop and bang on the TV screen and all over snowy Castlewych.

–

Readers, I made it.

I'm in the back of a cab heading to Frozen Falls resort. We were the last flight to get out, they said. Everyone else is grounded. My heart's still swirling around in my chest from the turbulence. We flew straight through a snowstorm and the Northern lights. If I hadn't been clinging to my seat and praying for a quick death, I'd probably have been awestruck by the beauty of the aurora out my window.

I definitely did the right thing. I followed the irresistible pull of the magnetic north and now I'm here and it feels absolutely correct.

And I can tell you this, right? You won't think I'm crazy? For a minute, once we landed at the airport, I had a moment of doubt. I'd stumbled outside and there wasn't a taxi to be seen, not a single vehicle for miles around, it seemed. And the snow was drifting in huge heaps everywhere and I realised I'm not properly dressed for this place, and I don't even have Niilo's number. But – and this is when you have to promise me you won't think I'm crazy – I was entering the terminal again, ready to rethink the whole thing over a hot chocolate, contemplating going back to England, when I saw a bear. In the airport. A huge brown grizzly bear.

I know, I know, it must be lack of sleep or those in-flight G&Ts or the surprise at finding myself alive after that awful storm. I'm probably in shock. But I saw a bear.

People were just walking straight past it, so I'm pretty sure it was just me seeing him. And he was looking at me, his big, black, glassy eyes staring straight at mine. And he walked right past me, out into the snow. And I followed him, and then he wasn't there any more. I mean, he never was there, right? But you know what I mean? And then a taxi pulled up by my side, and I got in.

#WhereisNiilo #LoveQuest #LaplandDash #AFricken-Bear?

–

After a bit of screaming and dancing around the flat in my pyjamas – I hope Piero's asleep downstairs or the sound of the fireworks masked my elated cries – I find myself climbing into bed, breathless and sobbing, actual, proper, howling sobs.

I scroll through the photographs on Nari's blog, just to drive in the very last nail and make sure I really am profoundly unhappy. There we all are: Niilo and Nari, me and Stellan, me and Toivo.

I'm throwing the empty tissue box by my bedside to the floor with a big weepy sniff and wondering if there's any loo roll in the bathroom when another notification pops up on my phone, just minutes after the last one. A text this time, from Nari.

> I hope you get this. I'm nearly at the resort. What do you want me to say to Stellan?

> And, look at this. I had it in my hand all the way home on the plane and couldn't show it to you in case I cried, sorry! It was all just too much at the time. It's the song Niilo wrote for me, in case you think I'm doing the wrong thing. Actually, I know you don't think that. And I'm sorry I couldn't bring myself to tell you about Stephen either. I told him I couldn't see him at New Year. It wouldn't be right when I love someone else. Tell me what to do about Stellan. Nari, xx

Attached to the text is a photograph of a piece of pale blue paper with creases folded into it. I zoom in on the handwriting, and the tears start again as I read.

> *Sorry, my translation is not good. Some things there are no English words for. But this is your joik, Love Niilo.*
>
> *Nari. Nari Bell.*
> *I was waiting for you.*
> *I knew you before we met.*
> *Did you recognise me?*
> *The first person to see me clearly.*
> *Nari. Nari Bell.*
> *The clearest sound.*
> *The brightest light.*
> *You deserve to fly.*
> *See the world.*
> *See the world.*
> *Encircle it like the moon does.*
> *Always moving on.*
> *Think of me kindly.*
> *Think of me kindly,*
> *And how I'm still here.*
> *And how I'm here waiting and loving you.*

I desperately type my reply, and click send, instantly hearing a sharp sound.

Message not sent. Retry?

And so I do retry, again and again. There's no way it'll get to her, she's too far away. There'll be no signal.

There's nothing for it but to roll into a ball on the bed and just let the tears fall.

Ping! Then another. *Ping!* And another. *Ping! Ping! Ping!* I sit up, wipe my nose on my sleeve, and try to focus on the screen.

> **Minä rakastan sinua**

I scroll.

> **Jag älskar dig**

There's another one.

> **Je t'aime**

I'm shaking now.

> **Te amo**

> **Ich liebe dich**

> **Is breá liom tú**

And I keep scrolling, and they keep arriving in every language until I see it.

> **I Love You**

> **I should have said it fifteen years ago. I should have let you say it to me every day in any language you wanted. I'm telling you now. I Love you. Stellan.**

I realise I'm gasping for air and holding the phone to my chest as I throw open the bedroom window and take deep gulping breaths. My head spins and the phone pings into life again. I can't take much more of this!

> **He isn't here. Stellan isn't at the resort! Nari.**

And that's when I drop the phone, just as I hear the sound of insistent knocking at the door of my flat.

Stumbling into the hall, I stand looking at it, unsteady on my feet, my mouth open, still fighting to fill my lungs. There's a silhouette behind the glass, and I just know.

I pull the door open and he looks at me in amazement as if he didn't expect it to be me; as if he hasn't just flown a thousand miles to get here.

'Stellan.'

'Sylvie! I've spent the last twenty-four hours on three different planes and on the floor of two airport departure lounges, and I got a cab all the way from Heathrow, but I'm here. Did you get my messages? I couldn't get a signal for ages.'

'All of them,' I say quietly, gazing at him in amazement.

'I mean it. I love you.'

Reaching for him, I pull him into the flat, letting the door close behind us. Stellan's kiss is like a balm, healing all the sadness and regret.

But he pulls away, like he always does, and I want to weep and say *no, not this again*, no more hesitating and picking at old wounds, but his words come out in a flurry.

'I'm sorry I couldn't bring him with me. He's booked on a flight in February.'

'Who? Niilo?'

'No, the last I heard, Niilo was heading to his cabin with Nari. He read her blog out on the trail and rushed back to Frozen Falls to meet her. He's full of ideas about all the places they're going to visit together, said he was planning on taking Nari to meet his cousin's family and some of his old friends in the South before they fly to Seoul. I guess he's earned some time off, don't you? And I was wrong about Nari. I should have known if she's a friend of yours, she must be good, and she's a perfect match for Niilo. I'm sorry I misjudged her. But, no, I'm talking about Toivo. I got his passport and his quarantine sorted and he'll be coming to live with his new owner in England in two months. That is, if you want him?'

'Of course I want him!' I let out a sharp breath. 'Come here.'

This kiss feels twice as sweet, and when Stellan pulls away this time, he keeps his lips close to mine as he says with a smile, 'You know, I don't want him to miss me. We're like family, me and the little guy, so I thought I'd fly back here with Toivo, maybe take a long vacation, see the sights and help him settle in? I heard there's some real nice open country round here for dog walks. Would you like that?'

'No, I'd *love* that,' I say.

'*Minä rakastan sinua*,' he says, before he kisses me once more, and this time I know he won't stop, and I'm dimly aware that there are fireworks exploding and snowflakes falling from here to Saariselkä.

A Letter From Kiley

Hi, it's me again, Kiley Dunbar.

I'm so excited you've found my book. *Christmas at Frozen Falls* is my second novel and it was a total joy to write. For a start, it's about my favourite time of year. As I type this letter to you, I'm sitting at my desk beside bookshelves festively decorated with fairy lights, and I'm wearing my cosy Christmas robin pyjamas, and I have a big slice of gingerbread and orange cake and a steaming cup of cocoa in front of me. It's June.

If my story happens to get you into the Christmas spirit too, it would give me so much happiness and encouragement if you could (pretty please with a dusting of icing sugar on top) take a few minutes to rate and review it. Your reviews really do make a big difference to me and help other people discover my books. So *Thank You* in advance for spreading the love for *Christmas at Frozen Falls*. Whether it's a blazing August day, drizzling autumn time, or a cold, crisp December, dive in and Have Yourself a Merry Little Christmas on me.

If I could get away with it, I'd be listening to Michael Bublé's festive songs and watching *The Vicar of Dibley* Christmas specials (the one with the Brussels sprouts is especially brilliant) all the year round, but I can see how that might be testing for my family. So I channel my love of all things wintry into reading lots of Christmas romances, even at the height of summer. And now I get to *write* Christmas love stories too. How lucky is that! It's like all my Christmases have come at once.

I really enjoyed matchmaking for my heroine, Sylvie Magnusson, who you'll meet when she's recovering from a broken heart (her ex-fiancé, Cole, is most definitely on the naughty list) and dreaming about her first love from her uni days. I adore a 'one that got away' reunion story, and in *Christmas at Frozen Falls* that's exactly what you'll get: a love story that spans fifteen long years of reminiscing about sexy Stellan Virtanen and wondering 'what if?'

And there's a whirlwind romance too for Sylvie's best friend, Nari Bell, all taking place in the winter wonderland of Finnish Lapland at Christmas. And there are husky pups! Loads of them. *Ooh*, I'm fizzing with excitement for you to read this book! I hope you love it.

I wrote this novel with you in mind, my amazing readers. I wanted to transport you to another world of cosy snowed-in cabins, crackling fireside kisses and dreamy winter landscapes under magical aurora skies. And I wanted to make you properly belly laugh, swoon for our heroes, and sigh for Christmas.

I know you have high standards when it comes to Christmas romances and I'm quietly hopeful *Christmas at Frozen Falls* won't disappoint, so make yourself a hot chocolate, grab a blanket and get snuggled up, because we're off to Lapland. Have fun!

Oh, and if you fancy a festive book chat (at any time of the year) get in touch @KileyDunbar on Twitter. I'll be right here, in my Christmas jammies.

Love, Kiley x

Acknowledgments

As always, the first people I want to shine a big loving light upon are the Dunbar babies and my lovely Nic. Thank you for loving me. I adore you all, and I'll always treasure our happy memories of Lapland.

Michael, you are an exceptional human being, my favourite writer and my biggest supporter. Thank you for twenty-one years of love, kindness and giggles.

The Dream Team, big and little, get a great big 'Thank You' hug too.

Liz is always there to discuss breaking Keanu news, and for that and lots of other things, I'm grateful. Thanks, love.

Clare Horrocks loves romantic fiction, and I really hope she loves this book! Thank you for all your support, Clare, x

Since my first novel *One Summer's Night* came out in March 2019 I've been blown away by the support of new friends met on Twitter who have encouraged me in a million different ways, so here's a *Golden Girls* style group hug for: everyone at \@UKRomChat, Jeanna Louise Skinner, Eilidh K. Lawrence, Lucy Flatman, Lucy Keeling, Dominique Simpson, Mark Desvaux, Mark Stay, Katie Ginger, Shelby, Julian Barr, Rebecca Duval, Pernille Hughes, Lucy Mitchell, Sandy Barker, Kim Nash, Ian Wilfred, Ella Hayes, Gem – Bee Reader, Jeevani

Charika, Emily Royal, Rachel Gilbey, Jane Lacy Crane, Alix Kelso, Sheila Riley, Win Kelly Charles and Ritu Bhathal. I'm so sorry if I forgot you this time around! There are so many of you out there, just being amazing, bookish Lovelies!

And I'm so glad I have the opportunity to thank all of the incredible book bloggers who helped me spread the love for my first novel as it made its way around the world on its Blog Tour. I *literally* couldn't do this without you all. You're incredible. Thank you times one million to: *Jan's Book Buzz*, *Donnasbookblog*, *Varietats*, *Coffee and Kindle Book Reviews*, *Stacy is Reading*, *On My Bookshelf*, *Jen Med's Book Reviews*, *A Little Book Problem*, *Sarah's Book Reviews* and *Kelly's Book Space*. If you don't yet follow these kick-ass book bloggers, I urge you to get online and check them out!

Thank you Sue Moorcroft and the *Romantic Novelists Association* for the bursary which allowed me to attend all three days of the RNA summer 2019 conference at Lancaster: yet another example of how book people are the best people.

I have a decade's worth of gratitude for all of my brilliant students and colleagues (especially Orlagh, Rachel, Joanne, Angi, Neil, Jennie B, Dominika, Susan, Jeongmee, David and Nicola) at Man Met Uni, Cheshire. I miss you and our beautiful, leafy, bustling campus so, so much. We did a good job and I'm proud of everything we achieved together.

Jason and Vanessa helped me with Finnish translations when I was just staring at all the letters and scratching my head. Thank you so much! Any mistakes are my own.

Diane Meacham designed this beautiful book jacket and it's just as eye-catching and wonderful as her cover art for *One Summer's Night* – I'm so grateful, thank you. And thank you to all the Hera Books family too, including Annabell and Jennie for proofing and editing with such care and attention.

I'll never get tired of saying how much Keshini Naidoo and Lindsey Mooney at Hera Books have changed my life, so I'm saying it again here. Thank you for putting so much love and care into our books and for giving me a fresh start at forty. I hope *Frozen Falls* does you proud. x